Irresistible You

Victoria Connelly

Published by Cuthland Press
in association with Notting Hill Press
All rights reserved.

ISBN-13: 978-0956986696
ISBN-10: 0956986692

To my dear friend Bridget

ACKNOWLEDGEMENTS

To Ken Howard and Dora Bertolutti for letting us stay in their wonderful Venetian home. To Mario and Michela at Ca'macana, and to Susanna Ensom at Flavia for answering all my questions about the magical world of mask making.

To Clare Donovan and Benita Brown for having so many wonderful Italian facts at their fingertips! Also to Stephen Bowden and all at FAW for encouragement and friendship. And to Catriona, Giselle, Henriette, Deborah, Hsin-Yi and Sue.

To Val, Pat, Tonia, Francoise, Kassandra, Carol, Barbara, Jennifer and Amarjit for sharing the great pleasure of writing.

And many many thanks to my wonderful friends in Germany: Frauke, Carola, Brigitte, Doris and all at Diana Verlag.

And to my wonderful husband Roy for carrying my laptop around Venice for me!

PROLOGUE

There's magic in the heart of Venice but not everyone can find it.

In Dorsoduro, there is a little mask shop called Viviana's. It's like many of the mask shops in Venice with its pretty window display of bejewelled faces; its scarlet walls are covered in the same jolly jesters and sparkling sunbeams, and a little bell tinkles merrily as you open the door. But the masks in this shop are different. It isn't anything you can see or touch; it's something that you feel - the curious connection between a mask and its wearer that cannot be explained.

Rows of alabaster faces await their fate - a date with colour. And what colour! Rubies, sapphires, silvers and golds, cerises, amethysts and jades – richer than a jeweller's window and far more precious.

There are beautifully feminine feline masks decorated in rich damasks and studded with sequins and pearls, and sombre, tubular-nosed plague doctors who stare down eerily from their home below the great black beam. Each mask seems to have a life of its own - a life first born in the imagination of its creator.

Stefano Cazzaro.

He's working in the shop now. What else would he be doing? For him, there is no life outside Venice, and Venice, for him, is Viviana's.

'Viviana?' he calls, and his wife soon appears, holding an espresso for her husband. 'It's from Cassandra,' Stefano announces, waving a letter that has just arrived.

'Oh!' Viviana says, 'I liked her. How is she?'

'Married.'

'Wonderful!'

'And pregnant.'

Viviana claps her hands to her mouth. 'It worked, then?'

'Of course it worked!' Stefano says with a little chuckle.

'And who is this one for?' Viviana asks as she watches her husband's paintbrush glide gently over the fresh golden skin of a new mask.

'Elena,' he says.

'Is she coming soon?'

'She'll be arriving next week.'

Viviana looks anxious for a moment. 'Will it be ready?'

'Will it be ready, she asks me! *Of course* it will be ready! Since when have I not been ready for a visitor?'

Viviana laughs and leaves him to it.

Once again, Stefano focuses on the little mask before him, his bright eyes narrowing in concentration as he holds his paintbrush like a magic wand. He loves this moment best of all. He could take his brush anywhere and create all kinds of wonders. There are such possibilities!

For a moment, he thinks about Elena.

'She's in a terrible muddle, isn't she?' he says.

The mask stares back up at him, its hollow eyes seeming to understand.

'I think she's going to like you,' he tells it, holding it up to the light for inspection. 'Yes. You'll be ready for Elena,' he says. 'But will Elena be ready for you?'

CHAPTER 1

Elena Montella woke up with her heart racing. She'd dreamt it again - the same dream that had been tracking her down and haunting her for days now. She shook her head, trying to free her mind of the image of herself stood in the church in a wedding dress. It always started so beautifully with music and flowers and smiling faces but, somewhere amongst the vows, it started to turn ugly.

'Elena. Do you take *this* man to be your lawful wedded husband?' the vicar would ask.

'I do,' Elena would say, her voice low and reverential.

'And do you take this man to be your lawful wedded husband?'

'I d-' she'd pause. 'Pardon?'

'And do you take *THIS* man to be your lawful wedded husband?'

'What?'

The vicar's eyes seemed to spear her with their intensity. 'Well?' he'd say impatiently. 'Who's it to be?'

Elena would turn around and see three grooms lined up behind each other.

'Come on, Elena!' one of them would shout.

'Yeah! Make up your mind!' the second would yell.

'Are you sure it's me you want?' the third would say.

'What's going on?' Elena would scream.

'*You* tell *us!*' one of the grooms would bellow, and it was at this point that things really started to get out of hand. Fists flew across faces, bouquets bashed heads, bibles were stuffed into bemused mouths and it would all end in a huge food fight - the congregation chucking wedding cake around in lieu of confetti. Elena could never quite explain that part. But she had a pretty good idea what the rest of it meant.

Swinging her legs out of bed, she got up and showered, hoping that the warm needles of water would wash away the remnants of her trio of bridegrooms. Some women collected shoes, she thought. Others preferred lipsticks, earrings or miniature teapots. But she had to go and be different. Her own particular collection was fiancés and, at that moment, she had three.

Men had always been a little weakness of hers; she just loved them but three at once could prove problematical from time to time. Her answerphone was usually chock-a-block with messages, and she had to think of all sorts of excuses to avoid treble-booking herself. Her diary was always a mass of colour because she used a different pen for each fiancé: Mark was blue, Reuben was red and Prof was purple. It should have been a simple enough system but she had been known to turn up at the wrong house at the wrong time and then have to explain herself to the fiancé she'd stood up. But, believe it or not, she hadn't deliberately got herself into this situation; it all happened quite by accident.

Prof had been the first to propose, Elena remembered as she lathered her hair in apple shampoo, and she'd been so surprised that she didn't really say anything at all as he'd pushed a ring onto her finger. And then Mark had proposed on the very night she was going to break up with him and, shortly after that, Reuben had gone down on one knee and done the same thing. Words had completely failed her. She loved each one of them and didn't want to hurt their feelings and so, to avoid any kind of confrontation, she'd accepted. She knew it was weak-willed of her and that she wouldn't be quite so popular if the truth ever came out, but it also felt overwhelmingly wonderful to be loved by three gorgeous men.

Nevertheless, things had got to change and she knew she was going to have to choose just one man if she was ever going to banish her nightmares and lead a normal life.

'Elena, my babe,' Mark had said to her at the beginning of the week, 'we really should start thinking about fixing a date.' He'd stroked her dark hair in that annoyingly sensuous way of his and she'd tried to push him away. They were, after all, in open view of the students on the way to class and she really didn't want to encourage the teasing that was already going on.

'I think the end of July would be perfect,' he'd continued, his fingers stroking the oh-so-sensitive place behind her ear. 'What do you think?'

Elena had looked at him in quiet bewilderment. 'I - er - I have to get these worksheets photocopied,' she'd said, ducking underneath his imprisoning arm and running into the office before he could stop her.

Mark, Elena felt, was the best friend a girl could wish for. He was sweet, attentive, boyishly handsome with bright mischievous eyes, and he didn't get all huffy when she was in a bad mood like some men did. But, on the negative side, he had the bank balance of a Benedictine monk. She really had tried to look passed this unfortunate obstacle but one look around his flat had sent a shiver of horror down her spine.

A couple of weeks ago, after he'd presented her with dinner in his dingy kitchen and they'd sat snuggling on the sofa of a thousand stains, she'd tried to break it off with him. Was this what she really wanted out of life? she kept asking herself. But, just as she was going to tell him things weren't really working out, he'd presented her with the ring. How could she have disappointed him? His eyes were so warm and full of love that she didn't have the heart to say no.

But it wasn't just Mark who'd been putting pressure on her, she thought, stepping out of the shower and drying herself with a fluffy pink towel. Her evening class professor had also been dropping very heavy hints in between lectures on nineteenth-century heroines.

'Mother's been asking again, you know,' Prof told her last week. Elena knew she shouldn't have asked him for an extension on her Emily Bronte paper. He always made conditions with such things.

Prof was Elena's older man. She called him Prof because she just couldn't cope with his ribbon of names: Sigmund Algernon Mortimer. They were far too posh and pretentious for her to use without bursting into hysterical laughter every time she did so. He was forty-nine years old, had a mind like Einstein and a mouth like a hungry porn star. He was handsome and self-assured; old-fashioned in the best possible way, dashing with threads of silver in his mahogany locks; and he was deeply protective - constantly checking up on her which could sometimes prove just a little bit exhausting. She was twenty-nine; she could look after herself. But he was the sweetest, tenderest man she'd ever met, and he always looked so cute in his little round glasses and paisley bow tie.

She wouldn't have felt quite so pressured with just Mark and Prof hounding her for an answer, she thought as she blow dried her hair upside down, but even Reuben had been getting in on the act.

'ELENA!' he'd shouted across the studio the other day, paintbrush poised in the most threatening manner. 'You're driving me crazy! I want to make an honest model out of you!'

Elena really did find it most off-putting to be told such a thing when naked on a chaise longue. She'd ignored him, as usual, because he was rather prone to these little outbursts. She thought it was all part of the artistic temperament. However, this caused him to become even more furious until, finally, he'd ripped his canvas with a palette knife and told her to go home without so much as a ravishment for her pains.

Elena had, on two separate occasions, walked out on Rueben and threatened not to come back. Sometimes, she felt that his ego was far greater than his talent and she wasn't at all sure that she could put up with him for the rest of her life, but something kept on pulling her back to him.

Men! They really were the most unpredictable of species, she mused, choosing a crisp white shirt and pair of black cotton trousers for the day ahead. She couldn't believe that she'd managed to pick, perhaps, the only three men in the world who wanted to sprint up the nearest aisle. Didn't anyone want to live in sin anymore? Her only explanation was that each of her paramours had come to the realisation that they might not be the only ones in her life, and that had brought their hunter-gatherer genes to the fore. She couldn't really believe that they had found her out, though, as she kept each one of them very separate.

Mark was Elena's work colleague at the foreign school she taught at in West London. She saw him four days a week when she was teaching, and kept Saturday morning's free for him.

She saw Prof every Thursday evening for her literature class at evening school and occasionally dropped by the university during Friday lunchtimes when she knew he wasn't tutoring.

Sundays were for Reuben and, because he had a whole posse of models, she didn't think he minded only seeing her once a week. He certainly hadn't questioned her about it. So, why the sudden urge for each one of them to get married? Whatever the reason for their Mrs Bennet behaviour, it spelt trouble for her. Hence her decision to make some life changes.

She was going away. Her bags were packed and she was just about ready to leave for the airport.

It was the Easter holidays and her flight to Venice was in three hours' time and she was going to stay with her sister, Rosanna, who was sitting an artist's apartment there and getting paid for the privilege.

She'd phoned Rosanna the week before but she hadn't sounded too pleased to hear from her.

'What do you want, Elena?' she'd asked.

'I want to come and see you,' she said in her sweetest sister's voice, but Rosanna wasn't having any of it

'What for? Are you in trouble again?'

'Yes, I am,' she said matter-of-factly.

'Dio Mio! I *knew* it.'

'I was joking!' Elena said. 'I just want to see you. What's wrong with that?'

'Nothing,' Rosanna relented.

'Good! I'll book a ticket, then,' she said, laughing at her little sister's bossiness.

Elena had a distinct memory of Rosanna wagging her finger at her from her cradle, but maybe she was mistaken.

Sitting on a plane can be a very soporific experience for some people, and Elena happened to be sat next to such a person. No sooner had they taken off from Gatwick than the woman in tartan beside her was snoring sonorously. Her glasses had fallen half-way down her nose, and her mouth hung open like a dog's on a hot day. Elena looked down at the lady's left hand, and saw two gold rings: a stunning emerald surrounded by diamonds, and a thick gold wedding ring. She wondered who had placed them on her finger and if they'd known she snored as they'd done so.

Mark had seen Elena off at the airport. That was why she was wearing his ring - a classic diamond solitaire. It was a bit smaller than she'd hoped for but she knew he didn't have much money. Her other rings were hidden in a red velvet pouch in one of her stockings. There was Reuben's row of rubies, and Prof's antique amethyst. All of the rings were so beautiful, and all so very different, just like the men who'd given them. So, how was a girl meant to choose just one?

She closed her eyes and tried to switch off her brain, which wasn't easy with the hippo-snorter beside her but, gradually, she felt herself drifting into a dreamless sleep and was only woken up by the announcement that they were about to land and, less than an hour later, she was on a boat ploughing across the open waters of the lagoon, sitting up high in her seat in anticipation.

And there she was: La Serenissima. The Pearl of the Adriatic. Venice.

In the deep haze of sunshine, everything looked milky-blue. Sunlight danced happily on the water like notes from a Vivaldi concerto. There were bell towers, church domes, houses and bridges and, as the boat pulled in to its stop, Elena breathed a long, contented sigh.

It felt so good to be back in the country in whose language she dreamt.

CHAPTER 2

There were a pile of unmarked essays on Prof's desk, there were five mugs of unfinished tea in varying states of decomposition around the room, and the answerphone had three messages which all needed responding to, yet all he could do was to sit and think of Elena. It seemed an age since he'd last seen her yet she had only been there last week, he thought, tapping his silver pen against his jaw.

He switched his lamp on as he endeavoured to make a start on the essays. His eyes weren't as good as they'd once been. He had to wear glasses now which, his last girlfriend told him, made him look like Indiana Jones before he set out to become a hero. He wasn't sure if that was a compliment or not. Wouldn't one rather be a hero than an academic - when it comes to looks, anyway? Still, he supposed it was better than being told he looked like Woody Allen.

Elena actually loved the glasses. She'd said they made him look distinguished and he supposed his grey hair was also being referred to when she made that remark. It used to be a rich brown but now it was threaded through with silver as if he'd walked through a city of spiders' webs. He wouldn't have cared so much but the grey had begun its sabotage long before his thirty-third birthday.

'I like older men,' Elena had told him, her warm kiss convincing him completely. So, there were some advantages to ageing, Prof thought.

Ah, Elena! Every time she was there, she filled the room with joy. It was the only time the place felt alive. Normally, it had that musty library-crossed-with-a-morgue smell that came from being stuffed with old books. Prof could tell that that's what Elena had been thinking when she'd first walked through his door. She'd had him summed up with a blink of her brown eyes. And yet, she'd stayed.

Of course, Prof knew it was wrong. How many times had he been warned about the perils of passion with pupils? It was irresponsible, irrational and idiotic. But it was also pure bliss. She made his heart leap within his chest. She made his head spin when she kissed him. She turned his walk into a waltz and his sleep into a heavenly haven. And his brain had been alliteratively addled. He felt as if he'd swallowed *The Golden Treasury of English Verse* as he kept thinking and talking in similes and metaphors. He'd be brushing his teeth and suddenly think, *she's like a rainbow*, or he'd be under the shower and remember a line of poetry which perfectly described her and run, dripping through the house to find it.

She was a true heroine. She could have walked straight out of a nineteenth-century novel. She was Eustacia Vye and Bathsheba Everdene rolled into one and he was sure Thomas Hardy would have fallen head over heels in love with her had he met her, and then punished her to within an inch of her life in one of his novels.

Prof would never forget the time Elena had first asked him his name. She'd made an appointment to see him about her essay on the Byronic hero but, instead of listening to his words of advice, she'd insisted on cross-questioning him.

'Professor Mortimer is such a stuffy name, don't you think?'

'I beg your pardon?' he'd peered at her over his glasses, feeling exceptionally stuffy.

'What's your first name?' she asked, crossing her legs and leaning across the table most alluringly.

He cleared his throat. 'Sigmund,' he said.

'*Sig*mund! As in Freud?' Elena laughed. But it wasn't a mocking laugh, rather a perplexed one, as if she had trouble believing he'd told her the truth. 'What were your parents thinking of?'

'It's a family name,' he said, picking up her essay again, ready to point out her lack of relevant quotations.

'It's terrible!' she went on. 'What do you think of me calling you Siggy?'

He frowned at her across the desk and shook his head. 'About this essay - I really think there's room for-'

'Have you got a second name?'

His frown was set in by this stage but he was obviously not going to win her concentration until he'd answered all her questions in a satisfactory manner.

'Algernon.'

Elena's eyes suddenly became very round and her mouth dropped open. 'Algernon,' she repeated, as if it were the punch line to a joke that wasn't particularly funny. 'Algie?'

'I beg your pardon?'

'Can I call you Algie?'

'I'm not sure that's a very good idea,' he said. 'Now, getting back to Byron-'

'What do most people call you, then?'

'Professor.'

'Well, I can't call you that!' she said, and that's when the name 'Prof' materialized.

Prof had always been an old-fashioned sort of man. He opened doors for women, he liked to pay for dinner and he never really believed in women chasing after the man of their choice. However, that was exactly what Elena had done. He really didn't get any say in the matter and, strangely, he'd found it a rather refreshing experience. He'd pretend to be outraged by her up-front behaviour but he knew she saw right through him from the start.

'Don't pretend you're not enjoying this, Prof,' she said as, many dinner dates later, which he most certainly insisted on paying for, she began undressing behind his filing cabinet. 'I know you're not really reading that Tennyson, so put it down and start paying *me* some attention.'

He slammed the book shut. 'He would have written about you, Elena,' he told her, crossing the room and loosening his bow tie.

'What about Shakespeare?'

'Sonnet after sonnet. He would have run out of ink writing about your beauty.'

She smiled at this and her fingers found the buttons of his shirt. 'Will you write about me?' she asked.

'Making love to you will be my poetry.'

She pouted prettily. 'Can't I have both sex and poetry?'

'Not at the same time,' he said.

'Okay,' she said after some careful thinking. 'Sex now; sonnet later.'

Prof had never fallen for somebody so quickly or so wholeheartedly. He had always loved rationally which was a bit of a contradiction, he knew. Love should be spontaneous and unhindered by thought. Wasn't that what years of being consumed by poetry should have taught him? Still, it wasn't in his nature to abandon himself quite so completely - until he'd met Elena. It was as if she'd unlocked him and set him free.

He gave her his grandmother's antique amethyst ring. He didn't think it was worth very much, but its mellow beauty had always struck him, and he'd so desperately wanted Elena to wear it. Sure enough, it looked stunning against her olive skin. The only thing they had to arrange now was a date. Mother couldn't have been happier.

'It's about time you found somebody to take care of you,' she said, still believing that he couldn't possibly survive in the world on his own, despite him being forty-nine and having been independent for the last thirty-one years.

'You need somebody to love. And somebody who loves you,' she said. And, he believed he had found her.

CHAPTER 3

Rosanna had said a prayer for her sister earlier that day. She'd said, 'Please, Mary, mother of Jesus, help to guide my sister. Give her the wisdom to know herself.' And then she began to wonder if she really should be praying to Mary. Was there a suitable saint to help incurable flirts? Should she pray to Saint Christopher as Elena journeyed through so many love affairs, or to Saint Anthony as she lost her heart to yet another man? They never taught you the really useful saints at school: who to pray to if you'd run up a huge debt or who to pray to if you were failing miserably in your private life. And then Rosanna remembered Saint Rita, the patron saint of desperate causes.

'Please, Santa Rita, help my sister out of her desperate situation as you yourself were helped.'

She sighed. She'd done her best, and only hoped that it would do the trick because she would be spending the next couple of weeks with Elena and she wasn't as prepared to put up with her amorous antics as she had been when they were teenagers.

It was always Rosanna who had to pick up the pieces and nurse the broken hearts of Elena's dumped suitors. She remembered Marco, the sweet nineteen-year old student who fell in love with Elena when they were staying outside Rome one summer. Unfortunately, it was nothing more than a *Roman Holiday* for Elena who, Rosanna believed, loved Marco's Vespa more than him. It was the feel of the wind through Elena's hair as they'd sped by The Coliseum that turned her on, and not the feel of his kiss. Then there was Massimo - Mama's best-friend's son. The mamas had always hoped that the two of them would get married but Massimo's mama didn't appreciate Elena three-timing her boy.

There'd been so many of Elena's suitors over the years that the names of the others had blurred in Rosanna's memory. Anyway, comforting the broken-hearted wasn't a role she relished and she was not prepared to play it in their adult lives. That was why she was a little reluctant to her staying. A fortnight was a long time when you were a female Casanova in Venice and Rosanna dreaded to think what Elena would be up to. She also had the feeling that Elena was running away from something and that could only be a relationship, or three, that wasn't working out quite how she'd anticipated.

It wasn't as if Rosanna had nothing better to do than sort out her sister's problems. She had problems enough of her own. She'd been sitting an artist's studio in Cannareggio. It was a quiet residential area of Venice and Rosanna loved strolling next to the lagoon, looking out across the water to San Michele - the *island of the dead* - where Venetians from forgotten times lay in peace behind the apricot walls and dark cypress trees. Mama had once told her that a great-great uncle of theirs was buried there and so, one day, she'd taken the boat across the short stretch of water, her black-ribboned chrysanthemums in her hand, and spent two hours walking up and down the rows of graves, peering into the ornate tombs and squinting at old photographs on the stones. She had found several Montellas but had never found her great-great uncle so had laid her flowers on the grave of Lucia Montella 1892 - 1938, saying a prayer for the woman who might well have been a long-lost relative.

There was definitely something about having Venetian relatives. It was as though they had the very water of the lagoon running through their veins. As soon as Rosanna had returned, she'd felt the connection immediately and knew that she had found her home even if she was staying in somebody else's in the meantime. She felt as if she could never go back to a land where cars tore up the roads with deafening speed; she needed to be surrounded by the water - to feel its peace and absorb its reflections.

So, she'd been absolutely delighted when she was asked to house-sit the studio of the well-respected artist, Sandro Constantini, who had set his sight on world domination no less. But, no matter how much he adored being in demand, he hated leaving his home and his cat, which Rosanna secretly called *cat-child*.

'*Bimba!*' Sandro would coo in an excruciatingly embarrassing manner, cradling it in his arms and pouting his lips as if he meant to kiss it. Rosanna didn't care for cats herself and had taken to leaving cat-child's food and drink bowl in the enormous sunken bathroom at the far end of the house. That way, they didn't have to pretend to tolerate each other.

'You will look after her, won't you?' he'd asked for the hundredth time before leaving for the States.

'As if she's my own baby,' she'd lied, smiling convincingly. Rosanna would have done anything to get that apartment for the summer. Her own horrible rented one on the mainland was a nightmare when it was hot. It heated up like a sauna and, if she'd dared to open a window, it would fill with a thick fog of fumes from the road below. Sandro's apartment was a dream in comparison. She felt like a princess floating around the enormous studio, her feet cool on the stone floors, draping herself on the cream-coloured sofas. It was heaven and, if heaven came complete with the cat-child, then she'd have to put up with it. Besides, this was a job; she was actually getting paid to stay there. It was probably the easiest money she'd ever earn. She didn't have to do much more than take care of the house, feed cat-child, field telephone calls and deliver a couple of canvasses. Other than that, she could attend her own sittings.

To be honest, it was a welcome relief to be free to choose her own work again although she had to be selective because Sandro could be quite a jealous artist. He liked to monopolise his models.

'I don't want to see my women in other people's paintings,' he would tell her, his dark eyes stern and serious. 'It's artistic adultery!'

Just as well he paid her enough not to need to work but her clients were safe bets whilst Sandro was abroad and this was her chance to put some money away for a deposit on her very own apartment.

She was really very proud of making her own way in the world and one would have thought she'd be respected for earning her own money and not being reliant on a man but respect was a word that the man in her life had obviously never heard of. Corrado Taccani may have been tall, dark, and handsome but he was also a male chauvinist pig. Rosanna hadn't known that, of course, when she'd first met him. He'd kept it well hidden, along with a few other unpleasant surprises. Like his mother.

Irma Taccani was the sort of mother-in-law you wouldn't wish upon your worst enemy. Bridges shook and canal waters quivered when she was in the vicinity, and shop blinds would be pulled down all of a sudden in an attempt to escape a possible unwelcome tirade.

Rosanna remembered when she'd found out that Corrado still lived with his mother.

'Who can afford their own place in Venice?' he'd shrugged, and it didn't really bother her too much until she met the mother in question.

She soon came to realise that it wasn't only Corrado's inability to fend for himself in Venice on a labourer's salary that was holding him back, but that Irma Taccani had him held in a boa constrictor grip.

So, where did that leave Rosanna? Did she really want Corrado enough to fight for him? There were days when she could think of nothing but Corrado - when she couldn't imagine her future without him even though he didn't want the same things as he did. He longed to move away from Venice to set up a little small-holding somewhere in Umbria where he could grow his own food and have his wife cook it for him and his seven children. Yes, Corrado wanted to turn her into a big fat Italian mama and that didn't really fit into Rosanna's scheme of things. She didn't want to live in the middle of a field and tread her own wine - she wanted to be able to book a table at the best restaurants and choose from a wine list.

She knew that procrastinating was just making matters worse, and what made her feel worse still was the fact that Elena would feel the same way. As she tidied round the apartment, Rosanna realised that she was dreading her sister's arrival because it would, inevitably, lead to talking about relationships, and what was she going to tell her? She knew Elena would force her into making some sort of decision about her future and she wasn't sure if she was ready for that.

CHAPTER 4

Elena wheeled her suitcase along the waterfront, groaning when she reached the Ponte Panada.

'Turn right after the bridge,' Rosanna had told her and it was lucky she remembered because she'd lost the directions she'd jotted down. Taking a deep breath, she picked up her suitcase and struggled to the top before almost falling down the other side under the weight of her entire wardrobe.

Turning right down a wide alley, she noticed lines of washing stretching overhead: vibrant displays of knickers, T-shirts and dusters. She turned into a narrower, darker alley where she could no longer hear the sound of the water taxis speeding across the lagoon. Everything felt hushed and sleepy.

Her suitcase dragged behind on its insufficient wheels but it wasn't long before she found the turning she was looking for: an anorexic alley with a tall building on one side which had been turned into apartments, and a two-storey building on the other side. This was the one she wanted and she soon spied a big brass bell and the name *S Constantini* engraved above it. Elena pressed the bell and waited, stepping back to look at the building. From the outside, it looked more like a derelict warehouse than a luxurious artist's apartment: the plaster on the walls was crumbling away to reveal the brick below. Most of the buildings in Venice were like that, she knew, but at least they were painted in sunny ambers or rosy reds; this building was a dull grey and the only window she could see was obliterated by iron railings making it look more like a prison than a home. She grimaced. What was Rosanna doing in a place like this?

She pressed the bell again and looked down the tiny alley to the canal. You had to be careful in Venice. If you were walking home drunk and took a couple of steps too many, you could easily end up in the water.

At last, she heard a key scraping on the other side of the heavy wooden door, followed by a bolt being drawn. This really was like a prison, she thought, as the door finally opened.

'Rosanna!' she yelled, seeing her sleepy-faced sister for the first time in nearly a year.

'Elena! Are you early? I was just having a little siesta.'

'So I can see,' she said, flinging her arms around her and kissing her cheek. 'Are you working too hard?' she asked with a touch of sarcasm.

'I think I must be,' she said in all seriousness. 'Come in,' she said, making no attempt to help her with her suitcase. She obviously remembered the time she'd once offered to lend her a hand and had almost dislocated her shoulder in the process.

Elena entered a cool stone lobby and turned right, following Rosanna up a small flight of stairs. 'I hope it's better inside than the outside,' she said.

'You must know Venice by now,' she said, and she was right. The most opulent of palaces could lie behind walls which often resembled nothing more than a public convenience, and this artist's studio was no exception. Reaching the top of the stairs, Elena took in a long, low gasp of wonder.

'My goodness! Look at this!'

Rosanna turned around and smiled. It was a smile which said, *I told you so*.

Elena nodded. 'You've landed on your feet here, haven't you?'

'For a while,' she assented. 'It's better than Mestre.'

Elena laughed, remembering her one visit to Rosanna's appalling apartment on the mainland, with fleas the size of rodents and rodents the size of dogs. 'This is *enormous!*'

Rosanna beckoned her to follow with an excited flap of hands. 'This part is open- planned. That's the studio,' she motioned to the left where two easels stretched up to the ceiling and an enormous wooden workbench sprawled its way towards the opposite wall. 'Living room here,' Rosanna said, her hand gliding along the back of an enormous cream sofa - one of two. 'Dining room,' she said, 'and kitchen there.'

Elena shook her head. 'It's amazing!'

'Through here,' Rosanna continued, 'is the bathroom.'

Elena followed her through and her mouth fell open at the sight of a sunken bath you could wash a small army vehicle in. 'It's a jacuzzi!'

Rosanna nodded, a twinkle in her dark eyes. 'There's a shower too and a sauna.'

'Where does that door go?'

'There's a small bedroom and some stairs leading to the basement. Sandro keeps all his old canvasses down there.'

'So where do I sleep?' she asked, suddenly remembering how tired she was.

'This way,' Rosanna said, getting into her stride as a tour guide. They walked back through to the main room and there was an open stairwell she hadn't noticed before which led up to a bedroom. 'I thought we could share. There's plenty of room.'

Elena nodded. 'It will be like being back at home when we used to stay up all night gossiping.'

Rosanna giggled. 'And I can keep an eye on you.'

'What do you mean?'

'I know you!' she said, turning around and narrowing her eyes at Elena. 'I know what you're like, but you're not bringing any of your boyfriends back here. Sandro trusts me and I don't want to upset him.'

'But I came here to see *you!*' Elena protested. 'What makes you think-'

'Then you *are* on your own?'

'Of course I am! I said I would be.'

'There aren't going to be any unexpected guests showing up?'

'*No!*'

'So, why are you here?' she asked.

'Gosh! Rosanna! I've just got off a plane! We haven't seen each other for almost a year. I'm parched. I'm tired. Can you at least offer me a cup of coffee before you start attacking me with questions?'

Rosanna's face softened with a smile and Elena smiled back. She had missed her so much. Walking across the room, she hugged her again, breathing in the musky perfume she wore and feeling her thick curls tickling her nose.

'I promise I'll tell you everything,' she whispered. 'I need your advice on one or two things.'

Rosanna pulled away from her and examined her with curious eyes. 'I thought you might.'

'But first, *please* can I have a coffee?'

*

Elena managed about two sips of coffee before Rosanna started twitching for information but Elena was able to divert her with a few questions of her own first.

'So where's this Sandro, then?'

'New York.'

'And he didn't take his muse with him?' Elena teased.

Rosanna tutted. 'Somebody has to stay and look after cat-child.' She nodded to a space in front of her.

'Good heavens!' Elena said, turning around and noticing the cat for the first time. 'It's enormous!'

And it was. Four times the size of the ferals which stalked the alleys of Venice, she looked as if he dined out on pizza every night.

As if reading her mind, Rosanna said, 'She's going on a diet whilst I'm in charge.' Rosanna pushed the toffee-coloured cat away from her before it had a chance to wind around her legs. 'She makes me sneeze,' she said. 'Anyway, how's the teaching going?'

Rosanna was just like mama, Elena thought, always asking about work, as if a person could only be defined by the job they did.

'It's okay. It pays the bills - just. But it's nice to get away for a while.'

'And your students are good?'

'Yes,' she said. 'They all work hard.'

'So, this Mark you mentioned the other day - is he someone you work with?' Rosanna asked.

Elena stifled a sigh. She really didn't want to launch into her extra-curricular activities just yet. She'd already taken off Mark's diamond ring and placed it in her velvet pouch to avoid questioning.

'He teaches at the school, yes,' she said. 'You'd like him. He's very clever and he goes to church.'

'What's that meant to mean?'

'Nothing!'

'You're making fun of me again?' she accused.

'No! I'm not!'

'You could do with a few Sundays in church yourself, you know.' Rosanna stood up and took Elena's half-drunk coffee away from her and marched into the kitchen.

Elena puffed out her cheeks and sighed. What had she let herself in for? She'd thought she could turn to her sister in times of need but she'd forgotten that her answer to everything was rooted in Catholicism and Elena hadn't been to church since she was a teenager.

'Rosanna!' she called after her across the expanse of studio. 'Be nice to me. I've had a horrible journey.'

She could hear her clattering cups in the sink as if she meant to break them up for a mosaic. She could be so Italian when she wanted to.

'Rosaaaaaanna!' she called, waiting patiently for her to emerge.

'What?'

Elena widened her eyes and put on the softest, most helpless of smiles hoping that, like most of the men in her life, Rosanna would relent and be sweet with her.

'I've missed you,' she said.

For a moment, Rosanna stood fixed to the spot as if she were carved from marble but then a wave of sisterly emotion flooded her and she ran over to the sofa, pulling Elena into a suffocating embrace.

'I've missed you too!' she sobbed, her curls poking Elena in the eyes and tickling her nose again. But Elena didn't mind. At least, for now, she'd got out of saying prayers under her sister's supervision.

CHAPTER 5

Mark clearly remembered the first time he met Elena. He'd taken one look at her and thought, she's not the sort of girl who'd ever look at me. And then she'd looked at him, and he'd been blown away.

She'd been wearing a pale red dress and was perusing the notice board. The man who ran the English school for foreign students, Tomi, the very thin Finn who lived entirely on a diet of coffee and cigarettes - never made a habit of introducing new members of staff to each other, so this was Mark's chance to introduce himself. He made sure his shirt was tucked in and ran a hand through his hair. After quickly examining his hands for whiteboard pen, he was ready for action.

'Excuse me,' he said, 'can I help you? You're new, right? I'm Mark Theodore - Upper Intermediate and Advanced.'

'Hello,' she said. 'Elena Montella. Elementary and Pre-intermediate.'

He nodded and smiled. She was the most beautiful woman he'd ever seen and that was saying something because there were some stunners at the school. Most of them were Finnish or Swedish with platinum blonde hair and summer-sky eyes but this raven-haired contessa arrested him immediately with her hypnotic dark looks.

His ear, trained to detect any form of accent, told him that she was Italian.

'Which room are you teaching in?' he asked.

'Room six,' she said. 'I haven't found it yet, though.'

He nodded. 'That's Geraldine's old room. She was the teacher before you.'

She nodded. 'I hope the students won't be disappointed at having me instead.'

It was on the tip of his tongue to say, nobody could be disappointed at having you, but he bit it back and merely grinned. 'Trust me - they will be delighted! Just follow me and I'll show you where it is.'

He led the way up the rickety staircase. There was an old banister rail lying on the first landing from the previous term, and paint flaked off the walls as if it were making a bid for freedom.

'It's a bit of a tip, I'm afraid. The refurbishment is always "Next term",' he said, quoting Tomi who didn't like spending the school's profit on fripperies such as décor. 'But it's a nice room,' he said, ducking his head to avoid a low beam and opening the door for her.

She nodded and smiled and Mark smiled too because he noticed a pile of photocopied sheets on the table at the front of the classroom. Elena had already found the room on her own.

'It's very nice,' she said, tucking a long, dark strand of hair behind her ear, revealing the most slender neck.

'I'm in room three so I'm right underneath you,' he said, and then felt his face heat up as he realised what he'd said. 'If you need anything,' he stumbled. 'I'm usually around. If not in the classroom, then in the staff room.'

She raised a dark eyebrow; it was the sexiest, most suggestive eyebrow he had ever seen and it made him wonder why he hadn't noticed women's eyebrows before.

'Then, I'll see you around,' she said and, almost banging his head on a low beam, he backed out of the room, feeling himself grinning like an idiot.

Seven weeks later, they were engaged. Mark still couldn't believe it. He'd never had a girlfriend for more than a couple of months at a time and yet here he was, an engaged man, planning a mortgage and a honeymoon. He felt the luckiest guy in the world.

So, when she told him she was going to Venice for the Easter holidays, he was a bit surprised. He'd tried not to show his disappointment, of course; Elena didn't like disappointment, and he knew that she had to go away and do some sister stuff. So, he shrugged. 'Okay. Send me a postcard,' he'd told her.

The thing with Elena was that she was a free spirit; she didn't like to be pinned down and he had no intention of doing that. She was as elusive as a butterfly: just when you thought she'd settled long enough for you to get a proper look at her, she'd flit away to another, more distant flower. But she'd never flitted as far as Venice before.

Sitting on the sofa of a thousand stains in his flat, the thought of two weeks without Elena was unbearable. He walked over to the window, looking out on a wet afternoon in Harrow. It wasn't very inspiring. He thought about Elena and what she'd be doing in

Venice. Was it raining there? He picked up the piece of paper that had fallen out of her pocket as she'd run for her plane. It was the address of the studio her sister was staying in.

Mark had never been to Venice. When he came to think of it, he'd never been anywhere much. His parents were very much into holidaying in the UK.

'There's nothing in the south of France that you can't find in Cromer,' his mother would insist. So, they'd inevitably spend the whole of their week's holiday locked away in a caravan on the Norfolk coast sheltering from the rain.

Elena had told him lots of stories about Italy: of her holidays in Rome, Umbria and Capri. It all sounded so exotic when you compared it to East Anglia. What puzzled him, though, was that she'd never mentioned any boyfriends. Now, in his experience, there were two reasons for not mentioning your past love-life: either you'd had more than your fair share of relationships or you'd had none at all, and Elena wasn't the sort of girl to be in the latter category. Which made him worry about what would be happening in Venice. Wasn't it meant to rival Paris when it came to romance? Would Elena be swept away by a gondolier?

He looked at the grey street outside. People rushed by, hiding under umbrellas and dodging the splashes from a never-ending stream of traffic. It was a grim scene and he grimaced at it. And then a crazy thought entered his head - the sort of crazy thought that was also brilliant and might just work.

Picking up his wallet and keys, Mark left the flat, shrugging into his jacket and running through the rain to the cash point in the next street. Pushing his card into the machine, he waited for his balance to flash up. Four hundred and seventeen pounds, ninety-two pence. Well, that put paid to his brilliant, crazy idea. April's pay cheque from the skint Finn hadn't yet cleared and he couldn't risk making a withdrawal when his rent was due in the next couple of days, and he didn't have any other source of cash. Unless …

He pulled up his collar up against the rain and legged it down the street. It was a five-minute run to the flat he was going to visit - a flat which, believe it or not, was in a street even grimmer than his one. Buzzing the intercom, he waited. It was gone three in the afternoon so was probably the best time to catch Barney Malone at home. Barney worked evenings in one of the local clubs and, when he wasn't doing that, he was out with his band, *No Name*. He was allergic to mornings but you could usually catch him around in the afternoon when he'd be wandering about his flat in his slippers and housecoat with a mug of tea and a bacon butty dripping ketchup down his front.

Mark buzzed again but the intercom didn't seem to be working so he stepped back into the street and peered up at the window through the rain.

'BarNEY!' he yelled. 'BARNEY!' Rain had just begun to find its way down his collar when a window from the second floor opened and a pale, unshaven face poked out.

'Hey, man! Come on up, man!' Barney shouted down to him.

Mark was buzzed in and he legged it up the stairs to his friend's flat.

'Come on through,' Barney said, ushering him in.

Trying not to trip over the drum kit in the hallway, Mark asked, 'How's it going, Barney?'

'You know what it's like, man,' he said, his pale legs sticking out of a holey housecoat. 'Do you want a cup of tea, man?'

Mark shook his head. Barney's cups were a regular penicillin culture. 'No, thanks. I can't stop long. I've actually come to ask a favour.'

'You have? Well, anything to help - ask away.'

'It's about that three hundred pounds.'

'Shit, man! Do he still owe you that money?'

'Yes.'

'God! I'm sorry.'

'So, you've got it then?'

'Er - no!'

'Barney - I really need that money.'

Barney ran a hand through his lanky hair and sighed, shaking his head and looking around his living room as if the money might magically appear from somewhere. 'I don't know what to say, man. I don't have it. If I did, it would be yours - right now - I promise you. But it ain't that simple.'

Mark could feel one of Barney's protracted stories about to materialise. 'It's been seven months,' he began.

'I know, man, but things are difficult. In fact, you couldn't have picked a worse time,' he said, falling backwards onto the sofa.

'Linda's going to have a baby.'

'What?'

Barney nodded. 'It's due in July.'

'Shit!'

'There'll be plenty of that,' he joked but his face was grim.

'What are you going to do?'

'I don't know. I've been applying for jobs.'

'What - *regular* jobs?'

'Yeah.'

For a moment, Mark tried to picture Barney Malone wearing a suit and working in an office but it was absurd. 'What about the band?'

He shook his head. 'It's dead, man.'

It was Mark's turn to shake his head. If he were perfectly honest, he'd never really expected *No Name* to reach the top of the charts but it would be sad if it were just to die out. It was Barney's life-force. Mark had never known him talk about anything else since they'd met at high school.

'Then you haven't got the money?' he said, aware that his voice was an ugly mix of despair and blame.

'What did you want it for, man? Was it something important?'

Mark nodded. 'You could say that. I need to get to Venice to see Elena.'

'Elena?'

'My fiancé.'

'Wow, man! You're engaged? That's like – mega!'

Mark couldn't help smiling at his enthusiasm.

'This is serious, then?'

'Yeah. I'm worried about her. I don't know – I've just got a bad feeling. I know I have to see her straightaway and that bloody skint Finn at the school hasn't paid me yet this month. And I still owe my credit card for that hideously expensive diamond I bought Elena. I'm stony broke.'

Barney shook his head, managing to look an even whiter shade of pale than normal.

'Here!' he said suddenly. 'I feel real bad about owing you, man. Have you got a mobile?'

Mark reached into his pocket and handed it to him wondering why he didn't use the phone on the table next to him.

'Got cut off last week,' he said as if following Mark's train of thought. 'Hello? Linda, it's Barney. I've got Mark here with me. Yeah. I know I do. That's why I'm ringing you. Listen, babe, I want you to lend me that three hundred quid. I'll pay you back - I've got an interview next week and the job's practically in the bag.'

Mark stood up and walked across to the window.

'Okay,' Barney said a few seconds later. 'That's sorted. She'll meet you by the cash point on the corner in ten minutes.'

'Yeah? Are you sure that's okay?'

Barney smiled. 'Hey, man - it's your cash and we're grateful for you helping us out.'

Mark grinned at him. He felt just terrible about hassling Barney at a time when he was down on his luck but what could he do? He needed that money. His future, he thought, might very well depend on it.

CHAPTER 6

Rosanna was not sure whether she'd got through to Elena that first night but they went to bed in good spirits and she was happy to leave things like that. She knew she could be a bit bossy sometimes but it only came from caring deeply about her sister. She wanted Elena to be happy, of course but, most of all, she wanted her to be safe. If Mama was around, she'd be reeling in horror. She'd never approved of Elena's conduct with the opposite sex and would quiz her at every opportunity.

'No supper until you tell me who you've been with!' Mama would yell from her permanent position in the kitchen, waving a wooden spoon like a gladiatorial weapon.

Looking back, she couldn't really blame Mama. Having a daughter like Elena must have been a nightmare. The telephone would never stop and they'd seriously considered installing one of those rotating doors to ease the flow of all the boys who came and went.

It had been strange sharing a bed with her sister again especially a bed that was so intimate. Sandro had said she could use it but she couldn't help feeling a little bit strange about sleeping in his bed. Elena had been too tired to stay awake talking long into the night like Rosanna had hoped they would, but there was time enough for that, she reasoned. She'd listened to her light breathing and had felt the warmth of her skin through the white sheet that covered her. She'd smelt of primrose soap.

She looked at Elena in the darkness and wondered what secrets she was hiding from her this time. It wasn't something as trivial as wanting to catch up on sisterly gossip. Nor was it of catastrophic proportions as before - of that much, she was sure.

Rosanna often wondered if she thought of that time so many years ago. They never talked about it now but she knew Elena still felt it keenly. Rosanna would often see the old pain fleeting in her sister's glance or turning a smile downwards as quickly as a cloud swallowing up the sun. It was a grim truth that the past never left. Every moment of every life was only a memory away and, although the pain might be buried deep, nobody knew when it would surface again.

Rosanna stroked the dark hair which spilled out over the white pillow next to hers. Her dearest Elena. She'd come home to her and she wouldn't let her down.

Her little, big sister.

CHAPTER 7

Elena woke up to an apartment filled with spring sunshine. Rosanna was already up and she could hear her bustling around the kitchen. She'd certainly settled into the place and who could blame her? It was incredible. Elena could get used to it herself. Maybe she wouldn't want to go back to cold, grey London at all. Maybe she could find herself a little place in Venice and start again. But, even as the thought crossed her mind, she knew that that was the coward's way out of the situation. She also knew that she'd been there before. She didn't openly admit it to many people but there had been a few times in her life when, instead of facing a situation, she'd turned and run away from it.

It had been the same that summer. She hadn't wanted to face the truth and so she'd ran and, if she was absolutely honest with herself, she was still running. She'd even dreamt about it last night. She would have thought that sharing a bed with her little sister would have made her feel safe and, after a day of travel, she should have slept soundly, but the past had hunted her down, locking her in a silent nightmare from which she hadn't been able to escape.

It didn't happen very often - not anymore but, when it did, she was left feeling as if all the stuffing had been knocked out of her and there was only one thing that could get her back on her feet again.

'*Coffee!*'

Rosanna's voice cut through the fog of her brain with welcome relief. It was funny how that one word could act as a cure-all. A bad morning's teaching, a weary journey or dreams that had assaulted the very core of your heart could all be banished by a cup of good, strong Italian coffee.

Elena pulled on her dressing gown and treaded softly down the wooden steps before padding across the stone floor to the kitchen.

'Did you sleep well?' Rosanna asked, setting the table for breakfast. 'I didn't want to wake you up - you looked so peaceful.'

Elena nodded. What was the point in upsetting her? What was the point in saying that she wished to God she *had* woken her up and rescued her from the shadows of her past.

'I slept like a baby,' she said, pulling out a chair and sitting down.

'I've never slept so well as I do here,' Rosanna said, taking a sip of coffee. 'It's so peaceful. And that bed - it's like falling asleep on a big white cloud.'

'Not like your place in Mestre, then!'

'I never want to go back there again,' Rosanna sighed, sitting at the dining table. 'It was like trying to get to sleep in the middle of a Hieronymus Bosch painting.'

'But Sandro won't be away forever, will he?' Elena asked, forgetting her own problems and focussing on those of Rosanna. 'So, do you plan on marrying him so you can stay here?'

'Don't be silly,' she protested. 'I'm not in love with him!'

Elena laughed at her. She was so unlike her. There were so many reasons to fall in love with a man, she had found: he might have a kind smile or beautiful hands; a warm heart or sensitivity. But he might also have a very nice apartment on the right side of town and that, to her, certainly shouldn't be discounted just because his smile might not be quite as winsome as you wished. But Rosanna was of the opinion that 'the one' had to have all these things and, in Elena's experience, that just didn't happen. Take Mark, for example. Out of Elena's three fiancés, he was the best suited to her in terms of personality: he knew what she was thinking - some of the time - and he gave her the space she needed but, on the negative side, he hadn't got two pennies to rub together. Prof, however, had a beautiful three-storey Victorian house in a leafy street in Ealing, several healthy bank accounts, and took three holidays a year, but he wasn't on quite the same plane as her and she often saw the disappointment in his eyes when he recalled a television programme from his youth and she had to admit that she had no idea what he was going on about. Ruben was rather a mix. Emotionally, they were very similar: they liked their own space and wouldn't pry into each other's private lives. He was generous, attentive when she needed him to be but, on the negative side, he could be extremely volatile.

Elena wondered what Sandro Constantini, Rosanna's artist and owner of this apartment was like and if she really couldn't make some sort of compromise on the love front in order to move in permanently.

'That reminds me,' she said, 'how's Corrado?'

Elena flinched at the force with which Rosanna tore open her bread roll at the mention of Corrado's name.

'He's fine,' she said, her tone of voice instantly informing her that she was *far* from fine.

'Still living with his mother?'

Rosanna nodded, her dark eyes narrowing into angry slits. 'I don't know why I put up with it! It's like the umbilical cord was never cut!'

'Then why *do* you put up with it?' Elena asked, glancing around the massive studio again and knowing exactly what she'd do if she were in her position.

Rosanna pouted in exasperation which left Elena feeling frustrated. If she'd been Rosanna, Corrado would have been left in a cloud of dust about a year ago, together with his tyrant of a mother.

'Anyway,' Rosanna began, 'what would you like to do today?'

Elena took a sip of coffee. 'I'm not sure,' she said, although she knew she was desperate to get out and get some fresh air. 'Do you need any shopping?' she volunteered.

'You can run an errand for me if you want,' Rosanna said, walking to the far side of the room where she bent down and picked up a canvas. 'This is ready to deliver,' she said. 'It's an address in Dorsoduro. It's been paid for so you only have to drop it off. I'll wrap it up first.'

'You don't want to come with her?' she asked.

'You want me to?' she said, her left eyebrow rising into a question mark. 'I thought you wanted to be by yourself for a while.'

Elena smiled. She hadn't said a single word but her sister knew exactly what was going through her mind.

'Venice is the best place in the world for thinking,' she said.

'I know,' Elena smiled. 'That's why I came here.'

Bouncing out over the bright water, the water bus headed out into the lagoon. The air was fresh and nipped the edges of Elena's ears reminding her it wasn't quite summer yet, but it felt so glorious that she contented herself with standing outside on the bus, holding onto the rails as they skirted the island.

It took about half an hour to reach San Marco. Elena had forgotten how large Venice was. Everybody said how tiny it was but it was only when you were out on the water that you could see how big it really was. She could have caught another bus to take her to Dorsoduro, but she wanted to walk from San Marco. The painting under her arm was a little cumbersome but it didn't retract from the pleasure of walking across the square. Music was playing outside Florian's famous café and grey clouds of pigeons landed at the feet of tourists armed with bags of feed. Elena felt a smile beginning to stretch across her face and a spring had definitely found its way into her step. She was in the heart of Venice on a beautiful April morning.

Leaving the square, she wound through the streets until she finally reached the Academia Bridge. A crowd of cameras were pointing at the white dome of Santa Maria della Salute but she didn't stop. She wanted to get the painting delivered. Then, and only then, would she afford herself the luxury of time.

Rosanna's address was easy to find and Elena left the painting with its new owner, wondering where he'd hang it as his walls were already a Piccadilly Circus of pictures. She thought of her own bare, rented walls back in London and how nice it would be to have the money to spend on something beautiful to look at. But Sandro's paintings were far too expensive on her teacher's salary and she'd have to be happy being a mere delivery girl of fine art.

With her mission accomplished, she decided to explore Dorsoduro. Tiny golden-stoned bridges, fine as cobwebs, threaded the streets together. People were eating lunch and drinking coffee at sunlit tables in the squares whilst gondoliers, in straw hats with jolly ribbons, flirted for business.

Elena gazed up at the houses and wondered how she could have chosen to live somewhere as drab as London where everything was grey and beige. There was no comparison when you looked at the colours Italians painted their houses. Tangerine, apricot, strawberry and cherry - Venice was a fabulous fruit bowl of colour. Balconies were stuffed with plants and dark green shutters were flung wide open in praise of the sun.

Only a few tourists had made it this far: the ones who had done their homework and knew where they wanted to go; those who wanted to buy something rather special. Not for them were the cheap, mass-produced masks with a tube full of glitter spilt lazily over them. Dorsoduro was home to the most beautiful mask shops in the world.

The streets were narrower and quieter there. They seemed darker too but for the bright windows of the mask shops. Elena had never been that fascinated by masks, she had to admit. They were beautiful and there was something rather compelling about the people who chose to wear them. Masks, she thought, were as much about what you revealed as what you concealed. Still, she secretly thought that they were a bizarre cross between a piece of jewellery and a muppet but there was something about one of the shops that drew her to it. It was called Viviana's and it wasn't anything out of the ordinary, in fact, it was probably the smallest and least enticing of shop fronts, but there was one mask in the window that caught Elena's eye. It was a plain gold half-mask with very little in the way of ornamentation but it had a warmth about it that made her smile.

Maybe it was just her natural magpie tendency but, before she knew what was happening, she opened the door, a little bell tinkling merrily over her head. There was nobody about and she shut the door behind her before taking a look around.

There was a huge wooden table at the back of the room which was choking with jars of brushes of every size from wisp-of-hair-thin to horse-tail thick. Behind these, stark white masks lay in wait for the colours that would bring them to life. Pencils, plant sprays, kitchen roll, scraps of paper, and boxes stuffed with rainbow ribbons jostled for space and, everywhere, mirrors which bounced back the light and made the room seem doubly filled with faces.

Every wall was covered by masks and it felt peculiar to be stared at by so many eyeless faces, and Elena was intensely curious to see the maker of these masks. There must have been dozens of mask shops in Venice where you can see the magic being created before your very eyes, and Viviana's was obviously such a shop.

The outside may have been rather unprepossessing but the inside was a feast for the eyes. It held colours you couldn't even imagine and shapes in which dreams - and nightmares - were formed. There were half-masks, cat masks, plague doctors with toucan-shaped noses, wood spirits, harlequins, clowns and jesters, sunbeams and moons. Elena's eyes couldn't keep still for a second.

Blues and silvers, reds and golds, feathers and leather, harlequins and sequins, velvets and damasks, golden braids, lacy veils, flowers, pearls and musical scores. It was a visual rollercoaster; a mass of magical mayhem. There was too much. She was spinning.

'Can I help you?' a voice floated from behind her and she spun around to see a tiny man with bright white hair standing behind the table. She stared at him for a moment. Where had he been? And then she saw a door she hadn't noticed before. It was slightly ajar, at the back of the shop. Had he been watching her? Waiting to see what she'd choose? She suddenly felt embarrassed; she hadn't come in to buy anything. She really didn't know what had made her come in at all.

'Is there anything I can help you with?' he asked again.

Elena bit her lip and felt herself blushing a scarlet to match the walls of the shop. 'No, thank you,' she said and, rather flustered, she left, the little bell tinkling as she closed the door behind her.

CHAPTER 8

The paintbrush was knackered and Reuben was laying the blame squarely on Elena. If she hadn't turned up at the studio in that red dress and danced around like some banshee then he would have cleaned it like a normal, conscientious artist. He couldn't afford to lose brushes like that, but he really couldn't afford to lose Elena either.

They'd argued just before she'd left for Venice and he felt bad about that now and, although he knew she'd be back in two weeks', and they could make up then, it wasn't helping him. Sometimes, he found conflict such as this helpful with his painting: it gave him a kind of nervous energy which would gnaw away at him until he put brush to canvas but, at other times, it would leave him as barren as an unprimed board. And, unfortunately, he was having an unprimed board moment.

He flicked through his sketchbook of Elena: Elena sitting, Elena standing, Elena clothed, Elena naked. His mouth felt dry and his palms felt wet as he looked at her. How cool she was and how hot she made him.

Reuben often wondered what had made him propose to Elena. He'd shocked the hell out of her when she'd presented her with that ruby ring. Her face was - well - a picture! He'd tried to paint it afterwards and it was rather reminiscent of Munch's *The Scream*. He'd probably exaggerated reality but that was what the best artists did: they took a model, found an interesting feature and made that their focus. With Elena, it was her eyes. He'd been immediately drawn to them: they held such light and intensity, such depth and emotion. He still hadn't worked out what she was thinking half the time, of course, and she never told him which always wound him up but he believed artists should have passion. A mate of his at art college used to annoy the hell out of him. He could never work up a sweat about anything. He was so bloody calm about everything he did, and his paintings, Reuben found, were always executed with the same bland brushstrokes. There was no vitality, no *lifeblood!* They were as listless and lifeless as he was. Well, Reuben was never going to let that happen to him.

He was Reuben Lord, an artist on his way up. His portfolio, even if he said so himself, was rather impressive, and he already had a client list that included an up-and-coming Hollywood actress and the latest It Girl. He was ambitious and obsessive about his art and poured all his time and energy into it. At least, he had done until he'd met Elena. She'd entered his world with the warm ease of a southern wind. He was sure she didn't know how much she rattled and riled him and he was finding it increasingly difficult to concentrate on his work especially since their latest fight.

He'd decided that he really had to sort this mess out with Elena and that meant an impromptu trip to Venice. They were engaged, for God's sake. How could she just run out on him like that? Well, he was going to show her that he wouldn't stand for that sort of behaviour. Knowing Elena, that was probably the plan: to work him up into a jealous frenzy which would show him how much he loved her.

Anyway, even if he didn't get things sorted with Elena, Venice might actually be good for the painting. He thought of Canaletto, Turner and Monet. Why not him? And, the beauty of it was that it would be tax-deductible.

CHAPTER 9

Books. Books. Books. Sometimes, there were just too many. Prof had been collecting books since being given his first pocket money over forty years ago, and not one had seen the inside of a charity bag: he'd kept every single one and, sometimes, it all became a bit too much. He was surrounded wherever he went. First of all, there were the books in his room at the university: floor to ceiling novels, dictionaries and critical appraisals; he was surrounded on all sides. It was a prison of print and there was no escaping it when he went home. His front door would never open to its full potential owing to the towers of paperbacks stacked along the length of the hallway, and it didn't get any better in the living room.

This extended library didn't stop downstairs. Oh no! The two flights of stairs were, themselves, furnished with a stack of paperbacks on each step, leading to the landing where his much-prized collection of travel guides lived. In the bathroom, there was always a selection of paperback novels, their spines cracked and their pages crinkled by wet thumbs after lengthy reading sessions in the bath. The bedroom was less indiscriminate: fiction from his boyhood years, through teenhood to early adulthood.

All in all, it was a bit of a fire hazard but he just couldn't bear to part with any of them. Each was a photo album of thoughts and feelings, of memories and moods. Whichever volume he chose to flick through opened up a forgotten world to him. It was like time travelling into his own history and it wasn't at all unusual for him to remember where he'd been when reading a particular volume. Every book held myriad memories and he'd never thought to get rid of any before but that was because it had only ever been him rattling around in this house. But wasn't all that about to change? He was engaged now and that would mean getting married before too long which meant sharing, and what woman in her right mind would want to live in this place?

No, he thought, he should really do something about it. He didn't want to give Elena any more reasons to postpone the wedding. It would only be a matter of time before there were even more than the two of them. That, he thought with a smile, would mean a whole new collection of books to begin, and the sooner they began that collection, the better. But they couldn't possibly fit any more books in this place before he got rid of some first.

He walked through the house, grimacing at the task ahead. It wasn't that he was particularly lazy, it was that he just didn't know where to begin and, in his experience of these things, when you don't know where to begin, there was only one woman to call: Betty Beaton. She'd been cleaning his mother's house for the last thirty years but he hadn't dared let her near his for fear of word getting back to his mother.

'Oh my God! I've never had such an experience as your son's house, Mrs Mortimer. I got through twenty-eight dusters and my vacuum cleaner broke – *actually broke!*'

Prof shook his head. He'd avoided her for as long as he could but he just couldn't think of another way out of this mess.

'You should have called me sooner, Professor Mortimer,' Betty Beaton admonished as soon as she walked through the door – or rather squashed through the door. She was a rather portly woman and didn't thank him for the fact that the door wasn't able to accommodate her.

'Sorry, Mrs B,' he said. 'But, as you can see, I need your help.'

She nodded and ran a tentative finger along the spines of some of the books in the hallway and then tutted.

'I'll pay you double what you're used to, of course.'

'It's not a question of money, Professor,' she said. 'What about my poor back? I'm not as young as he used to be, you know.'

'But you're only a girl!' he said, ashamed of himself for stooping to flattery.

She shook her head again and, for one terrible moment, he thought she was going to leave but she looked up at him, her mouth pursed so tightly that it was just a pink full stop, and her eyes narrowed as if to prevent herself from seeing even more unpleasantness.

'Where's your vacuum, Professor?' she asked sternly and he breathed a sigh of relief.

*

It took nearly a whole day before Mrs B was satisfied with the place. Prof looked around in wonder at her work

'You're a true miracle worker,' he said. 'What would he have done without you?'

'You'd have probably drowned in your own dust,' she said.

'I kept thinking you were going to uncover Stig,' he laughed.

'What?'

'Stig! *Stig of the Dump*,' he explained. 'It's a book where –'

'I don't have time to read,' she said.

'No. Of course not,' he said. 'Too busy keeping the nation spick and span, I dare say.'

She glared at him as if he'd insulted her rather than given her a compliment.

'Well, here's your money,' he said hastily, keen to get the house back to himself again.

'And when do you want me to come again?' she asked.

He was on the verge of saying *four years next Saturday*, but resisted. He hadn't planned on having a weekly cleaner but it looked as if he was stuck with her now and maybe that wasn't such a bad thing.

'How about Thursday morning?'

'Busy.'

'Tuesday?'

'Busy.'

'Er - ' he scratched his head. 'What about -'

'I can fit you in on Monday afternoons between four and six,' she said, folding her money into a voluminous purse. 'You'll need to get some new cloths and bath cleaner. I can't work with the ones you use.'

Prof nodded. 'Okay.'

'And you might think of investing in a new vacuum cleaner. Your one's had it.'

He bit his lip in an attempt to stop himself from laughing. 'I'll have a look this weekend,' he said, opening the front door and trying desperately not to push her through it. 'Thanks again, Mrs B.'

'Beaton,' she said, and he felt as if he had been.

CHAPTER 10

'You're *engaged?*' Rosanna exclaimed, her eyes doubling in size with what looked like horror rather than happiness. 'But you've only known him for - how long is it?'

'I don't know,' Elena lied. 'A few months. Anyway, it's long enough. I feel like I've known him all her life.' At least that part was true, she thought.

'But do you really know him? Trust him? Have you met his family yet?'

Elena sighed wearily. Of course, they were only talking about Mark. She hadn't dared break the news about the Reuben or Prof yet. One fiancé at a time, she thought.

'No. I haven't met his family but I don't necessarily think that's a bad thing. I mean, what if he turns out to have a mother like Irma Taccani?'

'Good point,' Rosanna conceded. 'But you have to go through these things – if you're making a lifelong commitment to someone, you can't get away with not meeting his family.'

'I just don't see the point in rushing. We just want to be us at the moment - is that so dreadful?'

Rosanna chewed her lip. 'Is he Catholic?'

'Rosanna!'

'Well, is he?'

'No! But neither am I.'

Rosanna tutted. 'What a way to talk! You show such little respect.'

There was a moment's silence.

'I thought you'd be pleased.'

Rosanna shifted uneasily on the sofa. She didn't look at all pleased; she looked as if she'd just discovered a porcupine in her knickers.

'Look!' she said, 'I have to go and meet a client and, when I come back, I want you to have thought long and hard about this, Elena. This is a life-changing decision, you know? You don't just get engaged on a whim. I know you! I know what you're like with men but you can't treat them just as you want. There has to be respect and truth and love.'

Elena sat perfectly still and perfectly silent. She didn't dare say anything, not when Rosanna was this worked up, but, boy, was Rosanna going to be furious with her when she found out the truth - that she had not only committed herself to one man but to *three*. What would she say then? Elena wondered, dread filling her heart.

With a sigh the north wind would have been proud of, Rosanna got up.

'Right. I'm going now. I want you to sit here and think about what you've just told me. *Really think!*' she said, waving her hand just like their mama used to wave her wooden spoon at her.

Elena's mouth dropped at her words as she watched Rosanna spring up from the sofa, and she couldn't think of anything to say in response so she simply watched as Rosanna swung her handbag over her shoulder and left the house. What a nightmare, she thought. Who did she think she was to talk to her like that? She'd forgotten how completely overbearing her sister could be.

Elena got up from the sofa and walked through to the kitchen. It was a relief to have the apartment to herself for a while. She looked out of the kitchen window onto a communal garden which was overlooked by other apartments where washing hung out of windows to dry in the bright spring sunshine. An old woman's hand shook a duster out into the garden but, other than her and cat-child, who Rosanna had let outside, there wasn't a soul around. It was so unlike her flat in London which looked out onto a high street that never slept. She loved the peace of Venice. The water seemed to absorb sound and some of the back streets seemed to be in a permanent siesta. It was just what she needed.

Elena closed her eyes to absorb the silence around her. There hadn't been many moments like this for a while. Life had been rather noisy. Her head had slowly been filled up with so much stuff that her thoughts had had nowhere to go but round and round in circles. Mark. Reuben. Prof. Three very special men who deserved nothing but one hundred percent of her attention. But they weren't getting that, were they?

There has to be respect and truth and love.

Rosanna's words swam in front of her again. She was right, wasn't she? Elena hadn't really thought this through at all. There was love, of course - her own interpretation of it which was obviously something different from her sister's - but respect and truth? Her three engagement rings showed nothing but her contempt for each of her fiancés. She had taken their tokens of love knowing that they were pledging themselves to her and her alone and, now that she thought about it, she could see how wrong it all was.

The funny thing was, it hadn't seemed wrong at the time. She'd thought that, by having three fiancés, she was giving more love and not less but she was sure Mark, Prof and Reuben wouldn't see it like that. But that was getting far too philosophical for her first day in Venice. She could allow herself at least one day off before she got down to the serious business of decision making.

She was just pouring herself a nice big apricot juice when the door bell rang. It was probably Rosanna, she thought, coming to say, 'and another thing …' and Elena was ready to give her a piece of her mind this time. But it wasn't Rosanna. It was Reuben.

At once, Elena's mind somersaulted into action. Reuben was in Venice. The man who wouldn't put his brush down to make her a cup of coffee after three hours' of her sitting for him had got on a plane and travelled a thousand miles to see her. If *he* had done that, then Mark and Prof were even more capable of turning up unannounced.

Elena looked nervously passed Reuben's shoulder in case all her fiancés were travelling together. What a horrendous thought! *Elena's Fiancés Tour Group. Discounts when three or more travel together.*

'Aren't you going to welcome me?' Reuben asked, obviously put out by Elena's puzzled expression.

'Of course!' she said, kissing him quickly. 'I'm just so amazed to see you! How did you find me?'

'You told me where you were staying,' he said, frowning. 'It wasn't that hard to find.'

Elena's eyes widened. So she had and, for once, he'd actually been listening to her.

He held her tight for a moment before he came into the entrance hall and followed her up the stairs.

'Bloody hell!' he said, his eyes taking in the sweeping splendour of the apartment. 'I mean – good grief! Does all this belong to one guy?'

Elena nodded. 'Sandro Constantini.'

'Never heard of him. Can't be that good if I haven't heard of him,' Reuben said, walking right into the room as if he owned it.

'Jealously will get you nowhere,' she chided.

'I'm not jealous,' he said, his eyes scanning the canvasses on display with the cautious scrutiny of a fellow artist. 'They're all pretty average, anyway. He must have a benefactor or something.'

Elena smiled. 'Reuben?'

'Yes?'

'Why are you here?'

He turned around and grinned, walking towards her and folding his arms around her waist. 'I came to see you,' he said, pushing his tongue into her ear.

She pushed him away. 'I know.'

He sighed. 'Okay,' he said, 'I felt bad about before - you know?'

She nodded, but already her mind was racing ahead to what Rosanna would say when she came back and found she'd smuggled a man into the apartment. 'But you didn't have to come all this way, you know. You could have just called me.'

'It's not the same though, is it? Anyway, I thought I could get a bit of painting in.'

Ah! Elena thought. The truth was coming out.

'This place is brilliant!' he continued. 'Do you think this Sandro guy would mind if I used his easels?'

'You can't stay, Reuben!'

'What? Why the hell not?'

'It's not my place! *I'm* not even meant to be here.'

'But who's going to know? Who's going to tell on us?'

'Rosanna! She's really strict about these things.'

'Elena, she's not even met me yet. I'm sure I can persuade her,' he said, his voice dark and silky.

Elena sighed, knowing it was going to be hard trying to convince him. 'She's not the sort of woman who can be wound round your little finger, you know.'

'But there's loads of bloody room here! I really don't see what the problem is.'

She looked at him. How could she tell him that her real worry was Prof and Mark turning up as well?

'The thing is,' she began, 'Rosanna doesn't know when Sandro will be back. He could turn up any day and I don't think he's the sort to welcome a group of strangers in his home.'

Reuben grimaced.

'I'm sorry,' she said, 'but why don't you book into a hotel somewhere?'

'You'll come with me, then?'

She bit her lip. 'Reuben, I came here to see Rosanna. I don't get to spend much time with her.'

'You're staying *here*?'

'Yes. You don't mind, do you? You'll get more work done without me hanging around, you know you will. And we can always meet up for lunch or dinner,' she said, trying to be as persuasive as possible.

'God!' he sighed. 'I don't know why I bothered coming!'

'Yes you do,' she said, aware that she had to change his mood pretty quickly or else they'd have another scene on their hands and Rosanna was bound to walk in right in the middle of it. 'It's because you love me.'

His frown eased a fraction and she wound her fingers through his hair.

'Okay,' he said at last. 'I'll book a hotel. *But*, I want to see you every day. I don't want you disappearing on me like you do back at home.'

'Whatever you say, Lord Reuben!' she smiled. His name was Reuben Lord but, with his slightly pompous nature, she'd always thought Lord Reuben far more suitable.

'All right if I have a shower?' he asked. 'Mr high and mighty wouldn't begrudge me that, would he?'

'As long as you're quick. There are towels under the sink, but only take one. I don't want Rosanna having an excuse to get worked up.'

Reuben groaned. 'God, I'm only having a shower. I'm not throwing a wild party!'

'I know. I know! It's just – well – you don't know what Rosanna can be like.'

He bent down to give her a kiss. 'And you'll get into something slightly more attractive, okay? I'm going to take you out to dinner.'

Elena hadn't really brought anything suitable for dining out in as she hadn't planned to do anything but eat pizza. She went upstairs and opened the wardrobe, whistling as she saw the collection of clothes. Rosanna had moved in good and proper.

Elena's hand pushed through the rich velvets and sumptuous silks. She was spoilt for choice. Besides, she reasoned, Rosanna hardly ever wore any of it which was a great shame because she could look like a movie star when she put her mind to it, but she chose to wear nothing but neutrals during the day. Elena had lost count of the number of black skirts and white shirts Rosanna owned. Occasionally, she'd break out into blue but nothing got more exciting than that, which was why Elena was so surprised to find crimsons, amethysts and golds in the wardrobe.

She pulled out a long velvet indigo dress and held it up for inspection. It was lucky that they were the same size because Elena didn't have the sort of money to buy such nice things at the moment.

She was just pulling the dress over her head when she heard voices downstairs. Rosanna was back. And she was talking to Reuben.

Elena rushed out of the room and ran down the stairs as quickly as was possible in the tight dress.

'Rosanna?' she called. 'Is that you?' It was a silly question but she just wanted to stop her from talking to Reuben.

'Yes! Of course it's me! Who else could it possibly be?'

Rosanna was standing in the middle of the living room, her hands on her hips and a deep frown etched across her forehead. She was staring at Reuben who was wearing nothing but a towel. And a scowl.

He turned and glared at her, his eyes dark and full of anger.

'Elena – *who the hell is Mark?*'

Elena's heart beat faster than was healthy as she stared at Reuben. 'What's she been saying to you?' she asked.

'Does it matter what Rosanna's said? I want to hear what *you* have to say, Elena!'

'He says he's not Mark, Elena, yet he's engaged to you!' Rosanna cried. 'How can this be? I don't understand!'

'Shut up a minute, Rosanna!'

'Don't you tell me to shut up! I go out for five minutes and come back to find a naked man in the apartment. A naked man who says he's your fiancé but who says his name's Reuben! I need to know what's going on here!'

'So do I!' Reuben shouted, his arms folded across his bare chest and his dark hair dripping down his shoulders.

'Reuben! I think you should put some clothes on,' Elena said, her voice incredibly calm considering she had no idea what she was going to say. 'Put some clothes on and I'll explain everything to you.'

'Talking of clothes,' Rosanna shouted, 'what the hell are you doing wearing my dress?'

CHAPTER 11

Rosanna had got the shock of her life when returning to the apartment.

'Elena?' she'd called as she'd walked up the steps into the living room. 'I hope you've been thinking about things whilst I've been out.'

Rosanna stopped in shock at the top of the steps at the sight of a half-naked man in the living room wearing nothing but a towel. Her mouth opened wide but no sound came out. She just stared. Who the hell was he? And what was he doing in Sandro's apartment? She'd only been out a few minutes and, as far as she knew, Elena hadn't left the apartment at all, so this man couldn't possibly be a burglar who just happened to have taken a shower.

'Who are you?' she managed at last.

'You must be Rosanna,' he said calmly, in perfect English.

'Yes,' she said, trying to work out who this drenched god was. And then she remembered her words of warning to Elena. How she'd explicitly told her not to go inviting anyone to stay. Of course! This must be her fiancé from England. Well, it seemed obvious to her that Elena had planned all this before she'd even come out here. She could see it all now - Elena had come on her own first and, what was the delightful English phrase she used - to *butter her up*? Then, her fiancé would show up and the two of them would have a fabulous free holiday at Sandro's expense. Elena hadn't wanted to spend time with her at all, had she? Rosanna was just part of some scheme of hers.

'I'm sorry about this,' the man said. 'I didn't plan this as an introduction.'

Rosanna shook her head. There was a slight blush around his cheeks and along his throat. She swallowed hard, trying not to let her eyes slide down his chest. He was incredibly attractive: raven-dark shoulder-length hair, wet from the shower - the water droplets sparkling like jewels; eyes dark as any Italian's but set in an alabaster face - not a sickly, pasty white like some English men's but that aristocratic white you see in old portraits in stately homes. Whatever Rosanna suspected about Elena, she couldn't blame *him* for it. He probably had no idea what he was letting himself in for by getting engaged to her.

'It's okay,' she said. 'Do you want another towel?' she asked and then bit her lip. What sort of a thing was that to say?

'I am dripping a bit, aren't she?'

'Oh! I didn't mean -'

'It's okay. No, I'd love another towel. Thank you.'

At least that had given her something to do - some temporary distraction from his half-naked godliness. It wasn't every day that she got to meet such attractive men, and without even having to leave the apartment. The men she usually got to meet were overweight, overpaid businessmen with great, fat hands and stomachs that bulged up against their easels. She couldn't help feeling just a little bit envious of Elena.

Rosanna peeped at his reflection in the bathroom mirror and he caught her eye. She felt herself blushing. This was ridiculous. What was she thinking of? This was her sister's fiancé and here she was having all sorts of impure thoughts about him! About how masculine his arms looked, and how his waist was so slim, how long his fingers were and...

She shook her head and bit her lip. She wasn't going to go there; she refused to let her mind wander into realms it had no business wandering in. And then she remembered her manners.

'I believe congratulations are in order,' she said, the fact that this was her future brother-in-law standing before her dawning on her at last.

A beautiful smile crossed his face and his dark eyes glittered. 'Oh! Elena's told you already?'

'Yes!' she said, pulling a white towel out for him.

'Thank you,' he said, roughly drying his hair before brushing the towel over his chest and arms.

'Have you set a date yet?' she dared to ask.

'Er - no. Not yet. That's kind of why I've come out here,' he said, suddenly looking quite shy.

'Oh? Are you thinking of getting married in Venice?'

He smiled. 'I hadn't thought about that, but it's a great idea.'

She smiled back at him, trying to picture him in a gondola with

Elena. 'It would be very romantic,' she said, a wave of jealousy engulfing her. Corrado hadn't once talked about getting engaged let alone setting a date for a wedding but she couldn't really blame him. She hadn't exactly been the most loving of girlfriends of late. Still, it was strange to think of Elena getting married. Rosanna had always known she would, of course, but this was all happening so fast. Hadn't she just met this man?

'You work at the same college as her, don't you?' she asked, trying to steer the conversation back to small talk.

He frowned, his dark eyes seeming darker all of a sudden. 'No,' he said. 'I'm an artist.'

'Really? Oh!' she blinked in surprise. She'd obviously got confused somewhere along the line. She'd thought Elena's fiancé was a teacher - like her. 'So you teach art at the college?' she asked, taking his wet towel from him and walking back through to the living room.

There was a pause before he answered. 'No! I'm an artist,' he said again.

She stared at him and she could feel her mouth dropping open once more. 'But you're Mark, no?'

'NO!' he shouted. '*I'm Reuben.*'

'*Reuben?*'

'Yes!' he said, his hands firm on his hips and his face set rigid.

'Oh!' she said. What else could she say? It was one of those moments when you wish to become instantly invisible, when you'd give anything to take back what you'd just said. But there was no getting out of this now. Her words were out and this Reuben guy, whom she'd thought was Mark, was expecting some kind of explanation from her and she didn't have one.

'What *the hell's* going on? I thought you said Elena told you we were engaged?'

Rosanna's heartrate accelerated. Something was terribly wrong here. Had she made a huge mistake? Was she confused? She looked around the apartment, wondering where on earth Elena was, and it was at that moment that she waltzed down from the bedroom. It got a bit confusing then because, for a few minutes, they were all shouting at each other at once.

'Elena! Who the hell is Mark?'

'Mark? What have you been saying, Rosanna?'

'Don't blame me! What am I meant to think when I come back to find a stranger in the apartment wearing nothing but a towel?'

'Is this Mark someone you work with? Is that why you never let me meet you at the school?'

'Don't be ridiculous, Reuben! Mark has got nothing to do with-'

'Your sister seems to think that you're engaged to him!'

And on it went: questions, threats, recriminations until:

'*QUIET!*' Elena suddenly yelled.

Rosanna bit back what she was about to say next and decided it was probably better to say no more until this was sorted out - one way or another.

'Listen!' Elena began. 'There's been a dreadful misunderstanding here. Reuben - please don't look so serious. I told Rosanna about our engagement this morning.'

'So, what's all this about some bloke called Mark?' he interrupted.

It was exactly the question Rosanna wanted to ask her.

'He's just someone I work with. I don't know, we were just talking about my job and he came up. But that's it.'

Rosanna glared at Elena but she fired back a look which warned her away from their discussion of that morning.

'How come Rosanna thought you were engaged to this Mark, then?'

Elena shrugged. 'Rosanna?'

Great! It was pass the buck time. Rosanna might have guessed. She felt so angry. How was she meant to know that the half-naked man in the middle of Sandro's apartment wasn't Mark, her sister's fiancé? One minute, Elena was telling her about this man she'd met at work and, after what seemed to her to be an extraordinarily short space of time, got engaged to. She'd shown her the ring too - a beautiful diamond solitaire. A little smaller than she'd imagined Elena ending up with but lovely all the same. Then, after chiding her for her behaviour, she went out for a few brief moments and came back to find a semi-naked man padding around the apartment. A man called Reuben to whom her sister was engaged. Was she going mad?

For a few tense moments, she let them stew whilst her mind tumbled. Half of her wanted to expose and embarrass Elena - to flush out her lies and find out exactly what was going on; the other half - the sisterly half - got the better of her and, like a fool, she heard herself backing her sister's ridiculous story.

'I'm sorry,' she heard herself saying. 'I must have got confused.

We had a few drinks last night and, what with not getting enough sleep, I had the most horrendous headache this morning. I've obviously got everything muddled.'

Reuben nodded sagely. Rosanna was an appalling actress but her lie was obviously what he wanted to believe.

'You see?' Elena said, her tone jovial but jarring to Rosanna's ears. 'You can be so silly and jealous sometimes,' she said, hugging Reuben and kissing his cheek.

Rosanna couldn't quite believe what she was witnessing and she had an uncontrollable urge to slap her sister. She didn't know what was going on but she'd wager Elena was up to no good.

CHAPTER 12

Mark wasn't savouring his flight to Venice. There weren't many people in the world that could get him on a plane and, even though it was only a two-hour flight, he couldn't help wishing that Elena had a sister in Norfolk instead of Italy.

Barney's girlfriend had come good with his three hundred pounds but he wasn't likely to see much change from it if he had to find a hotel. He was really hoping that Elena would let him stay in the apartment. He smiled to himself. Venice was meant to be one of the most romantic cities in the world. He had visions of them walking through the streets as if they were honeymooners. They might even want to go back for their honeymoon, he thought, trying not to think how many thousands of feet in the air he was at that precise moment and also refusing to think about how much this wedding and honeymoon were going to cost. It would mean taking out a loan and the thought of that made his stomach flip. But Elena deserved nothing but the best. For a moment, he tried to imagine her in a wedding dress – something floaty yet elegant – like Liv Tyler in *Lord of the Rings*. Yes, he liked that idea. He'd already been checking out venues for the reception and had found a perfect coaching inn in the Thames Valley with the prettiest garden looking out over the river. Well, if you were going to get into debt, you might as well do it with style, he reckoned.

They hadn't talked much about where they were going to live but it was pretty obvious that his grim flat wasn't in the running. He'd never been to Elena's. She'd assured him that her flat was worse than his and that it wouldn't do at all as a marital home so he guessed they'd be looking for something else over the summer.

Mark had wondered about asking Tomi about a pay rise but he'd thought better of it when he was told by another of the teachers that the last person to do that had been 'let go' and replaced by someone half his age for, presumably, half the salary. They'd have to come up with something else. Maybe they could teach some private lessons. He'd always been rather keen on the idea but couldn't possibly think to do it in his present accommodation.

He closed his eyes and tried to picture the kind of apartment he imagined them living in: a light, spacious loft conversion with pale wooden floors, white walls and windows looking out over more expensive suburbs than his present flat did. Three or four bedrooms would be nice: one for them, a spare for friends and family, a study, and one for – he grinned – the future.

Maybe they could use the study as a classroom – setting up their very own school in miniature. They could charge a better hourly rate and there wouldn't be the hassle of early mornings on the tube and the stress of actually getting Tomi to pay them at the end of each month. They could stumble out of bed after an early session under Egyptian cotton sheets, share a shower, cook breakfast in the sleek steel kitchen and then greet the students who'd all be incredibly well-behaved and stinking rich.

Mark fidgeted in his seat as he began to get excited about his dream future with Elena. That was the great thing about dreams – you could have the most expensive taste in the world and it wouldn't cost you a penny. He dreaded to think what the reality would be but he wasn't going to think about that now. Instead, he focussed on the next few days ahead and what he was hoping to achieve.

It was only over the last couple of weeks that he'd become aware of Elena's multiple persona. He didn't really know how to explain it but he got the feeling that she was many different people all at once. He knew everybody could be like that: who didn't become the downtrodden child when talking to a parent, or a sycophantic sop when speaking to a bank manager? But it was more than that with Elena.

For the most part, he got the vibrant vixen who was so full of energy that it practically spilled out of her but there were times when somebody else would flash from her eyes – a distant, more thoughtful person – somebody she tried to keep hidden but who, nevertheless, kept trying to escape.

'What's the matter?' he'd asked her the first time he'd seen her with a look in her eyes of such mournful proportions that it had almost made him cry.

'Nothing!' she'd said, and her mouth had heaved into a huge smile again and the look was gone. He'd caught her off-guard but she refused to acknowledge it, and that wouldn't do. If they were going to be married, if they were planning a future together, then he needed to know all about her.

There was nothing about his mundane life she needed to know. An only child with divorced parents who'd both gone on to marry perfect replicas of their exes, he'd spent all his life in West London with a quick detour to Edinburgh University before becoming a teacher. He felt dull, dull, dull, and he wondered what somebody as vibrant as Elena was doing with someone like him. They said opposites attracted but he felt as if he were a bungalow next to her palace. But this palace obviously had hidden hallways – maybe even a prison or two – and it was up to him to find out exactly what she was hiding behind so perfect a façade.

CHAPTER 13

Reuben had to admit that Elena argued a convincing case as to why Rosanna thought she was engaged to some teacher called Mark rather than an artist called Reuben, but he still had his suspicions. After all, she hadn't exactly greeted him with open arms. He thought he could've at least expected a warmer welcome from her after having travelled such a long way - or at least a welcome somewhere above tepid - but no - she'd been suspicious and, unless he was becoming really paranoid, she'd looked guilty. She'd kept looking over his shoulder as if she'd expected him to have brought somebody with him and, when he'd kissed her, it had felt tense and awkward.

As they left the apartment, he confronted her.

'I don't think you're telling me the truth, Elena,' he said, kicking his suitcase which was also behaving badly.

She rolled her eyes at him. 'You can think what you like but I *am* telling you the truth. I'm engaged to *you!*'

'Me and me alone?' he asked. Was it his imagination or did he see a very pronounced swallow when he asked her that question?

'Of *course* you alone! What do you take me for?'

'Then where's my ring? Why aren't you wearing my ring?' he asked, noticing the missing rubies.

'It's *my* ring,' she corrected. 'And I never wear rings when travelling. You don't know who might be eyeing up your valuables.'

Reuben supposed that was a fairly reasonable argument and yet he couldn't help feeling that she was hiding something.

'I've got the ring upstairs,' she said. 'I can go and put it on – right now – if you want me to,' she said, turning around and making to return to the apartment.

Of course, he shook his head. 'Don't bother,' he said. 'But make sure you have it on tomorrow'

'I will!' she replied and her eyes flickered with sudden mischief. 'I'll be wearing your ring and nothing else if you manage to find yourself a hotel.'

He smiled. Elena always knew exactly what to say and he felt his suspicion ebbing away. He even let her persuade him to book into the Hotel Danieli which was extravagant even by his standards. The Venetian-red palazzo seemed to glow in the rich afternoon light and he had to admit that it was beautiful.

'It's *so* romantic,' she cooed as they entered through the revolving doors and took in the sumptuous splendour of the foyer. So he booked a double room with a view out across the lagoon. As he took in the Murano glass chandeliers, the antiques, the pink marble and the gold leaf columns, he knew that he'd be able to knock out a few pictures during his stay and thus recoup any money spent.

Once in the room overlooking the Bacino di San Marco, they had sex. He couldn't use the phrase 'making love' because that, to him, implied something long and luxurious, and what Elena and he had was fast and furious; it left them breathing heavily and sweating profusely.

As he was gazing up at the ornate ceiling, Elena propped herself up on an elbow and, stroking an idle finger through his hair, asked, 'You do believe me, don't you?'

'What?' Reuben was still lost in the land of lust.

'That you're my one and only.'

'Yes,' he said but, quite frankly, at that moment in time, he would have said anything she'd wanted him to say.

They kissed and fell asleep and, after she left, he showered, towelling himself dry for the third time that day. Despite the sumptuous surroundings, he felt uneasy and restless and there was only one way out of that. Picking up his sketchbook, he began to draw. Black, silken hair. Soft, dark eyes. Gentle curves of shoulders and breasts. He drew them quickly and confidently because he'd been paying them so much attention.

He filled page after page until the light in the room turned into the rich amber of early evening and then he flicked back through the pages. She was beautiful, he thought, as he looked at the images he'd caught with a few brief strokes of charcoal.

Finally, he closed the sketchbook before closing his eyes but it wasn't any good because the images were burned into his brain. She was beautiful. It was the only word he could think of to describe her, and, at that moment, he felt as if he couldn't live without her.

He sighed a long and weary sigh as he whispered her name under his breath.

'*Rosanna!*'

CHAPTER 14

Elena had to admit that she was shocked and shaken by Reuben's unexpected visit and felt sure she had betrayed herself terribly. Normally, her life was beautifully orchestrated; with three fiancés, you couldn't live any other way. Of course, she could never fully predict what Reuben, Mark and Prof were going to request from day to day but she was always the master of control. A quick: *I'm sorry, I can't see you today – something's come up at work*, usually did the trick. She'd never really found herself in any sticky situations, which was lucky, she knew. Maybe she'd subconsciously chosen three very understanding men but, with Reuben's arrival, it seemed that things were beginning to unravel and that her past might be about to catch up with her. It was something that certainly seemed to preoccupy Rosanna.

'What the hell is going on here?' she'd hissed under her breath as soon as Reuben had disappeared to get dressed.

'Shush! He'll hear you!'

'I don't care. I think he should be made aware of what's going on here - whatever it is!'

Elena pushed Rosanna to the far end of the living room and they sat down on one of the enormous sofas.

'Just listen - *quietly!*' she said.

'You lied to me, Elena! You lied to your own sister!'

'I didn't lie to you,' she said, trying to remain calm. One of them had to be calm.

'How can you say that? How can you try and cover one lie with another? You told me you were engaged to some guy called Mark - some teacher at your school. That's what you said! You think you can play games with me? You think you can make fun of me?'

'I'm not! Rosanna - just listen, will you?'

'And then you tell me that this Reuben is your fiancé! And he's under the impression you're engaged too.'

'We *are* engaged,' she said quietly.

'So why did you say you were engaged to this Mark person, then?'

'Because I am.'

Rosanna blinked and then her eyes stretched wide and her mouth fell open. 'What are you saying?'

Elena took a deep breath before she answered very slowly and very calmly - to make sure that she was understood this time. 'I'm saying that I'm engaged to Reuben and to Mark.'

There was a dreadful moment of complete silence.

'Say something,' Elena said at last.

'What do you want me to say?' Rosanna said in a voice that was so cold and quiet that it made Elena's whole body chill in response. 'You're about to become a bigamist - what is there for me to say?'

Elena sighed. 'I'm not going to become a bigamist! I'm only engaged to them. I'm not going to marry them both!'

'Then what do you think you're doing? I don't understand it! I don't understand *you!*'

'Do you think I did this on purpose?' Elena asked. 'You think this is some sort of game of mine? Well, it isn't! It's just a situation I got myself into and I thought you might be able to help me out of it. That's why I came here in the first place. I wanted *your help*. I was going to tell you about it all. I'd never lie to you, Rosanna!' she said, wincing at her hollow words as she thought about Prof and how she hadn't dared to reveal his presence in her life yet.

'You want me to help you with this mess?' Rosanna asked and her tone was finally a little calmer and a little less chilly.

'Yes,' Elena said, appealing to the virtuous side of her sister's character; the side that would want to save her soul at whatever cost to herself. 'I've messed up - big time - and really don't know what to do. I love them both, you see.'

Rosanna's forehead crinkled and Elena could almost read her thoughts: her shock, her anger, her great disappointment and, finally, her musings as to how she could save Elena from yet another sinful situation.

'Are you sure?'

Elena nodded. 'It is possible, you know.' Rosanna shook her head but Elena took her hand in hers and repeated, 'I love them both.'

Rosanna looked completely stunned for a moment, as if she couldn't have been more surprised if Elena had told her she was really a mermaid and that her time had come to head back out into the lagoon. But she didn't get a chance to respond as Reuben, fully clothed, walked through from the bathroom.

'Ready?' he asked, walking towards the sofa.

Elena let go of Rosanna's hand and, for a moment, she sat perfectly still and Elena half-feared that she was going to say something.

'Are you all right?' Reuben asked Rosanna with a gentle smile.

Rosanna stared back at him. 'I'm fine, thank you,' she said.

'It must be strange for you,' Reuben said, 'having a complete stranger turn up and tell you he's your sister's fiancé.'

Again, there was an agonising pause before she answered. Elena really wished she wouldn't do that: it made her so nervous.

'It's *all* very strange,' Rosanna said, holding Reuben's gaze with hers but aiming her words at Elena.

'Okay!' Elena said, getting up. 'Time to find somewhere for you to stay.'

Reuben and Elena had left the apartment and, as soon as they were out of earshot, he started with the questions. It didn't take long for her to persuade him that he was her one and only and, when she saw the relief and belief flooding into his eyes, she sincerely wished that she was telling the truth.

Dear Reuben. Her passionate artist who followed her out to Venice to say he was sorry. There weren't many men who'd do that and yet she'd been lucky enough to find one and look at how she treated him, She didn't even have the decency to two-time him like a normal floozy, but three-timed him instead. How low could a girl go?

She was delighted when he'd booked into the Hotel Danieli because it was conveniently placed on the opposite side of Venice from Sandro's apartment. That, she thought, would allow her the space she needed.

'I'll come and see you tomorrow,' she'd promised him after a marathon sex session and vowing to herself that, in the meantime, she'd have done her best to sort things out.

Leaving the Danieli, she turned right and walked the short distance to San Marco. She looked out to the island of San Giorgio Maggiore. The early evening light had turned the water bronze and gave everything an ethereal glow. She'd never seen such a beautiful light before and she felt tears pricking her eyes as if she didn't deserve to see such beauty. She blinked them away. Tears weren't going to solve any problems. Tears were for the hopeless and she wasn't hopeless: she was a rational woman who'd stumbled into a rather unusual situation but, surely, if she could get herself into such a situation, she could jolly well get herself out of it?

Yes, she thought, *think rationally, think positively* but, most of all, *think!* She smiled - she was beginning to sound like Rosanna.

It was strange but Elena's feet seemed to know where they were going long before she did. She left San Marco, leading lightly through the shop-lined alleys before climbing the wooden steps of the Accademia Bridge. Then, she wound her way through more alleys and over smaller canals until, finally, they stopped – outside Viviana's, the mask shop.

She hadn't thought to go there – not consciously anyway, and her eyes widened in surprise when she realised where she was. She hadn't really wanted to go in the first time so why had she come there a second time? And then, her eyes fixed on the golden mask – the very one that had arrested her attention before. It wasn't alone in the window, of course, it had to jostle for space like the smallest child in a large family, but it was the only one she took any notice of.

Her hand hovered over the door handle for a moment before she opened it, hearing the merry bell tinkling again, and closing the door behind her.

Silence.

She looked around, half-expecting to see the old, white-haired man again but, like the time before, there was nobody about. She took the opportunity to walk over to the shop window and stretched her hand out over the myriad masks to reach the golden one. No sooner had her fingers closed around it than she heard a familiar voice behind her.

'Can I help you?'

Elena turned around, dropping the mask back into place.

'Sorry,' she said automatically, feeling awkward at having tried to help herself to this man's goods.

'Is there a particular mask that *draws you*?' he asked and she was immediately arrested by his use of the phrase draws you. He didn't say, 'Is there a particular mask you like?' His phrase, 'draws you' was very precise, very perceptive, she felt.

'Actually, yes,' she said, pointing to the golden mask.

He joined her and, peering slowly into the window as if he were afraid he might startle the mask if he moved any quicker, he looked at the one she'd singled out.

'Oh, no!' he said, shaking his head vehemently as if he meant to rid himself of it.

'But that's the one that draws me!' she said, repeating his own words for emphasis. 'That's *the one!*'

'No, no,' he said again, and she'd never heard the word 'no' said quite so emphatically. 'Not *quite* right for you.'

'How do you mean?' she asked, secretly thinking he was rather mad and that he was merely steering her towards something more elaborate and more expensive.

'I have just the mask for you,' he said and, with that, he walked towards the door at the back of the shop and disappeared just as she heard the bell tinkle above the main door.

'My husband is serving you?' an elderly woman with a shock of white hair asked her.

Elena nodded, marvelling at the fact that the woman looked like a perfect copy of her husband only with flaring hips and a fine bosom at right angles to her tiny frame.

'*Stefano!*' she called and Elena's eardrums trembled at the power of her voice. How could tiny people boom so, she wondered? Surely there wasn't enough room in her frame to house such a huge voice. 'You have a lovely lady waiting for you!'

She heard Stefano muttering something to himself as he came into the shop again.

'My husband!' the lady said, shaking her head from side to side. 'The only man in Venice who could leave the side of such a beautiful woman!'

'Is she?' Stefano said. 'I hadn't noticed,' he added, winking at Elena before kissing his wife. 'What man could notice other beauties when he has a wife like you?'

'Ah! You great fool!' she laughed, pushing him away and shaking her head again. 'I'm Viviana,' she said turning to Elena once again.

'Elena,' she said, and shook the tiny hand she proffered.

'And what is Elena looking for?'

She shrugged her shoulders, not really knowing how to answer. But she needn't have worried because Stefano answered before she had the chance to concoct something suitable.

'Elena was looking at the mask in the window,' he said, and his wife nodded immediately.

She frowned. There were dozens of masks in the window. How could she possibly know which one she was interested in?

'The gold one,' she explained.

'Yes,' Viviana said. 'The little half-mask.'

Elena could feel her frown deepening in a most unbecoming manner. 'Yes. How did you know?'

'Viviana knows everything!' she chuckled. 'But that's not quite the mask for you, is it?'

'That's just what I was telling her,' Stefano said.

'And what did you find for Elena?' Viviana asked.

Stefano stepped forward and offered up a plain white box for her inspection and Viviana nodded in agreement as if she could see the mask contained within.

'Open it,' he said, so she did. She pulled away a couple of layers of tissue paper to discover an almost identical mask to that in the shop window, so why had he made such a fuss about finding this one for her? She picked it up and smiled as the gold shone brightly.

'It's a mezza neutra,' Stefano explained. 'Do you like it?'

'I do,' she said, turning it around in her hands. 'It's so light and,' she paused, 'it feels - warm!'

Stefano nodded as if he'd expected her to say those very words.

'Almost human,' she added, a child-like excitement suddenly overwhelming her. 'Can I try it on?' she asked, lifting it up to her face before he had a chance to answer but, quick as lightning, his hand stopped her.

'No, no, Elena. Not yet. It is my gift to you. You can try it on later but not here. Not in the shop.'

'But how do you know it will fit me?'

He smiled a tiny, knowing smile. 'It will fit you,' he said. 'But you must try it on when you are alone.'

His answer perplexed her and confirmed her opinion that he was completely mad.

'Please, you must let me pay for it,' she said.

He shook his head.

'Never turn down a gift from Stefano. It would be very bad luck,' Viviana explained.

Elena smiled. She already had quite enough to contend with, she thought, without inviting a dose of bad luck too, so she graciously accepted his gift.

'All I ask is that you'll let me know how you get on with it.'

She smiled again. 'I promise,' she said before leaving the shop with the golden mask tucked under her arm.

CHAPTER 15

Mark's eyes were dazzled by it all. Everything around him seemed golden. Perhaps it was because he'd left behind a particularly grey day in London, but he felt as if he'd landed in paradise. When he got off the boat, he pulled his rucksack onto his back and stood absolutely still for a moment, looking out across the lagoon. The last of the sun's rays streaked across the water like a comet's tail. It was mesmeric, and the water looked so inviting, you could almost be lulled into jumping right in for a swim. You wouldn't, of course. This was Venice, after all.

He felt rather pleased with himself for having the bright idea of visiting. It was going to be a great week, he thought, and that sunset was very auspicious.

The apartment was easy to find as he had Elena's directions from her sister. What he hadn't got, though, was a phone number, so he hadn't been able to ring ahead and check that firstly, someone would be in and, secondly, that he'd be welcome. Ringing the bell on the wall of the rather ugly exterior, he prepared himself for disappointment. If she wasn't in, he'd just have to find a cheap hotel, if there was such a thing in Venice.

It didn't take long before he heard the door opening and he quickly raked a hand through his hair. At least he'd remembered to shave for once.

He smiled as a woman greeted him. She had the same lustrous dark hair as Elena and her eyes were large and a deep, deep brown. She was about the same height but her figure was fuller.

'Rosanna?' he enquired, his eyes taking in her face which was quite lovely if a little sullen-looking.

'Yes,' she said. She didn't look at all welcoming.

'I'm Mark. Mark Theodore. Elena's fiancé.' He smiled at her but he didn't receive one in return. 'I work with Elena,' he explained.

'Yes! Yes!' she said at last. 'Elena's told me.'

'Phew! I was beginning to get a bit worried then!'

She stared at him for a moment more. 'You'd better come in.'

'Thanks,' he said. 'Look, I know this is a bit unexpected.'

She turned around from her position ahead of him on the stairs. 'Don't worry. I'm used to the unexpected with Elena.'

Mark laughed but he noticed that her tone was deadly serious. 'She *can* be unpredictable,' he agreed.

Rosanna said something but it was in Italian and he couldn't make out what it was and didn't like to ask in case he wasn't meant to have heard.

'Blimey!' he said as they reached the top of the stairs into what could only be described as the biggest living space he'd ever seen. It was the size of his entire flat and the thin Finn's English school rolled into one.

'Yes,' Rosanna agreed.

'How come I've never heard of this artist before? If he owns something like this, he must be pretty well-known.'

'He's still working on the getting well-known bit but his art sells for a fortune here.'

'I can see,' he said, dumping his rucksack and walking over to look at some of the canvases.

'Please, don't touch anything over there. Most of the oils are still drying.'

Mark nodded as his eyes roved over the pictures stacked up against the wall. They were mostly nudes and, looking closer, he noticed that they were mostly of Rosanna. He cleared his throat, suddenly feeling rather hot and uncomfortable. It felt almost incestuous looking at nude paintings of his future sister-in-law and he hurriedly looked for something else to comment on in the room.

'Those are his latest,' Rosanna said as he examined some paintings on a long trestle table that looked like a fallen oak tree.

'Yeah?' Mark peered closely. 'What's this business with the cat?'

There was a moment's pause before Rosanna suddenly burst out laughing. Mark looked up at her, wondering how, one minute, she could be statue-cold and, the next, sound like she'd just heard the funniest joke in the world.

'What is it? What did I say?'

'The cat!' she said, her hysteria subsiding slightly and her features rearranging themselves back to normality. 'That bloody cat!'

'What about it?' he asked, feeling thick. He didn't quite understand what she'd found so funny.

'It's Sandro's pet. His darling *Bimba*. Horrible animal - appears in all his paintings - even the portraits. It makes me sneeze but he insists on having it in the house.'

'I don't see it.'

'No,' she said. 'When Sandro's away, the cat will play - *outside!*' she said and then started laughing again.

This time, he couldn't help but join in. Her face fell apart when she laughed and her joy was contagious. If they hadn't both heard the door open then, they might both have ended up in a heap of helpless tears on the floor.

'Elena?' he said quietly to Rosanna.

She nodded.

'Listen. I want to surprise her,' he whispered, grabbing his rucksack from view.

'Oh, I think you'll manage that,' Rosanna said, the laughter banished from her face once more.

'Rosanna? Is that you?' Elena called from the lobby and Mark felt himself smiling at the sound of her voice. It felt an age since he'd last heard it.

'Yes.'

'Who's that with you?' Elena called, her feet clicking on the stone steps.

Mark waved his hand at Rosanna in a shushing motion.

'Nobody,' she said. 'I was just laughing at something on the television.'

Mark blew a kiss to Rosanna, hid behind the great oak desk, and waited.

CHAPTER 16

Somewhere between leaving Viviana's and the Campo San Giovanni e Paolo, Elena must have taken a wrong turn but the strange thing was, she didn't feel at all anxious - not like she would have back in London. It was probably all part of the romance of being in a different city. She guessed tourists never knowingly looked for the danger lurking beneath the fine architecture and magnificent views. Who wanted to think about pickpockets in the middle of paradise? Anyway, she knew she was fairly close to home now and it wasn't as if she were alone: she had her mask with her for company.

Elena looked at the box stashed safely under her arm and couldn't resist taking a quick peek. In the light of a small campo, she opened the lid and let her eyes feast on the golden face gazing up at her from out of its bedding of soft tissue. She couldn't help but smile. What was she doing with a mask? She'd always laughed at people who'd worn them. Yet something had burned within her and she simply hadn't been able to think about leaving the shop without it.

She wondered why, with all the beautiful and fantastical masks at Viviana's, she had been drawn to one of the plainest. Even though it was the most beautiful gold she'd ever seen and was edged with the most delicate of details, and boasted a fancy scroll above its left cheek, it was fairly plain compared to the rest that had been on display.

She let her finger trace along the scroll and, for a moment, she swore her fingers took on a golden hue. Should she try it on? Stefano had seemed keen that she should. Hadn't that been the condition of the gift - that she try it on and let him know how it went? She smiled. What on earth did he imagine would happen to her by simply putting on a mask? He was a funny man. Still, the temptation was proving too much.

Her fingers fastened around the mask and she was just pulling it out from its bedding when a dog, no bigger than a rat, ran right between her legs. She was so startled that she almost dropped the mask in shock. Quickly replacing it and putting the lid back on the box, she couldn't help feeling rather self-conscious as a man lumbered by in pursuit of his rat-dog. She mumbled a quick apology as if it was her fault and then decided to get her map out. It was time she found her way back.

At least it would be nice and quiet when she got back, she thought, realising she was only a couple of streets away. She'd probably have a few more pressing questions from Rosanna but she was hoping that she'd had time to calm down by now. With any luck, she might even have thought of a way for her to get out of her prickly predicament.

She thought of Reuben back at the Danieli. He'd wanted her to stay with him, she knew, and she was mean not to, but she had told him that she'd come away for some space and that he had to respect that. Besides, she could tell that he'd been itching to get his sketchbook out. And dear Mark. What would he be doing back in Harrow? Probably down the pub with his mates before going back home to one of his horrible microwaved meals. She couldn't really blame him, mind. Nobody would want to cook on that disgusting cooker in his flat.

And sweet Prof. What would he be doing now? she wondered, as she found her way into the long, thin calle that would lead her back to the apartment. He'd probably be having dinner at his favourite restaurant, a pile of essays to read next to a bottle of red wine. She hoped he wasn't reading her latest attempt and wondering where her bibliography was because she hadn't written one.

Out of her three special men, Reuben was the one who'd made the effort when it counted and that meant a lot to her. But did it mean that he was *the one*? Did getting on a plane to Venice constitute true love? Or were his motives jealousy, lust and a realisation that, if he did some painting, it could be tax deductible? But wasn't all that part of what she loved about Reuben? His drive, his passion, his ambition and dogged determination were so admirable. Prof had those very same traits but his were hidden under the surface. He wasn't in-your-face like Reuben; he was subtle, silent and self-assured.

Elena couldn't help getting a warm feeling when she thought of Prof and her heart went out to him sitting on his own with nothing but a pile of essays for company. Digging in her handbag, she found her mobile phone. It was a well-kept secret from her fiancés as she couldn't quite contemplate three men being able to find her wherever she went. She dialled Prof's number and waited.

'Hello,' he said a moment later.

'Prof? It's Elena!'

'Elena! How are you? Is everything okay?'

'Yes - fine! I'm in Venice.'

'I know. I miss you!'

She bit her lip. He missed her. 'I miss you too. I wish you were here. You'd love it. Everything's so beautiful.'

'Have you been sight-seeing yet?'

Her mind tumbled back to the interior of the Danieli and she could feel herself blushing with guilt. 'Not really. Not yet. I went to Dorsoduro today and bought a mask.'

'A mask?' she heard him chuckle. 'Whatever for?'

'I don't know,' she said, suddenly feeling silly for sharing that with him. 'Where are you?'

'At *Reggie's*,' he said.

'I had a feeling you'd be there.'

'You've caught me in between a very fine pasta dish and tiramisu - in honour of you. I'm with you in spirit.'

'And I bet you've got your essays with you,' she said and then promptly wished she hadn't. Why had she tempted fate like that?

'Ah! Yes. Elena, I'm glad you mentioned that. I wanted to have a word with you about your essay.'

'Pardon?' she said.

'It's about your bibliography. You don't appear to have-'

'Sorry! I can't hear you? There's something wrong with the line.'

'Elena?'

'Prof? Look, I'll ring you back when I can,' she said, and hung up, turning her phone off in case he tried to ring her back. Putting it away, she headed for the apartment without any further delays.

Letting herself in with the spare key Rosanna had given her, she could have sworn she heard voices from upstairs.

'Rosanna? Is that you?' she called.

'Yes.'

'Who's that with you?' she asked, climbing the stairs.

'Nobody,' she said. 'I was just laughing at something on the television.'

Elena reached the top and she greeted her with a kiss. 'I'm sorry I'm back so late.'

'I was getting worried. I thought you'd got lost.'

'I did for a bit,' she admitted, stopping as she noticed Rosanna rolling her eyes. 'What? What is it?'

Rosanna jerked her head in the direction of the oak table and her face contorted in the strangest of manners.

'*What?*' Elena asked, puzzled by her curious behaviour.

'*SURPRISE!*' a voice suddenly shouted from behind the table. And she was. In fact, for a moment, she was sure her heart had stopped. It was Mark.

'Rosanna!' he chided. 'You spoilt the surprise! What did you go and do that for?' he asked. But Elena knew exactly why she'd done it. It was to prevent her from casually talking about Reuben.

'Mark!' It was all she could manage for a moment.

'Elena!'

Elena's heart was thumping in her ears as he hugged her.

'God, Elena! It's so good to see you!'

Think, Elena, think, Elena, think, think, *think!* She mustn't act too surprised. She mustn't try and throw him out at the earliest opportunity. She mustn't mention Reuben!

'This is such a surprise!' she said.

'I found this!' Mark said, producing a piece of crumpled paper from his pocket as if it would explain everything.

Elena took it from him and recognised her own handwriting. 'It's the address of this place. I wondered where it had got to!'

'You must've dropped it on purpose, eh?' he said with a wink.

She smiled up at the way his mind worked. Never, in a million years, would she have dropped it on purpose. But she couldn't tell him that - not after he'd travelled all that way and spent money she knew he didn't have on the air fare. 'A Freudian slip - right out of the pocket?' she suggested to him.

He grinned. 'That's what I reckon. Anyway, what man would let his fiancé get away with a trip to Venice on her own?'

Elena didn't dare catch Rosanna's eye at that comment. 'You're right,' she said. 'I should have asked you to come with me.'

'Yes. You should've!' he chastised, bending forward and kissing her.

Elena felt his arms wrap around her and she had to admit that it felt good. This was Mark, after all. Dear, sweet Mark who would do all her photocopying for her at school so that she could nip out to buy new lipsticks during break time.

'But where are you going to stay?' she asked, practicality raising its ugly head.

Mark's eyebrows rose a fraction and she saw his glance take in the huge apartment. 'Well, I was kind of hoping-' he stopped, looking across at Rosanna.

He was right, of course. How could they think of making him find a hotel at this time of night? Elena turned and smiled at Rosanna, hoping, for once, that she could read her mind.

'It's pretty dark out there. I wouldn't want Mark to get lost like I did. We can find him somewhere to stay first thing tomorrow.'

Rosanna chewed her lip and sighed. 'Okay!' she relented. 'But,' she added, holding a baton-like finger up in the air in warning, 'if Sandro comes back, you'll have to do the explaining.'

'Thanks, Rosanna!'

'There's a single bed through there,' she said, pointing to a door that led to the spare bedroom.

'A single, eh? Won't that be a bit of a squash?' Mark whispered to Elena.

'Mark!'

'Where are you sleeping, then?'

'Upstairs, with Rosanna.'

'Oh!' Mark said, looking crestfallen. 'That's sounds like much more fun. Can't I share with you two?'

Elena slapped him on the back and led him through to the spare room. It had low beams and he had to duck to avoid cracking his head, but it was cosy and he soon made himself as home, emptying out the entire contents of his rucksack even though Elena reminded him that he'd be leaving in the morning.

'God, Elena, I've missed you,' he said again. 'I was going out of my head in Harrow on my own.'

'You mean, you've only come out here because you were bored?'

He shook his head in mock anger. 'That's not what I meant and you know it! I *missed* you! I'm no good without you,' he said, and his arms were around her again.

Elena rested her head on his shoulder and hugged him close to her. She felt so confused. First Reuben and now Mark. What was going on here? Was she being tested? Wasn't it enough that she'd come out here to sort things out? Why were these extra obstacles being thrown at her? Or were they here to help her? Was Prof's absence a sure indication that he wasn't the one for her? But hadn't he been thinking of her - eating Italian as he'd read her essay?

'You're very pensive, aren't you?' Mark whispered.

She looked up at him. 'Not pensive,' she lied. 'Just happy.'

'Good,' he said.

'Come on,' she said, taking his hand, 'Rosanna will be thinking we're up to no good.'

When they went back through to the living room, Rosanna had cooked up some pasta and they all ate at the table as if they were one big happy family. For a few minutes, nobody said a word but concentrated on the food, although Mark made many appreciative noises as he ate. Elena had to laugh at her earlier image of him sitting in his flat eating a ghastly microwave meal when, all along, he'd been on his way to her.

'It's great to finally meet you,' Mark told Rosanna as he all but scraped the pattern off the plate with an eager fork. 'I've heard so much about you.'

Rosanna looked up at him and gave the tiniest of smiles. 'And I've heard all about you,' she said with great control.

Mark laughed. 'I dread to think what you've heard!'

Elena glared at Rosanna, making sure she didn't elaborate. She had a devilish glint in her eyes.

'So, Rosanna, what's it like to be a model?' Mark asked before Elena could think of anything else to say. Elena almost choked on her mouthful as she saw Rosanna flinch. Nobody asked her about her work. She was always incredibly secretive about it as if she were ashamed of what she did.

'It's - er,' she stumbled, staring down at her empty plate, 'good.'

'Yeah? Don't you get embarrassed? I mean, having people gawping at you all the time?'

Elena cleared her throat. Even though Rosanna had been threatening to drop her in it since the unexpected arrival of two of her fiancés, she decided to help her out.

'She only gets embarrassed when people ask her questions about it!'

'Oh!' Mark said. 'Sorry. It's just, I've never met a model before.'

'It's okay,' Rosanna assured. 'It's just there's not much to say. I sit there and they paint me. It's-' she gazed up at the beams in the living room as if hunting for the right words, 'calm,' she concluded.

Mark nodded, as if he understood perfectly. 'That is definitely something you can't say about teaching.'

Elena smiled. He was right there. Teaching was as far away from *calm* as Venice was from London.

'Anyway, the pasta was great. I haven't been cooked for in a long time,' he said, and Elena immediately felt like the worst fiancée in the world.

Rosanna, suitably flattered, smiled at him and blushed as she cleared the table.

'I'll do those,' Mark said. 'It the least she can do.'

'No, no. I wouldn't hear of it,' Rosanna said. 'Why don't you make yourself at home?'

Mark nodded. 'Well, I wouldn't mind a shower.'

Elena's mouth fell open at the shocking symmetry of the day and Rosanna caught her eye briefly but, this time, it was merriment twinkling their eyes rather than devilry.

'I'm not sure we have any clean towels left,' she said. 'I don't know how we get through so many.'

'I'm sure we can find one,' Elena quickly interrupted, knowing that Rosanna was enjoying her discomfort immensely. 'I'll go and have a look.'

Mark followed her through to the bathroom and gave a long, low whistle.

'I know. Imagine having a place like this.'

'I'm imagining,' Mark whispered, squeezing her to him and kissing her neck.

'Mark! My sister's in the next room!'

'She could join us if she wants to.'

Elena glared at him. 'I hope you're teasing!'

'She's very cute,' he continued.

'Cute? Cute is not a word I'd ever think of to describe Rosanna,' she said, thinking of her sister's scolding tongue and her tempestuous temper.

'That's because she's your sister.'

'Are you going to have this shower or not?'

He raised his hands in defeat and began to get undressed.

'It's late,' she said. 'I'll see you in the morning.'

They kissed goodnight and she left him to it.

Walking back through to the living room, Elena sat down next to Rosanna on the sofa. Rosanna looked up from her magazine and Elena was ready to receive a tirade on the appalling day she'd put her through but Rosanna surprised her.

'Did you see Reuben off okay?'

She nodded. 'He's in the Danieli.'

'Can he afford it?'

'I think so.'

There was a moment's silence.

'He seemed nice,' Rosanna confessed.

'He is.'

'And this Mark - he seems nice too.'

'Well, you didn't think one of them a monster and the other being a prince, did you?' Elena groaned. 'Now do you see how difficult it is? It's not as easy as eeny, meeny, miny mo! They're both wonderful - in different ways.'

Rosanna nodded. 'But you're still only one person. You can't split yourself in two. I mean, how have you been coping with two fiancés?'

Elena stifled a giggle. 'It's not been easy,' she said, thinking of dear Prof and what Rosanna would say if she knew she was juggling three.

'And now you've got me involved,' Rosanna said. 'I've never known a day like today.'

'I'm sorry,' Elena said because, believe it or not, she was. 'It won't happen again,' she added.

Rosanna stared at her. 'It had better bloody not!'

And then they both burst out laughing.

CHAPTER 17

Prof's tiramisu tasted bland and bitter after he got cut off from Elena and he couldn't concentrate on the next student's essay. All he kept thinking about was Elena in Venice. It had been echoey and there'd been some street noise and he had an awful image of her wandering around the dark alleys of the city on her own. What was she doing out on her own? There was no excuse - he should have been there with her. She'd even told him that she'd wished he was there. So what was he doing eating alone in *Reggie's*?

He took one last spoonful of tiramisu, collected his essays together and asked for the bill. Leaving the restaurant, he remembered how cold it was and cursed having taken neither car nor coat. A brisk walk and thoughts of Elena would have to do their best to warm him up, he thought.

He didn't know why he hadn't thought of going with her before. Of course, she had made it clear to him that this wasn't a holiday for her but he should have read between the lines. If an English professor couldn't read between the lines then who could? She'd probably wanted him to be more forceful and he wasn't very good at that. If a woman told him that she was happy to go alone then he believed her. He wasn't used to being dominant and taking control but Elena had definitely said she'd wished he was out there with her.

There was only one small problem. He didn't actually know where Elena was staying. He'd been very lax in not making her write down the details for him but he really hadn't considered following her so he'd let it go. All he could remember her saying was that she was in the residential area. She'd mentioned The Island of the Dead being fairly close by too. His knowledge of Venice was pretty sketchy but it couldn't be that big, being an island, and they were bound to run into each other sooner or later if he frequented the right area, and he could always ask around. His Italian was a little rusty but he could ask if anyone had seen two stunning sisters recently.

Reaching home, Prof opened the door and put the lights on, once again admiring his new-look home. He had to admit that Mrs B had surpassed herself. He'd never seen so many shiny surfaces in his life and, after her big clean up, he felt it only fitting that *he* had a big tidy up, and had collected seven boxes of books which his sister and niece were going to sell at a car boot fair. This meant that you could actually get in the front door without having to lift your arms above your head.

He'd bought new bed linen, had all his curtains dry-cleaned, ordered a new three-piece suite to replace the two-seater sofa which had seen him through his bachelor years and had even bought a few pot plants to make the house seem a little more inviting. Mrs B had suggested some scented candles and potpourri but he wasn't sure if he wanted to go that far.

Yes, he thought, walking into the living room, he was very proud of his new-look home. The stage was set. All he needed to do now was to find the other player.

CHAPTER 18

'You *must* like one better than the other?' Rosanna said, clattering around the kitchen as she prepared breakfast the morning after the arrival of the fiancés.

'I've told you, it isn't that simple.' Elena put her head in her hands at the breakfast bar and sighed. 'I thought you understood that.'

'But you must - you know - *gel* with one of them more?'

'That's crazy, Rosanna! Are you seriously telling me that there's only one perfect person out there for us?'

Rosanna stared at her. 'Yes! I guess I am!'

'That's the most stupid thing I've ever heard! That would mean you could be wandering around forever trying to meet them! And what if you missed them? What then? Say if you got on the bus five minutes before they arrived at the stop or if you spent your entire life shopping at the wrong supermarket because you liked Waitrose and your perfect partner preferred Sainsbury's? Does that mean you'd have to spend your life on your own?'

'You're getting hysterical, Elena. Keep your voice down! Or do you want to wake Mark?'

Elena bit her lip. Mark was still sleeping and it had given her a chance to talk things through with Rosanna but she was beginning to wish she hadn't asked for her advice.

'I guess I just don't believe that there's only one perfect person,' Elena started again. 'I think there are lots of people you could be happy with - dozens, *hundreds* maybe.'

Rosanna's eyes widened and her mouth dropped. 'Dio mio!'

'There *has* to be! Think of all the potentially life-changing decisions we make each day. We take a certain route to work, we choose a shop for our groceries, we decide to go to a party - all these things involve meeting people and that means a potential mate.'

'God, you make it sound so animalistic!'

'I think it is. Do lions or bears or birds hang around for a perfect partner? I think they choose the best that's around at the time and get on with it.'

Rosanna crinkled her nose in obvious disgust. 'But we're not like that - we expect more.'

'I know.'

'But what you're saying is-'

'What I'm saying is that maybe both Reuben *and* Mark are right for me.'

Rosanna huffed. 'I think you're just making excuses.'

Elena shook her head. There was no point continuing with this conversation. Rosanna would never come round to her way of thinking and she didn't want to spend her holiday arguing with her.

There were a few moments' silence and she watched as Rosanna tidied the kitchen. She looked just like their mama when she did that.

'The thing we have to make sure of,' Rosanna said at last, in a much calmer tone of voice, 'is that, whilst you're doing whatever you have to do, they don't accidentally bump into each other. Reuben already has his suspicions about Mark, doesn't he?'

Elena cast her eyes in the direction of the spare room where Mark was sleeping. 'Yes,' she said, lowering her voice. 'He has a rather jealous nature.'

'I noticed,' Rosanna whispered back. 'How, exactly, did you meet him?'

'It was a bit like you and Sandro. I heard he wanted a new model and went along to his studio. I'd never modelled before that. I guess it must run in the family because he kept booking me and the money is definitely better than what I earn at the school - for the work involved, I mean. It's just a shame his studio isn't quite like this. I mean, it's not bad if you compare it to Mark's place, but it's a bit of a dump in comparison to this.'

'Oh? How?'

'It's a great building - one of those converted warehouses - but it's not in a very nice neighbourhood.'

'He can always move in time.'

Elena nodded. 'Oh, he plans to.'

'And what are his plans?'

She raised an eyebrow. 'You're very interested all of a sudden.'

Rosanna looked a little put out at her observation. 'Not at all,' she said. 'Shouldn't I show an interest in the man who proposes to marry my sister?'

She smiled. 'I suppose so.'

'I think he'd take good care of you.'

'You do? So does that mean he has your vote?'

Rosanna put down the tea towel for a moment and looked at her. 'I didn't say that. I only said I liked him.'

'So, you think I should go for Mark?'

'Elena! You can not ask these questions! What am I meant to say? I can not make these decisions for you!'

She sighed. 'I'm sorry! It's just, you're so wise.' Elena's comment instantly calmed her. 'You always seem to make the right decisions.'

'You think so?'

'Well, don't you?'

Rosanna echoed her weary sigh. 'I've got a problem of my own and, I'm afraid, it's of my own making.'

Elena bit her lip. 'What?' she asked in anticipation, relieved that she wasn't the only Montella girl who got herself into trouble.

'I've been invited for tea at *La Stronza*'s!'

Elena's eyes widened in sympathy. 'Irma Taccani?'

'Beetch!' Rosanna spat, finding it necessary to curse the woman in more than one language.

Elena stifled the urge to laugh. 'I don't understand. If you hate her so much, why are you going?'

They walked through to the sofa with bowls of muesli and Elena perched on the arm whilst Rosanna flopped on a heap of cushions.

'I'm going because Corrado wants me and his mother to be friends.'

'Then you must still love him? I mean, you *must* if you're doing this for him.'

Rosanna's face fell. Her whole expression seemed to sink before her very eyes.

'If you don't mind me saying so, you don't much look like a woman in love.'

'I don't?'

Elena shook her head and rested a hand on her shoulder. Putting her half-eaten cereal down, Rosanna took hold of a cushion and hugged it to her.

'I feel as if I've had a cold for the last six months.'

Elena frowned. 'What do you mean?'

'You know when your whole body aches and you feel listless and lifeless? That's exactly how I've been feeling. But this is far worse than a cold because I'm denied the pleasure of a good sneeze.'

Elena laughed.

'What?' Rosanna turned to her, her eyes wide with hurt.

'I'm sorry!' she said. 'I just had this image of Corrado being stuck up your nose!'

'It's not funny.'

'I know,' she said, and, putting her breakfast bowl down too, she nestled up next to her. 'So, we have three men to sort out,' Elena told her, doing her best to eliminate Prof from the love equation for the time being.

'I don't know what to do,' Rosanna whined.

'Corrado will be there, won't he? He wouldn't leave you alone with the old witch?'

'No, he'll be there all right. Mama's darling little helper.'

'Then, you should go. Go and have tea. Try not to throttle anyone. See how things go and come back and tell me all about it,' she advised.

'And you're going to sort things out with Mark and Reuben?'

'Well, that's rather a tall order for an afternoon's work but I'm going to try,' she said. 'I'll have to find Mark a cheap hotel. He doesn't have a lot of money.'

'Well, don't book him into the Danieli! Can you imagine if that happened? Dio mio! Do you think there'd be a fight?'

'Rosanna! They are *not* going to meet! Not if I have anything to do with it.'

Rosanna looked glum all of a sudden as if the reality of it all were just hitting her. 'Your situation makes me feel much better about having tea with *La Stronza*.'

'Thanks a lot! I'm glad I'm useful for something.'

Rosanna kissed her cheek. 'I've got an appointment in Murano.'

'Modelling?'

She nodded. 'A dirty old businessman who likes me to pose with a disgusting teddy bear.'

Elena grimaced and walked down the steps with Rosanna and watched her go.

'I'll be back for lunch - in time to get changed for this afternoon.'

'Okay!' she called after her. 'You've got your mobile?'

'Of course!'

Elena smiled, relieved that her sister carried it with her in her line of work. She really didn't know how she could do her job. She didn't think *she* could ever do it, and yet she had posed for Reuben. That was different though - she was in a relationship with him before she'd taken anything off. But she couldn't ever strip for strangers no matter how good the money was which was why she was so surprised at Rosanna for being able to do it. She'd always been the bossy sister - the one in control but, out of the two of them, she was also the shy one. Elena had to admire her, though. She was an independent woman making a good living in a beautiful city. All she needed to do now was to find the right man and Elena had a strong feeling that it wasn't Corrado.

CHAPTER 19

Rosanna always loved the brief boat ride to the island of Murano. It was normally packed with tourists and it was usually a squeeze to find somewhere to stand as few people wanted to sit indoors when you could watch the progress of the boat across the lagoon stopping, on its way, at the island of San Michele, where everyone would strain their necks to try and get a peek at the graves without actually leaving the boat.

The water usually helped her to think but she didn't think anything could have eased her mind that morning. She'd left Elena in the apartment with her fiancé, or, rather, *one* of her fiancés. The other, of course, was at one of the most expensive hotels in Venice. Two fiancés, Rosanna tutted aloud to herself. How on earth had she managed to do that? She knew Elena's track record but she'd never thought that anything like that would happen. And to have them both turning up at the apartment!

Rosanna thought of her first encounter with Reuben and could feel her face flushing as she did so. It wasn't because he'd been dressed only in a towel, which had been embarrassing enough on its own, but it was how she had felt. She closed her eyes and tried to recall it. It was warm, it was tingly, and it was incredibly disturbing because she hadn't felt like that since school. Yes, that was it, she thought: it was like having a crush - that strange phenomenon she'd thought you left behind once you became an adult, but here she was experiencing the self-same feelings - for her sister's fiancé.

This was terrible. Did she really have a crush on Reuben? It couldn't possibly be anything more than that, could it? She'd only met him yesterday. It was outrageous to suppose that the emotion was anything more. She'd be in dreadful trouble if it was. No, she reasoned, he was just a very attractive man who'd happened to be standing half-naked in front of her. What normal red-blooded Italian girl wouldn't respond to something like that?

But, the thing that was worrying her was that she couldn't remember ever having responded that way to Corrado. There'd been no adrenaline rush. Her heart hadn't fluttered inside her. Not once had she blushed when he'd looked at her. Was that normal? Did that mean she didn't love Corrado? Or, should the question be, did it mean she was falling in love with Reuben? *Oh!* Elena had got her so confused with her ideas about each person having so many possible partners and how impossible it was to choose just one but, even so, she shouldn't have been thinking about the physical beauty of one of her potential brothers-in-law. It wasn't right. In fact, it was probably illegal.

Leaving the boat, and attempting to put any illegal and incestuous thoughts firmly out of her mind, Rosanna made her way to the heart of Murano, towards the street where Signore Vapori lived. He owned a tiny apartment above an antiques shop which he ran and it was stuffed full of beautiful objects which he'd have her pose alongside. She'd been naked under a chandelier, naked on an oak chest, naked on an eighteenth century chair and, the latest one was naked with a teddy bear - antique, of course. She'd never forget her horror as he'd handed the bear to her last week and told her to place it in her crotch. She didn't want to think about where else this teddy had been. It didn't look as if it had ever been washed in its long lifetime, and she was sure she could smell something unsavoury on its fur. But, she was being paid to do this and, no matter how strange it was, she reminded herself that it was preferable to many other jobs she could've ended up doing.

There were two ways she'd found to cope with such situations: she would either pretend that this was the greatest living painter she was sitting for and that this painting was her passport to eternal fame or, and this was her favourite, she would work out how much she'd earned that month and what she could spend it on if she so chose. Her mind would drift over the latest lipsticks and expensive perfumes to velvet scarves she'd seen draped gently over a mannequin or the latest season's stylish boots. These thoughts would usually keep her occupied until she was given a tea break when she'd pull on her robe and have to make polite conversation. This too, she'd learned, was a necessary survival tactic. She'd soon discovered, after a couple of near-misses, that she should be polite but with an air of aloofness. A lot of her clients dabbled in art as a hobby and would forget that the woman who'd been sitting in front of them with no clothes on was actually doing it for the money and not to titillate them. Occasionally, if she felt a client was becoming particularly frisky, she would say something like, *And how is Signora Vassallo?* Or, *My fiancé, Corrado, got into a fight at the weekend! Can you believe it? A grown man fighting in the streets!* But she only used that one in extreme cases.

But, as she sat for Signore Vapori, she realized that he was far more interested in the old stuffed teddy than he was in her body and she felt herself relaxing or rather dwelling, once more, on the peculiar events of the last couple of days.

Reuben. Her mind wouldn't leave him alone. She didn't even know his last name. All she knew were the brief facts that Elena had told her. And that he was very handsome. She'd never seen a man with long hair before. Well, it wasn't long like hers but it was almost shoulder-length, and it was so dark. That was another thing, once he was dressed, she'd noticed that he was wearing black from head to toe. She'd always thought she was rather cautious with colour - going for muted tones and subtle hues but she'd never gone as far as that. Strangely enough, though, she quite liked it.

No! No! *No!* She mustn't keep thinking about him! She must put him firmly out of her thoughts.

'Miss Montella!'

A voice suddenly startled her out of her thoughts.

'Signore Vapori?'

'Could you please loosen your grip on the bear? You're strangling him!'

Rosanna looked down and noticed that, in her agitation, her hands were, indeed, throttling the poor teddy to within an inch of his already threadbare life.

After three hours of posing with the smelly teddy, Signore Vapori paid her. Luckily, he didn't deduct any money for her near-murder of his beloved toy, and she got the boat back to the mainland. Arriving back at the apartment, she couldn't help feeling a little relieved to find she had it to herself. She didn't think she could face Elena, not after the appalling thoughts had been having about Reuben.

She was just slipping out of her clothes for a shower before heading out for tea with *La Stronza* when the doorbell went. Grabbing her modelling robe, she ran down the stairs. Either it was Elena, having misplaced her key already, or another one of her secret fiancés, she thought to herself. But, she was wrong. It was Reuben.

Rosanna stood, transfixed in surprise. It was as if she'd conjured him up out of her thoughts but, now he was here, she wasn't at all sure what to say to him.

'Hello,' he said, sounding a little nervous.

'Hello,' she said back, sounding even more nervous than he did.

'Can I come in?'

'Elena isn't in,' she said quickly.

'That's okay. Actually, I wanted to talk to you.'

'I'm on my way out,' she said before realising how rude she sounded.

'Oh.'

They stared at each other for a moment.

'You look like a model in that robe,' he said.

'I am. I mean - this is my modelling robe. I model,' she explained very badly.

'You do? I was going to suggest you do. You've got a great figure.'

Rosanna's mouth dropped open. Had he really just said that?

'I'm sorry,' he mumbled, looking down at his boots and kicking them against one another. 'I shouldn't have said that.'

'No! It's okay,' she said, anxious that he shouldn't think he'd offended her. 'Elena didn't mention I was a model, then?'

'No. To be honest, she doesn't really talk much about her family.'

Rosanna nodded. 'No. I don't expect she does.'

'Why is that?'

Again, she was surprised by his question. 'Well, I'm not sure that's for me to say. Especially not dressed in my modelling robe on the doorstep.'

Reuben gave a slight smile and she noticed the dimples in his cheeks. She wished she hadn't because she couldn't take her eyes off them after that.

'Look, I'm sorry, but I have to go out,' she said again.

'Would it be possible for me to stay here and wait for Elena? I have a feeling that we're going to keep missing each other otherwise, do you know what I mean?'

Rosanna looked at him. He still had an edge of suspicion hovering around him, and who could blame him? But what was she meant to do? What if Elena came back to the apartment with Mark in tow only to find she'd let Reuben in?

'I'm not sure that's a good idea.'

'No? Why not?'

'I think you'd be better waiting for her at the Danieli. In fact, she's probably there now, wondering where you are.'

'You think so?'

'Yes,' she said, trying to dispel the image of her walking hand in hand by the Rialto with Mark.

'Look,' Reuben began, 'I don't mean to be rude about your sister, but I think she's doing her best to avoid me and I want to know why.'

Rosanna could see the pain in his eyes as he spoke. He looked as if he was speaking from the very centre of his being and she felt absolutely awful because she didn't know what to say to him.

'I'm sorry, but I really have to get ready to go out,' she said.

He examined his boots again like a lost schoolboy and it made her heart bleed. Her bloody sister! What did she think she was playing at - leading these two wonderful men on? For a dangerous moment, Rosanna wanted to tell Reuben everything about Elena. It would be an emotional scene, of course: she'd wring her hands and curse her sister to the sky and Reuben would probably tear up a few of Sandro's canvasses in his passion but then she'd comfort him and the tears would turn to kisses...

'Rosanna? Are you okay?'

Blinking hard to dispel the fictional image that was floating, so beautifully, before her eyes, she looked at Reuben.

'Look,' she said, 'why don't you come inside whilst I get ready? I'll make you some coffee.'

'Thanks,' he said softly, and followed her up the stairs.

CHAPTER 20

Mark wondered where they were going. They'd been on the go for twenty minutes and had walked over the Rialto Bridge and still hadn't reached their destination. But he trusted Elena knew where they were heading. Anyway, he was enjoying a bit of sightseeing on the way. The late morning sunshine sparkled like thousands of stars caught in the water of the Grand Canal. He had his first glimpse of a gondola and almost wrenched his neck out of joint at the precarious angle the gondolier was standing at whilst moving at such a great pace. He wondered how much it would be to hire one. They certainly didn't seem to be short of business, he thought, counting the number of couples out on the water, but he knew that they were outrageously expensive and that his wallet wasn't that well-padded.

They walked by dozens of shops which all seemed to be selling the same things: brilliant masks, glass in colours that blinded the eyes, and ropes of beads which glowed in the sunshine. But they didn't stop to shop.

'I like your sister,' he said as they left the shops behind and walked over yet another bridge in the bid to find a hotel he could afford.

'Don't start that again,' Elena snapped.

Mark blinked. It was, he thought, an odd response for what was meant as a compliment.

'What do you mean?' He looked at her. Her dark eyes were cast down and her brow looked as if it had been ploughed by a very angry farmer. It wasn't the sort of face you wanted to see on a bright spring morning in the middle of Venice.

She sighed. 'Nothing. I meant nothing. It's just that everyone likes Rosanna.'

'Oh. Well, that's good, isn't it?' he reasoned.

'Of course,' she said.

Mark couldn't think how his comment could have upset her. 'You are strange,' he said with a half-laugh.

She turned and glared at him. 'How?'

'The things you say sometimes. The way you look.'

'How do I look?'

They stared at one another. 'Confused.'

Bang on cue, she gave him her best *confused* look yet. 'That's stupid! How do I look confused?'

'You just do,' he smiled.

She tutted and walked on.

'Elena?'

'What?'

'What's the matter?'

She stopped and placed her hands on her hips and he knew he was in trouble. It was a stance every man dreaded. 'Nothing's the matter! Why do you think something's the matter?'

'Because you've hardly said a word to me all morning. I came out here to talk to you and you're doing a good job of preventing me.' Mark swore her dark eyes turned even darker at that moment and, if he hadn't been made of such stern stuff, he might very well have high-jacked the nearest gondola and fled there and then.

'I didn't ask you to come out here,' she said.

He wasn't at all surprised by her comment as he knew it would be flung at him sooner or later and he supposed sooner was preferable as it would give him a chance to sort things out.

'I know you didn't.'

'Well, stop blaming me for -' she stopped in mid-sentence.

'For what? For not being over-thrilled to see me?'

'That's not fair, Mark.'

'Isn't it? I've come a long way to see you, you know,' he said. 'I even got on a bloody plane. Do you know how terrified I am of planes?'

Her angry mouth opened into a circle of surprise and he instantly felt appalled at having made her feel so guilty.

'You're the only person in the world who could get me on a plane,' he added, wishing he hadn't mentioned it at all. He hadn't meant to but she could be infuriating at times and he wanted her to see what he was willing to do for her.

She looked over her shoulder at a stretch of murky canal. Mark thought about crossing the brief space and placing his hand on top of hers as she rested it on bridge but he also wanted to see what she'd do and hear what she'd say but, just as he was sure she was about to say something, a group of school-children filed between them, their voices loud and echoey. He watched Elena through the spaces that they made as they jostled and pushed each other, and he slowly convinced himself that she was never going to speak to him again.

When silence filled the streets once more, he said, 'You came out here for a reason, didn't you?'

She turned back to face him again. 'Of course I did. I told you. I came to see Rosanna.'

'No, no,' he shook his head, pleased that she was still speaking to him but annoyed that she still wasn't being honest. 'It's more than that.'

There was a few moments' silence as if they were both waiting for the other to speak first.

'Why are you being like this?' she asked at last.

'Like what?'

'Why do you keep asking me all these questions?'

'Why are you being so secretive?' he fired back.

A passer-by gave them an odd stare before walking on and leaving them facing each other across the bridge.

Mark scratched his head. 'I don't know what it is but I always get the feeling you're hiding something from me. I don't know how else to explain it. It's like I'm only seeing a little part of you and that you've locked the rest of yourself away.'

'I don't know what you mean,' Elena said. It was just the kind of bland, uninformative response he knew he'd get.

'I sometimes get the feeling that you don't love me enough. Is that what this trip is all about?'

Again, the silence between them was palpable but there was no taking the words back now. It was something he'd been dreading saying. He'd been holding it back and holding it back but the thought kept on surfacing and he had to have some kind of answer, even if it was an answer he really didn't want to hear. He loved Elena - more than he could possibly tell her - and he'd come out to Venice in an attempt to make sure that things worked between them but, ever since he'd arrived, he'd been dogged by doubts and threatened by fears.

'You asked me why I came out here,' she began in a subdued voice, 'but I think I should be asking you the same thing.'

'And I've told you - I wanted to talk to you about all this.'

'It looks like you came out here to break up with me. Well, it would have been cheaper if you'd waited for me to come home!'

'NO!' he yelled. 'Elena!' He could feel his whole face scrunching up in consternation. It was all getting out of hand and he felt he was making a real mess of everything. It wasn't meant to have snowballed out of control like this. 'I came out here to *stop* us from breaking up! The feelings I kept getting from you - I don't know - I'm not explaining it very well - but we don't ever talk at home. And I don't see you much outside of work. I don't even know what your flat looks like. I mean, what do you do when you're not at the school? I want to know!'

He could feel his heart racing. All these words - all formed from these paranoid worries he had about his relationship with Elena - were pouring out in an uncontrollable torrent. What was wrong with him? Couldn't he be a normal bloke and just make the most of what he'd been given? Why did he have to go and question everything? Things had been good between them. They had just as much chance as the next couple at making a go at things so why was he prodding and poking about?

'I'm sorry,' he said at last. 'You're right. I shouldn't be asking you all this.'

Elena shook her head. 'No,' she said very quietly. 'It's okay. You've got every right.'

Mark looked at her closely, watching as she blinked slowly, not once looking up at him. 'You're not angry with me?'

'No,' she said. 'In fact, I should have been honest with you from the start.'

Mark's mouth felt dry in anticipation. He wasn't quite sure what he was expecting her to say but it seemed an age before she spoke.

'I don't know how I feel,' she said at last.

Mark frowned. It wasn't exactly the sort of confession he'd expected. 'What?'

'You said you wanted me to be honest - that you felt I wasn't being open with you. Well, now I am.'

Her eyes met his and he could feel himself burning up with shock.

'God!' It was all his brain could come up with. But what had he expected? He'd confronted her, demanding an honest answer and he'd got one, so surely he should have been pleased? Except he hadn't really expected this reply.

Neither of them spoke for a couple of minutes. It was as if they were allowing their words time to settle before they examined them in any detail. To be honest, he was terrified of saying anything else. He could see they weren't going to get much further with things today. Elena looked tired and on the verge of tears and he felt he'd be pushing her right out of his life if he tried to talk to her anymore.

'Elena,' he said softly, crossing the bridge to stand next to her. 'I don't want to leave things like this today but I think we both need a bit of time to think things over.'

She nodded and he stroked her hair and the soft skin behind her ear which he loved so much. She looked so sad and he desperately wanted to kiss her but he didn't.

'Can I come and see you tomorrow?' he asked.

She nodded again. 'Where are you going to stay?'

He shrugged. 'Somewhere cheap. Not too far away from you.'

'Okay. Come over in the evening.'

And that was it. There were no kisses or hand holding or hugs. She simply turned and walked away from him and, for the first time since losing Marmaduke, his cuddly toy cat, when he was five years old, Mark felt like crying in the street in front of everybody.

CHAPTER 21

Rosanna made Reuben a cup of coffee and went upstairs to get changed. He took the opportunity to poke around the great Sandro Constantini's paintings and he was shocked to discover an alarming collection of nudes. Why hadn't he noticed them before, he wondered? He'd only noticed the scenes of Venice.

Bending down for a closer look, he noticed that they were all of Rosanna and his eyes fell upon her dark nipples and the gentle curve of her belly.

He put the paintings back and walked over to the kitchen to try and distract himself. There was a rack of washed plates and cups which should have been distracting enough but he started to imagine Rosanna's bare arms, elbow-deep in washing-up suds, her long fingers washing the plates with delicate ease.

'Bugger!'

'Are you all right, *down there?*' an angelic voice floated down from upstairs.

'Yes!' he said, clearing his throat. He left the kitchen and went to sit down on the sofa, wracking his brains for topics to take his mind off the naked Rosanna in the paintings - the one who was getting dressed upstairs at this very moment.

Drains. His drains at home probably needed cleaning. Yes. He must get that sorted. Guttering. Probably full of pigeon crap. He must give Mike, the handyman, a ring about that. A new exhaust pipe for the car - he'd been putting that off for ages too. Council tax. Wasn't he going to arrange direct debit for that?

It was working.

'I'll be down in a minute,' Rosanna shouted.

Drains. Guttering. Exhaust pipe. Council tax. Just keep chanting those, he told himself. Do not, under any circumstances, think of Rosanna in the bedroom above, and how easy it would be for you to follow her upstairs.

'Reuben?'

'What?' his neck almost snapped as he turned to see her standing beside him.

'You okay? You're a bit red.'

'I'm fine,' he said. 'You were quick.'

'I never waste any time,' she said, fixing him with her large brown eyes. 'Are you sure you're okay?'

'Yes,' he said

'I've got to go now,' Rosanna said, checking her handbag for something and then flicking a lock of thick hair over her shoulder.

'I don't see why I can't stay here and wait for Elena,' he said, suddenly remembering the reason he was there.

'I'm sorry,' Rosanna said, 'but it's not possible.'

'Why not?' He didn't like the tone of his voice; he sounded petulant, like a spoilt child, but he wanted to get to the bottom of this. Now, not only did he think Elena was hiding something but that her sister was in on it too.

'I don't make the rules here. This isn't my apartment,' Rosanna tried to explain.

Reuben looked across at her and he knew she was hiding something but, at the same time, her face was gentle, almost apologetic.

'I'm sorry,' he found himself saying. 'I'm putting you in an awkward position. I don't mean to. It's just that all this is very frustrating. I come out all this way to apologise for something that I don't even think I should be apologising for. I'm mistaken for someone called Mark, then packed off to an outrageously expensive hotel where I'm expected to wait until her ladyship calls for me. It's not bloody good enough!'

'I *know!*' Rosanna agreed and, at once, he felt terrible about sharing his thoughts with her.

'Look, I've really got to go now,' Rosanna said, 'but I'm glad you feel you can talk to me.'

Reuben raised his eyebrows in surprise. 'Really?'

'Of course I am. We're almost family,' she added. 'We should be able to be honest and open with each other.'

'Yes,' he said, that one word, *family*, putting him firmly in his place.

They left the apartment and Rosanna told him to hold tight at the Danieli and that she'd be very surprised if Elena wasn't there right at that very moment wondering where he was.

'And, if she hasn't tried to see you today, I'll have very strong words with her tonight,' she finished.

Reuben watched her head off to her appointment, her shoes clicking on the pavement. She had a fantastic figure, he thought, as she disappeared round the corner and her burgundy dress had looked stunning.

Perhaps he should have told her that.

CHAPTER 22

Once Rosanna left the apartment, her feet picked up such a pace that they very nearly flew right out of her shoes. She looked down and admired them: beautiful rich burgundy strappy heels - not the sort for crossing great distances in but she so wanted to look nice. She'd met Irma Taccani before, of course, but she'd never had a summons to tea before, and she thought she should make an effort even if she wasn't sure she was her son's intended.

Rosanna wasn't sure of anything anymore. She'd been in at least two minds about Corrado before Reuben had arrived and, now, she didn't know what to think. She'd barely stopped thinking about Reuben since the moment she'd first seen him dressed in one of Sandro's white towels. What was it about him? She was a rational woman; she didn't fall in love at the drop of a hat - or even the drop of a towel for that matter. Yet there was something about him that she couldn't shake from her mind even though she knew she had every reason *not* to be thinking about him. Or did she?

One of the reasons she thought she shouldn't be thinking about Reuben was that she was with Corrado but she still had her doubts about him, and that was one of the reasons she'd agreed to go over to his mother's today. The second reason was that Elena was engaged to Reuben. But she was also engaged to Mark so surely that put a new spin on things.

She groaned. Could she just wait around and see which man her sister picked and hoped it wasn't the one that she had fallen for? And, even if Elena chose Mark, Rosanna had no real proof that Reuben felt anything for her, even if she had felt his eyes burning into her when he'd been in the apartment.

Doing her best to put Reuben out of her mind, - she turned right into the calle that led to Irma Taccani's. The apartment was one of several overlooking one of the tiniest canals in Venice. Washing was strung across the canal, the brilliant colours reflected in the dim water, still as a painting. Like Sandro's apartment, this one was tucked away in a quiet spot far from the reach of tourists. This was the

Venice Rosanna loved but she wasn't at all sure that she was going to love her time here this afternoon.

Taking a deep breath, she pressed a golden buzzer. It took a couple of minutes before she heard an elderly woman's voice croak a response.

'Signora Taccani? It's Rosanna Montella.'

There was no reply.

'Corrado invited me. For tea!'

Still, she didn't speak but, after what seemed an age, she buzzed Rosanna in.

Her palms were beginning to sweat and she fiddled anxiously with her hair which, she was sure, was sticking out, giving her the appearance of a Gorgon, and she suddenly regretted her choice of outfit, believing it to be slutty rather than sophisticated, and the shoes, which she'd thought so beautiful just moments before, now looked wildly inappropriate.

Narrow stairs led up to the Taccani's and, reaching apartment number five, Rosanna knocked on the cracked white door and waited.

'*Corrrrraaaddoo!*' a voice called from behind the door. Rosanna waited. And waited. She was just about to raise her fist and bang with the whole weight of her body behind it when the door swung open and Corrado beamed a smile at her, pushing a hand through newly-washed hair.

'I thought you were ignoring me!' she complained.

'Mama doesn't like answering the door.'

'But she knew it would be me!' she pointed out, baffled.

Corrado gave an apologetic shrug. 'She doesn't like people,' he said.

Rosanna's eyebrows rose. Well, she supposed that made sense as most people didn't like her either.

'Well, can I come in or can't I?' she asked.

She stepped inside and Corrado gave her a smile which began in his eyes. They were the first things she'd noticed about Corrado. Well, actually, if she was absolutely honest, it was his arms she'd noticed first: his big strong labourer's arms, tanned by a thousand hours of sunshine. She'd imagined what it would feel like to circle his wrists with her fingers and to have his arms wrapped right around her waist and, when she'd found out, she hadn't been disappointed. But, back to his eyes. He had the largest, darkest eyes she'd ever seen. They were like autumn conkers and were far too pretty for a man to own. They held a brightness in them, despite being so dark, and yet were lazy too - as if they couldn't be bothered to focus on anything for long.

What she soon became aware of was that he couldn't possibly have inherited his eyes from his mother. Hers were like tiny, shrivelled raisins, barely daring to peep out of her face and yet seeming to miss nothing.

Corrado ushered her into the living room. It was small and dark but she was instantly aware of how clean it was. Every surface shone. It was the kind of room you dared not breathe in let alone sit down in, but Corrado motioned to a two-seater sofa by the window and, carefully inspecting her skirt, Rosanna sat down.

She instantly felt guilty as she thought about the state of Sandro's studio. There was a tarantula-like ball of hair at the bottom of the bath, bits of dried tomato on the kitchen tiles which Elena called her spaghetti western shoot-out, and a snow-like layer of dust on the plants. She'd have to have a major housecleaning session before he came back. Looking around the Taccani apartment, it was clear to her that dust never even got a chance to land, and dirt was a foreign species.

'Rosanna?'

'What?'

'Are you okay?'

'I'm fine,' she said. 'Just a little overcome by all the dirt in here. Doesn't your mama ever clean this place?'

'What?'

'Nothing. I was joking.'

Corrado raised dark eyebrows at her in bemusement. He was always a little slow on the uptake.

'Mama's been baking. Would you like some crostata?' he asked, sitting down on the sofa next to her and taking her hand in his.

Rosanna hesitated before answering. Wouldn't that make a lot of crumbs? But she nodded, knowing she couldn't win either way. She actually didn't like apricots, unlike most Venetians, but it wouldn't endear her to either of them if she turned Irma's baking down.

Corrado took Rosanna's hand to his lips and kissed it. It felt deliciously warm and she could feel spirals of desire shooting through her body. It felt ages since she'd last been kissed.

'Corrraaaadooo!' a voice called from the kitchen breaking their spell. Rosanna watched as he jumped to attention, dropping her hand as if it had suddenly caught fire.

'Coming, Mama.'

She bit her lip. She obviously wasn't the top woman in this particular household. Getting up from the sofa, she walked over to a dark wooden table where she had noticed a shoal of silver photo frames. There were no less than three baby photos - all of Corrado. He was an only child and, from the other photos showing his passage through childhood right up until adulthood, the collection had more of a shrine-like feel to it.

Rosanna had a sudden vision of Irma Taccani, duster in hand, polishing each silver frame with the utmost care. She picked one up: a sweet school portrait with Corrado wearing a smart navy tie. She held it towards the window as if she half-expected to see a great lipstick mark on it.

'What are you *doing*?'

A blunt voice startled Rosanna and she dropped the frame which crashed to the floor.

'I - I was-'

'*Mio Dio*!'

'I didn't mean to-'

'Mama!' Corrado interrupted. 'It was an accident.'

Irma stared at Rosanna, her raisin-like eyes shooting her down with disdain.

'I'm ever so sorry,' Rosanna said at last, daring to examine the frame as she placed it back in line on the table. Nothing was broken, thank god, but it didn't stop her from feeling stupid.

'Doesn't Rosanna look lovely, Mama?' Corrado said, as he led Rosanna back to the relative safety of the sofa and sat down next to her, holding her hand so that she couldn't do anymore damage.

Irma's tiny eyes squinted until they almost completely disappeared in her sallow face.

'Red,' she said, and that was all, but the word came out of her mouth as if it were a curse.

'Burgundy,' Corrado corrected.

The raisin slits opened a fraction and she eyeballed her potential daughter-in-law but there was no changing her mind. She thought she was a slut and that was that. Rosanna should have worn blue, like the Madonna, and then *La Stronza* might have been happier.

'We don't normally have tea,' she said, sitting on a chair opposite the sofa.

'Oh?'

'Too early. It's too English. I do not like to eat before eight in the evening.'

'But,' Corrado interrupted, 'it's nice to do things the English way for a change.'

'Pah!' Irma spat. 'Who wants to be Engleesh?'

'I'm not really English, you know,' Rosanna said in her defence. 'My father was English but we never really knew him.'

'I thought you were schooled in England?' Irma asked suspiciously.

'But that doesn't make me English. I don't live there anymore, do I?'

Irma frowned at her as if she was answering her back.

'I'm as Italian as you,' she dared.

Irma just shook her head and then disappeared into the kitchen and came out with a large plate of crostata. Rosanna winced.

Irma placed the plate on a small table in front of the sofa. Cut into neat slices, the apricot glowed like some form of alien ectoplasm. Rosanna could only thank her lucky stars that Irma was a little on the mean side and had cut a particularly small slice for her.

'That looks wonderful, Mama,' Corrado said, his voice fuelled with admiration. 'Mama is such a good cook,' he added.

'You cook?' she asked Rosanna sharply.

She tried not to gag on her mouthful of crostata. 'Not really,' she said, trying not to wince after her first mouthful of the vile apricot tart.

'What?'

'Of *course* she does, Mama! She just doesn't admit to it.'

'Every woman should cook.'

'Rosanna works hard too,' Corrado said, and she was impressed that he would defend her in front of his mother in that way.

'I've heard,' Irma said, her raisin eyes looking unimpressed.

Rosanna wondered how much Corrado had told his mother about her job and whether she knew that it involved her taking her clothes off but Irma didn't elaborate and Rosanna was grateful for it.

They ate in silence for a few moments. It was the most nerve-wracking few moments of her life. Part of her was aware of Irma's stare, another part was terrified of making crumbs on the immaculate sofa and carpet, and another part of her wracked her brains for something intelligent and unincriminating to say.

'This is nice,' Corrado said at last, and all Rosanna could do was nod, casting a quick look at her watch to see how long she had to put up with this before making her excuses and escaping for home.

CHAPTER 23

Elena couldn't get Mark's wounded expression out of her mind. Why did she keep shutting him out when he so desperately wanted to help her? He was the only one of her fiancés to have questioned her like that - the only one to realise that she wasn't being completely honest. But did he really want to help her? If she told him the truth, would he really understand? Somehow, she didn't think he would. Some people thought they could handle the truth - and would bug and bother until it was exhumed but, once in possession of it, would turn and flee faster than an athlete on steroids. It was like licking somebody else's wounds - it just wasn't natural. People's pasts, she'd always believed, should be left well and truly alone.

When Elena got back to Sandro's, it was late afternoon and Rosanna was out. Even with her mind in a maelstrom, she spared a thought for her sister and hoped she was coping with the pint-sized ogre that was Irma Taccani.

The apartment seemed so quiet with just her there. Of course, peace and quiet was part of the reason why she'd come to Venice but, now she had it, she felt restless and anxious.

She took her coat off and put the kettle on before bolting upstairs. When she reached the bedroom, she found herself standing in the middle of the room wondering what she'd come up for with such urgency. It wasn't like her to be forgetful. She looked around, trying to jog her memory but she just drew blanks. She thought about retracing her steps to the kitchen to see if she could pick up her train of thought, and she was just about to head back down when something caught her eye.

Gleaming gold in the dim light of the bedroom, the mask stared at her, empty-eyed, from the dressing table.

'Hello,' she laughed, not feeling quite so alone anymore.

Rosanna had stared at her in astonishment when she'd taken it out of the box and placed it there.

'What did you buy that for?' she'd asked.

'I don't know,' she'd replied, not wanting to try and explain that she'd felt as if she hadn't had a choice in the matter.

She thought it looked really at home on the dressing table, gazing blindly out at the room, its gently curving shape filling the space beside Rosanna's jewellery box perfectly.

She picked it up and, just like the night before in the calle, her hands seemed to glow with gold. She pulled her fingers along the smooth, cool black ribbons and toyed with the idea of putting it on. If only, she thought, I could wear the mask - hiding behind it so that nobody could see me. She smiled to herself. She was turning into a child again - running away from her fears and responsibilities. Yet, that was what she wished to do more than anything else in the world at that moment.

Elena held the mask up and smiled at it. 'I wish you could make me invisible,' she whispered, as if to a trusted friend.

The hollowed out eyes seemed to speak to her. *Put me on, they dared. Make me yours. I will not disappoint you. Put me on. You know you want to.*

And she did. She really did! Her heart was racing like a child's at a fairground. She felt a flow of excitement travelling through her body and couldn't stop herself from grinning widely.

Peeping around the door to double-check that there was nobody in the flat, she slipped the mask over her face and tied the black ribbons behind her head. She'd expected it to feel cold but it was pleasantly warm against her skin and fitted snugly around her eyes and over her nose. She was just about to take a look in the mirror when she suddenly felt nauseous. Her skin was burning up and her vision was beginning to blur and she had the startling sensation of pins and needles in her eyeballs. Something very strange was happening. She felt peculiar - as if she were dissolving. Her mouth felt dry and her heart was hammering loudly.

'Rosanna?' Elena called out in a hoarse whisper. She felt so helpless and vulnerable and sincerely hoped that her sister might have returned home early from her afternoon visit. But there was no reply. Elena was alone.

She didn't think things could get any weirder so, when the jolt came, she cried out loud. Her body felt as if it had been electrocuted and she was so shocked that, after the initial scream, she found she couldn't speak at all.

What was happening to her? Her hands flew up to behind her

head to try and rid herself of the mask but she couldn't feel her hands at all. Her mind must be playing tricks on her, she reasoned, or she must surely be asleep and having some sort of weird nightmare.

Wake up! Wake up! She told herself and then she heard a thud - she'd landed on the floor. Had she fainted? She still felt dizzy but not enough to faint, surely? Her eyes closed and she groaned as she slowly felt the tingling sensation leave her body.

And then - *bliss!* She felt unusually warm and relaxed, like those blissfully gentle moments before sinking into sleep. She could feel her heart rate slowly returning to something approaching normality. Letting out a deep breath, she opened her eyes.

Nothing. Elena panicked, shut them and opened them again, her vision flooding with the bedroom. For a few seconds, she just sat there, listening to herself breathing. Everything was okay. She'd just had some sort of funny turn, she assured herself. Maybe she was overdoing things and this was her body's way of telling her that she needed to slow down. But she couldn't shake the feeling that something wasn't quite right. Something, she thought, was missing...

HER!

She was missing!

'WHAT THE HELL?'

Well, at least her voice was still working, and she could still see. So what was going on? She tried to pinch herself with her unseen arms. 'Ouch!' She was still there, then, and not asleep. But maybe it would have been better if she *was* asleep, she thought. At least she could explain things then. But she was very much awake - awake and - *invisible!*

That was it! She was invisible!

She shook her non-existent head. Surely that wasn't possible? Surely the notion of invisibility only lived in fiction? Yet, here she was, standing in the middle of Sandro's apartment with nothing to show but her confusion!

This wasn't a trick, and it wasn't very likely that this was her body's response to stress, was it? It was the mask.

Her hands flew up to the ribbons tied around her head. She could still feel them and, loosening the little knot she'd made, she felt the mask slipping away from her face. She waited. Slowly, very slowly, the tingling sensation returned and she saw her body floating back into existence, appearing like a hazy mirage before settling into its usual solid self.

Oh my God! Mio Dio!

She looked at the golden mask in her hands, her eyes wide with wonder. What had she got hold of here? She was holding a little piece of magic - a miracle - something that wasn't meant to exist.

Elena turned it around, expecting to see some sort of explanation or warning: a sticker, maybe, saying something like: *wearing this mask can seriously injure your appearance*, but there was nothing.

She took a deep breath. Even though she'd experienced the most horrendous reaction when she'd put the mask on she wanted, more than anything, to try it on again - just to check - just to make sure she hadn't imagined it all. Placing it against her face, she carefully tied the black ribbons behind her head once more and waited.

She felt only a slow dissolving-like feeling this time which was a great relief. Perhaps the powerful reaction only came the first time. She had obviously lost her mask-wearing virginity.

Giggling, she walked across the room. She could still hear her feet on the floorboards and she obviously still took up physical space because she had to open the door in order to go down the stairs.

'Rosanna?' she checked to see that she still had the apartment to herself. The coast was clear so she walked down the stairs on invisible legs, grinning with an invisible mouth. She knew exactly where she was heading: there was a large, full-length mirror in the bathroom downstairs and she intended to get a good look at herself - if that made sense.

Walking into the bathroom, she stood in front of the mirror. It was true - she could see absolutely *nothing*. But she still wasn't completely convinced. She walked across and placed her hands on the mirror's wooden frame and, still, she could see nothing, even though the feel of the wood was very real underneath her fingertips.

'*Mio Dio!*' she whispered. She wasn't there at all! She was just air and space; she was a big fat nothing! And then, something dreadful occurred to her: maybe she'd died! Maybe she was able to turn invisible because she wasn't really there anyway? But her senses were still present: she could speak, see and hear. She picked up a bar of Sandro's primrose soap and sniffed. Yes. Her nose was still intact too. What about taste?

She ran through to the kitchen and poured herself a glass of apricot juice and drank, the liquid heaven filling her with relief. But were her senses only apparent to herself? There was nobody there to ask which meant one thing: she'd have to leave the apartment if she was to find out the truth.

Grabbing her coat, which instantly turned invisible the moment it was on, she left the apartment. It was a strange feeling to open the door into a world in which she was invisible. She was lucky that there was nobody around to see her or, rather, not see her, but observe the door opening and closing for no apparent reason.

She turned left and walked the short distance down to the Fondmenta Nove and looked out across the expanse of lagoon to the island of San Michele. It never failed to dazzle her with its beauty and, for a moment, she stood watching the water taxis bouncing over the waves, and the vaporetto leaving a huge white wake in its trail. People were out walking their tiny mascot-like dogs along the front whilst others shopped for groceries, and all were oblivious of her. It wasn't as though she'd stopped traffic before but they, quite literally, walked right by her without even noticing. She watched in amazement as a young couple walked towards her. They were linking arms and both wore sober expressions on their faces as if it would hurt them to smile. Could she make them smile, she wondered?

As they got closer, she wondered what she should do. The young lady was nearest to her and, as she approached, Elena stuck a foot out - just slightly- and watched as the lady tripped over it. Her eyes widened in astonishment as she clutched the arm of the man and looked behind her to see what had caused her to stumble, but there was no pebble or loose paving slab. The man shook his head and the young lady frowned.

Elena wondered whether to follow them and see what else she could get away with but she thought better of it when she saw a middle-aged woman approach. She was carrying one small carrier bag of groceries and was muttering to herself. Elena waited until the woman was parallel with her and then tapped her on the shoulder. The woman screamed and almost threw her bag of groceries into the lagoon in fright, and Elena had to cover her own mouth to stop herself from screaming too. Turning around, the woman looked down the length of the Fondamenta Nove to see who had assaulted her but, of course, there was nobody there.

Elena supposed she was lucky that she had only caused her to scream. This invisibility lark was beginning to give her a sense of power that could very well be her undoing.

With this thought in mind, she returned to the apartment and took the mask off as soon as the door was safely closed behind her and she'd made sure she was the only one inside. Again, she felt a tingling sensation spreading through her body until she was visible again. She laid the mask on the long oak table which Sandro used to spread out all his art equipment. It looked at home amongst the brushes and tubes of paint, and that was when she remembered Stefano. He'd created this mask so surely he knew what it was capable of doing? And why had he given it to *her*? He'd taken very great care to find this particular mask for her, but why?

Elena grabbed a carrier bag from the kitchen and placed the mask inside it and then left the apartment again. She felt too fidgety to queue and wait for the vaporetto so decided to cover the distance on foot.

Elena had never walked so fast in her life. She almost flew over the bridges and, to be honest, wouldn't have been a bit surprised if she actually had with the way things were going that day. Canals blurred as she broke into a run down narrow calli and across campi, questions flying around her heated brain. What had she been sold? What did she have in her possession? Did Stefano know what he'd given her? And, if he did, why had he given it to her?

Her feet pounded up the wooden steps of the Academia Bridge and she weaved in and out of groups of tourists, finding her way through the narrow streets towards Viviana's.

Allowing her pace to slow, she took a few deep breaths. She felt a bit dizzy but wasn't sure if that was from all the running or because of the strange experience of the mask. She checked inside the carrier bag and its blank eyes looked back up at her in complete innocence. It didn't seem right to put a magical mask inside a plastic bag but she'd wanted it to be well hidden.

Turning right into the tiny calle, she noticed the instant hush around her. There was nobody around. In fact, she couldn't remember seeing anyone much after she'd left the Grand Canal but she was in too much of a hurry to think about that.

She marched straight up and opened the door into Viviana's, the little bell announcing her arrival.

'Stefano!' she shouted before the door had closed behind her.

'Elena?' he shouted back, his white eyebrows arrowing across his nose as he appeared from his secret workshop.

'What kind of a shop is this?' she demanded, looking around her and gesticulating at the masks.

'What do you mean? Are you all right, Elena?'

'No! I'm not all right! What kind of masks are you selling?' She could feel her eyes popping out of her head at her question and her cheeks were blazing with fury. But, to her consternation, Stefano just nodded.

'Ah,' he said calmly, 'so you've tried on the mask!'

'Yes! I tried on this mask,' she said, thrusting the carrier bag under his nose, 'and it nearly killed me.'

He shook his head. 'No, no,' he said gently. 'It wouldn't have done that.'

Her eyes widened. '*No?*'

'The masks are always what the customer has asked for.'

'Are they?' She stared around the shop at the myriad masks hanging on the scarlet walls and her eyes rested on a tubular-nosed one. 'What about this one, then? What does this do?' she asked, plucking it from its position and holding it up to her face.

'You mustn't try on what you don't intend to own,' Stefano said calmly.

'Why not?'

'It's not your mask - trust me.'

'Trust you? I'm meant to *trust you*? Why should I do that? You gave me a mask that almost killed me!'

Stefano shook his head in a gentle manner as if she'd said something of mere irritation. Elena turned back to the masks on the wall.

'What would happen if I tried this on?' she said, taking another mask from the display. 'What would this one do to me? Turn me into a frog? Send me back in time?'

His hand reached out to retrieve the mask from her and he placed it back on the wall with gentle ease.

'It is not your mask,' he said again. 'You have yours - the one you requested.'

'But it wasn't the one I requested - it was the one *you* chose.'

Stefano frowned. 'You do not trust me at all?'

She shook her head but his eyes held hers firmly and she felt herself swallowing hard and looking away. 'I don't know,' she said at last in a quiet voice.

'Elena,' he began, 'I only give people the things that they have already decided they need.'

'But this mask -'

'Hush!' he said with absolute calm.

'But it's -' she stopped. His eyes seemed to silence her. 'I don't understand all this,' she said. 'It's too much! I need to know what's going on.'

'Why?'

'Because - ' she stopped without being able to finish her sentence.

'We do not always need to know the answers. Sometimes we must simply be.'

She bit her lip. 'Why do you always talk in riddles?'

'But I'm not.'

'And how can you remain so calm? You *know* what this mask did to me, don't you?'

He held his hands in the air and shook his head in a gentle manner which made her want to grab his shoulders and shake him. 'It did what you bid it.'

Elena frowned. And then she remembered the wish she'd made as she'd picked it up off the dressing table. She'd wished to become invisible.

She stared at Stefano. 'But these things can't happen - not really! They're impossible!'

A small smile spread across his face. 'You don't believe that, do you?'

'I don't know what to believe anymore!'

He shrugged. 'Some things can't be explained. Some things are just -' he paused, searching out the right word.

'Magic?'

He nodded. 'We all need a little magic in our lives, don't we?'

Elena watched as he turned and walked across the shop to the bench on which several masks awaited their fate.

'But the thing with magic,' he began, not looking up from the work bench, 'is that we must know when to use it. We must use it wisely. Don't you agree?' His eyes caught hers for the briefest of moments and she found herself nodding.

'Yes,' she said.

'Magic can be fun but it can also do great harm if its power goes to your head. You know what I mean?'

She nodded, and wondered if he knew about her little incident with the lady and the shopping bag on the Fondamenta Nove.

'You don't need to rationalise magic but you do need to *ration* it,' he said.

There were a few moments' silence. Elena waited for him to say something else. She wasn't sure what more there was to say and if she could actually absorb any more of Stefano's riddles.

'What should I do now?' she asked at last.

Stefano put down the mask he was working on and gave her his full attention again. 'You have some decisions to make, don't you?' he asked. 'Well, the mask will help you.'

Elena frowned. 'But how will I know when to wear it?'

'You'll know when the time is right,' he said lightly before picking up the unfinished mask from the bench and poring over it with great concentration.

It was clearly time for her to go. She turned around and walked towards the door, her mask swinging beside her in its carrier bag.

'Just one more thing, Elena,' he called after her.

'Yes,' she said, wondering which riddle he'd come out with next.

'Have some fun!' He smiled and gave a little chuckle. 'Have some *fun!*'

CHAPTER 24

There could be fewer sights in this world finer than Venice from a plane, Prof thought as they came down to land at Marco Polo airport. It was a real gem. No wonder it was known as the Pearl of the Adriatic, he smiled. And there was a pearl within the pearl too - Elena, his bride-to-be.

His wife! The thought made his heart pump madly and, for a moment, he felt as if he was about to self-eject right out of the aeroplane with joy. He had to find her! The thought of his little Elena in the middle of Venice without him was too much. But what if he couldn't find her?

As the wheels of the plane touched down, Prof tried to remain optimistic. He'd try not to give up hope even before he'd arrived. No, he thought, an hour later, as the Alilaguna made its stop for San Marco, he would find Elena and sweep her off her feet. But, ever practical, and always thinking about his stomach, he would check-in to his hotel, freshen up, and find something to eat before he started out on his great romantic quest.

It would be hard to estimate the number of hotels there were in Venice but it wouldn't be too difficult to guess which one Prof chose for his visit: the Danieli. As he stepped into the lobby, he gazed in rapture at the columns and arches that greeted him with regal splendour. It, quite simply, took his breath away. And his room was a symphony of splendour too and, if he hadn't been in such a hurry to have a drink and something to eat, he would have sat down and composed a couple of sonnets about it there and then.

Walking down the red-carpeted staircase, Prof felt decidedly underdressed for such a place. His old suit just wasn't up to these sorts of surroundings and he hoped he wouldn't be thrown into the lagoon for lowering the tone of the hotel. Perhaps he'd buy himself a new outfit whilst he was there. What were the labels he'd heard his students talking about so often? Gucci? Prada? Dolce and Gabbana? They all might have been ice-cream parlours for all he knew. A Prada pistachio. A Dolce and Gabbana double chocolate. But he'd have to smarten up a bit if he was to step out with Elena. He'd have to do her beauty and style credit. As much as she swore she loved his tired old jackets, he felt sure she'd adore him even more in the latest fashions.

Reuben hadn't dared to set up an easel in the lobby bar at the Danieli, but had found a quiet corner where he was getting on quite nicely with his sketchbook. People came and went - drinking, laughing, flirting and departing, without even noticing his busy pencil catching their secret moments. That was the way Reuben liked it. There was nothing worse than an inquisitive intruder who thought it their right to see a work in progress. Why did people think they could interrupt an artist just because they conducted their business in a public place? He didn't butt in to people's conversations when they were on their mobile phones or look over the shoulders of people who chose to work on laptops, so why should artists be fair game for public scrutiny? Art was not a spectator sport.

It was about three in the afternoon when a man walked right in front of the person Reuben was sketching. Reuben was just about to swear very loudly at the man but managed to check himself just in time. Besides, he thought, the man was a work of art himself and worthy of a sketch or two. He looked so awkward and out of place in his tweed jacket and bow tie.

Reuben span his pencil around and caught the man in a few light lines. He turned a page and watched as the man ordered a drink and sat down, craning his head back to take in the full splendour of the room. Reuben watched as his hand fiddled with his bow tie. He wore a gold signet ring on his little finger. He held his drink in his left hand and sipped it quickly as if he didn't intend on staying long.

And then he looked up and saw Reuben. Reuben looked down hastily but his pencil kept moving. He had almost finished. He knew that everybody moved eventually. It was one of those inconsiderate things people did with no thought of the artist struggling to capture them but that was part of the joy as well - trying to capture that elusive moment forever.

Reuben's pencil moved at lightning speed as he tried to finish the sketch whilst it was still fresh in his mind. He deliberately didn't look up again for fear of causing further embarrassment, and he was just putting in the finishing touches when he became aware of a presence at his shoulder. It was on the tip of his tongue to tell this most recent interloper to bugger off when he heard the words, 'It's really rather good,' and he was so taken by surprise that he put his pencil down and looked up.

'Thank you,' he said, staring up into the face of the man he'd been sketching. It was a kind, open face with bright, intelligent eyes winking from behind his round glasses. Reuben couldn't help but give a smile.

'I don't think I've ever been drawn before and, I must say, you've done rather a good job there,' the man in the bow tie went on. 'I mean, I really recognise myself!' he said, a small laugh in his voice as if he were surprised by what he saw on the page. 'It's quite extraordinary!'

'Thank you,' Reuben said again, watching as the man sat down opposite him and removed his glasses.

'I take it you're professional?'

Reuben nodded. 'It's taken a while but I can just about live off it now.'

'I should hope so too which such a talent,' he said. 'Sigmund,' he added, proffering a hand. 'Sigmund Mortimer.'

'Reuben Lord,' Reuben said, shaking it and nodding.

'I guess this place throws up some interesting subjects?' Sigmund said, looking around the room.

'Well, I've only been here a day but it looks promising so far.'

Sigmund nodded. 'It's extraordinary. Really extraordinary,' he enthused, craning his head back to take in the full splendour of the ceiling as he had when he'd first sat down.

'So,' Reuben began, deciding that it might actually be quite nice to have a bit of conversation, 'what brings you to Venice?'

Sigmund smiled. 'Romance,' he said.

Reuben grinned. 'Me too.'

The two men looked at each other as if sharing a wonderful secret and Reuben watched as Sigmund stretched his legs out and crossed one ankle over the other. He looked more comfortable now.

'Venice and romance kind of go together, don't they?'

Reuben nodded, surprised to be having such a conversation with a stranger, but he welcomed the temporary distraction from his concerns about Elena. And his rapidly growing fascination with her sister.

'I mean,' Sigmund smiled, 'everything is so beautiful. I don't think I've ever seen a place like it. Paris, Prague, Barcelona, Rome - they have nothing on this!'

Reuben watched him as he talked. He'd never seen anybody as enthusiastic or animated about the subject of architecture. It occurred to Reuben that it must be a part of his job. Maybe he was a travel writer or a historian.

'I'm a lecturer,' he said when Reuben asked him. 'English Literature.'

Reuben picked up his pencil again as his new companion talked on. He wasn't really listening as he drew but he wasn't really concentrating on where his pencil was taking him either so, when he finally stopped, it came as a complete surprise to see what he'd drawn.

'Shit!' Reuben exclaimed.

'What's the matter?' Sigmund asked, trying to get a look at Reuben's sketch. 'Not gone as you planned?'

'Not exactly.'

'Can I have a look?'

Reuben shrugged and held the sketchbook out to Sigmund who took it and gave a long, low whistle.

'She's beautiful,' he observed. 'Is this your romantic interest?'

Reuben wasn't sure what to say. He didn't have many friends and wasn't used to talking about his personal life with anyone other than those who actually made up his personal life. But this fellow looked trustworthy enough. Reuben wasn't sure if it was the tweed jacket, the round glasses or the bow tie. Maybe it was a combination of all three and the fact that he reminded Reuben of his old geography teacher. But he felt that he could talk to this man.

'You could say that,' he said at last.

'She's very beautiful,' Sigmund said, handing the sketchbook back.

Reuben took it. 'She is, isn't she?'

And then he sighed because he'd gone and drawn yet another picture of Rosanna.

CHAPTER 25

'Elena! Where have you been?' Rosanna yelled as her sister walked up the steps into the apartment.

Clutching the box with the mask in it, Elena looked up and saw her sister's dark scowl.

'I've been out.'

'Well, I know that! I've been worried about you. Have you been with Mark all this time? What happened? Where's he staying?'

Elena reached the top of the steps and walked into the living room. 'No. I've not been with Mark all this time. He's staying somewhere near the Rialto and I really don't want to talk about things at the moment.'

Rosanna shook her head in exasperation. 'Reuben's been here wondering where you've been hiding yourself.'

'Oh, dear. I meant to go and see him.'

'So, where have you been all day?' Rosanna demanded.

Elena sighed and flopped down on one of the large sofas. How could she explain what had happened since she'd last seen her? How could she begin to explain how mean she'd been to Mark and how, after arriving back at the apartment, she'd proceeded to turn invisible.

'Is that the stupid mask you bought?' Rosanna asked, sitting down next to Elena and peeping into the carrier bag.

'Don't touch it!' Elena shouted.

'Why not?'

Elena bit her lip in panic. 'It's still wet. I took it back and they fixed one of the ribbons.'

Rosanna screwed her eyes up in disbelief. 'You've been getting a mask fixed when you have two fiancés in Venice?'

'I don't know what else I can do at the moment,' she said. 'Anyway, Mark's coming over this evening.'

'And what about Reuben? He did get here first, you know, and he looked so upset when he was here - all agitated.'

Elena sighed wearily. 'I'll go and see him before this evening.'

There was a moment's silence as if the sisters were contemplating the possible complications of the evening ahead.

'How did your afternoon go?' Elena asked at last.

'Ah! *La Stronza*!' Rosanna spat, throwing her arms in the air before getting up from the sofa and marching through to the kitchen. Elena followed her and watched as she threw a cup of strong coffee together. 'She is such a bitch! I can't believe that woman! I should never have gone in the first place.'

'Why? What happened?'

Rosanna threw some lunch dishes into the sink before answering. 'She insulted me! She treated me like a whore!'

'How?'

'Pah! She didn't like my dress.'

'But it's a beautiful dress,' Elena assured her.

'She thought I looked like a prostitute.'

'She actually said that?' Elena said, startled. That was pretty rough, even by Irma Taccani's standards.

'Well,' Rosanna said, her mouth pouting and her neck drooping into her shoulders like a put-upon tortoise, 'not exactly. But I could see that's what she was thinking!'

'I'm sure she wasn't,' Elena said, in a vain attempt to calm Rosanna. The unfortunate thing was that she believed Rosanna was right. Irma was the nastiest piece of work Elena knew. Well, that she'd heard of.

'She doesn't want me to have anything to do with her little boy!' Rosanna said, firing a jet of water into the sink and squeezing half a bottle of washing up liquid into it.

'But you're not sure whether you want to have anything to do with him either,' Elena pointed out.

'That's not the point! I should be allowed to dump him in my own time.'

Elena shook her head. Rosanna wasn't being very practical. She was intensely proud and stubborn and it was obvious that Irma's Taccani's behaviour was making it harder for Rosanna to make her mind up when it should have been making it easier.

'So, you *are* going to dump him?'

'*Merda*! I don't know!'

Rosanna stalked out of the kitchen with her coffee cup and Elena followed.

'I wish I could help you.'

Rosanna pouted. 'I think you have quite enough to cope with at the moment without becoming involved in my problems too.'

Elena knew her sister was right but she was desperate to help her. She could see how miserable all this was making her. If only, Elena thought, there was another man who could take her sister's mind off things. That's what was needed: an injection of new love! But who? Elena knew how difficult it was to find a good man. Just look what had happened to her: she'd waited years and years then three had come along at once.

'Hadn't you better get along to the Danieli?' Rosanna asked.

'I've only just got back,' Elena said.

'But Mark will be coming over before long and-'

'All right!' Elena sighed, standing up with the mask in her hand. 'I'll go and see Reuben.'

'Good!' Rosanna said, nodding sagely. 'And be nice to him.'

'Of course I'll be nice to him! What do you take me for?'

'A two-timing, no-good, double-crossing madam!'

Elena blinked hard. She supposed she deserved that.

Elena caught the vaporetto to San Marco. Of course, she should have gone to see Reuben at The Danieli after visiting Viviana's in Dorsoduro but her head had been so crammed with confusion that she'd been able to do nothing but head back to the apartment. That had been a mistake though - with Rosanna there checking on her every move, she hadn't even had a chance to try on the mask again.

She wondered if she should have told Rosanna about the mask. Stefano had said to have fun with it and hadn't given her instructions not to tell anyone about it but it felt as if it *should* be a secret. She had it with her now, tucked inside her jacket. Not that she intended using it, oh no, it was just that she didn't want to leave it in the apartment in case Rosanna stumbled upon it.

Entering the Danieli a few minutes later, Elena placed a hand on her jacket pocket. She walked straight by the main desk, passing the grand staircase on her right and the bar on her left and headed towards the lifts, but then a thought occurred to her. There was a ladies toilet here. Looking around her, Elena headed towards it and locked herself in a cubicle. It was risky, she knew. What if she took a bad turn and drowned in the lavatory bowl? What if it didn't work properly and only half of her turned invisible? What would she do then? But the temptation was too great and she took the mask out of her pocket and tied it on.

It took a few seconds to begin but she soon felt the strange pins-and-needles in her eyes, and experienced the warm, melting sensation in her body but didn't experience the nausea or jolting electric shock that she had the first time she'd tried the mask on. She breathed a sigh of relief and then giggled as she looked down at her non-existent body. It had happened so quickly this time. She'd soon be able to tie the mask on and disappear within a few seconds. What fun she could have then!

In the meantime, how was she going to get out of the cubicle without raising alarm?

She cleared her throat. 'Hello?' she shouted through the locked door. 'Anybody there?'

There was no answer. The coast, she assumed, must be clear. Slowly, she opened the door and sneaked back out into the lobby. There was an elderly couple waiting for the lift, a man on the phone behind the reception desk, and well-dressed guests drinking in the bar. Absolute normality. Elena felt a delicious smile spreading over her invisible face. What chaos she could cause, she thought. What fun she could have here. Stefano's words tickled her ears and she felt she'd be disobeying him most ungraciously if she didn't have just a little bit of fun before seeing Reuben.

Walking into the bar, she took a look around the room. There were numerous couples, drinking and talking. Elena watched for a few moments before zooming in on her first victims. A couple in their forties were sipping drinks in the corner of the room. The man was browsing a tourist guide, his face frowning in concentration. Or was it annoyance? Elena walked towards them to find out.

'You're not listening to me, are you, Phillip?' his wife barked.

'I am,' he said, his voice weary.

'Well, what did I say, then?'

'You were talking about Murano.'

'About the glass chandelier we saw. We simply have to go back and buy it. We can have it sent over in time for our anniversary. It will look simply stunning in the dining room.'

'But there's nothing wrong with the one we have at present,' the man protested lightly. 'We've only had it two years.'

'You are joking, aren't you? Darling, it's *so* last year. No,' she said, her red mouth set in a solid, implacable line, 'it won't do. We'll go back in the morning and order the one we saw today.'

The man sighed. 'Very well.'

'Darling, you know it makes sense.'

Elena grimaced. The word *darling* sounded like poison on the woman's lips. Elena pondered for a moment and then spied the woman's handbag on the floor beside her chair. Bending down, Elena took the long strap in her hand and dragged it slowly across the floor until it was a good two metres from the woman's chair.

'Darling,' the woman said a minute later, 'where's my handbag? What have you done with my handbag?'

'Nothing! What would I want with your handbag?'

'Then where-' she stopped as she spotted it. 'What's it doing over there?'

Her husband looked up and raised his eyebrows in surprise. Tutting, she got up to retrieve it.

'I most certainly didn't put it over there!' she complained, her suspicious eyes narrowing further.

It was all in the timing, Elena thought, as the woman came back to the table to sit down. One swift movement. It was so simple, so childish, and yet so effective!

'Darling!' the man cried, real concern in his voice. 'What on earth are you doing on the floor?'

The woman looked up at him, dazed and angry, her legs askew and her very expensive-looking skirt exposing a great deal of pale leg.

'Well, don't just stare at me! Help me up, you idiot!'

Elena watched as he helped his wife up and led her out of the bar with the rest of the guests watching on in silent amusement. For a moment, Elena wondered if she should follow them. The woman certainly needed taking down a peg or two but, she decided, that now was not the time, and so let her victim go free. She really must go up and see Reuben.

'Where the hell have you been?' Reuben shouted as he opened the door to Elena.

'That's not a very nice welcome!' Elena said, having forsaken fun and games and run through to the toilet to take the mask of in her hurry to be with Reuben.

'And neither was the one you gave me when I first arrived!' he said.

Elena shook her head and pushed passed him to get into the room. He could be so childish sometimes but she supposed that she was the cause of it this time.

'Rosanna told you I'd been over to the apartment?'

'Yes. I'm sorry I wasn't in.'

'Where were you?' he asked, his expression thunderous.

'I don't want to be cooped up all day.'

'Then why didn't you come here to see me?'

'I might very well have done and we missed each other!'

'We didn't though, did we? You didn't come to see me here, did you?'

Elena shook her head. 'No.'

'Then where did you go?'

'Just out,' Elena said, sitting down on the edge of the bed.

'And I don't suppose you'll want to stay here for long either, will you?'

'Don't start, Reuben. I'm here now, aren't I?' He sat down next to her. 'You can be such an awful grump at times!' she said, ruffling his dark hair and kissing his cheek.

'It's you who makes me grumpy.'

Elena smiled. 'I know.'

He smiled back at her and they kissed. He put his arms around her and nuzzled into her neck and she felt herself floating away on a tide of bliss.

'What's this?' he asked a moment later.

'What?' she said, stirred out of her hazy state by his question.

'This!'

Elena looked down and saw the mask in his hands which he'd obviously found whilst exploring her clothing. 'Oh! It's nothing. It's just something I bought myself. A little souvenir of Venice.'

'I'll have to draw you wearing it later,' he said, winking at her.

Elena laughed nervously. 'It's only a cheap trinket.'

Reuben ran his fingers along the curved edge of the mask. 'You could wear it now,' he whispered in her ear.

Elena froze. 'No!' she said, trying to sound light-hearted - as if she couldn't care if she wore it or not.

Reuben frowned. 'Go on! Put it on. It'll be fun.'

'Reuben!'

'Don't be a spoil sport!'

Elena felt panic rising inside her. 'I'm not!'

'Then why won't you put it on?'

'Because-'

'What?'

'Because it's weird! It's kinky! And I'm not into that,' she said, her heart hammering loudly.

Reuben tutted. 'It was only for a bit of fun,' he said defensively.

'Well, it's not the kind of fun I'm into.'

He handed the mask back to her and she placed it in the pocket inside her jacket before taking the jacket off and throwing it over a chair.

'Well, that's certainly killed the mood, hasn't it?' Reuben groaned, flopping back on the bed in a world-weary fashion.

'I'm sorry,' Elena said.

'I don't understand why you bought a mask if you don't want to wear it. I mean, what's the point?'

'Can we stop talking about the mask, please?'

Reuben sat up. 'What do you want to talk about then?'

'I don't want to talk at all,' she said, her voice softening as the fear of her magical mask being discovered drifted away.

Reuben cocked a dark eyebrow at her and they began to kiss.

Prof hadn't been able to find a single restaurant open before seven o'clock and his stomach was rumbling like an angry volcano by the time he finally sat down to dinner.

It had been a very pleasant first day in Venice, he thought, tucking into a mountain of ravioli. How strange to have met an artist from London. He'd have to make sure he saw him again before he went home. Maybe he would commission something - a portrait perhaps. But did he really want a portrait of his myopic face staring down from his wall? Maybe he'd commission one of Elena. Or maybe not. If he sent Elena round to Mr Reuben Lord, he'd probably seduce her before he lifted a single paintbrush.

But where *was* Elena? The island was much bigger than he'd first thought. When people talked of Venice, they made it sound so small but it was a large labyrinth of streets and squares. A person could hide away for years and not be discovered and Prof had only a few days in which to find Elena.

Elena stretched back on the bed and picked up Reuben's sketchbook. 'You've been busy,' she said, flicking through the pages, a sated smile filling her face. 'Oh my God! You've drawn Rosanna!'

Reuben looked up from the pillow and snatched the pad from her with fingers faster than bolts of lightning.

'Reuben! Let me look! They're really good.'

'You know I draw everyone I meet,' he said.

'I know,' Elena said, the pad back in her hands. 'You should show her. She'd like them.'

Elena flipped through the pad. There were endless bridges and canals, a gorgeously detailed study of San Marco complete with a posse of pigeons, and a couple of sketches of Santa Maria Della Salute. And then her eyes halted on one page. There was a sketch of a man wearing a bow tie and little round glasses.

'When did you do this?' she asked, her voice sounding hollow.

'What?'

Elena showed him the page she'd found.

'This afternoon. In the lobby bar.'

'Here?'

'Yes. He's a guest. English. Quite a nice bloke, actually.'

Elena felt the colour drain away from her face. It couldn't be, could it? Maybe it wasn't. Maybe Prof had a double. She shouldn't jump to conclusions.

'Are you okay?' Reuben asked.

'I'm - er - fine.'

'What is it? Do you know this guy or something?'

'No!' Elena said, trying to laugh it off. 'He just reminds me of someone.'

'Who?'

'Oh, someone I knew years ago at school.'

Reuben took the sketchbook from her and closed it, seeming to believe her lie.

'Look, Reuben, it's late. I'd better be off,' she said, getting up and feeling her legs quaking beneath her.

'Why don't you stay here, Elena? I don't understand!'

'Because I'm staying with Rosanna. I've told you.'

'But I'm paying for this amazing room! I can't believe you'd turn down a room like this. And it's so late now. I don't want you walking about in the dark.'

Elena looked at her watch. It was late, wasn't it? Mark would be waiting for her at the apartment by now.

'I've got to go, Reuben. Don't worry. I know my way around.'

'And just when am I going to see you next? We haven't had a chance to talk properly yet.'

Elena smiled at him. He was right. Every time they met, they seemed to do nothing but make love. 'I'll give you a call tomorrow.'

'Tomorrow? When? I might be out.'

But Elena was out of the room before he had time to protest further.

Doing her coat up in the lift, she looked at her watch nervously. She hadn't actually set a time to see Mark, had she? He'd wait for her, wouldn't he? As long as Rosanna didn't get all heated up and angry at her absence and start divulging information which Mark shouldn't know, everything would be fine.

The lift door opened and Elena stepped out, walking into the hotel foyer. And that's where she saw him. It was Prof. Sigmund Algernon Mortimer really was in Venice. It hadn't been his double - he really was here - in this very hotel. He really had spoken to Reuben! And he really was staring at her - right now.

'Elena?'

Elena froze for a vital, stupid moment and then darted, like an arrow from a bow, to the ladies. The mask! She had to get the mask on. There was nobody in the ladies and she reached for the mask and tied it on. She couldn't take a chance on becoming trapped in the cubicle - invisible or not. She had to risk it here.

'Elena?' Prof's voice was outside the door.

Her heart drummed madly as she tied the black ribbons around her head with shaking fingers and waited for the tingling to begin. She counted silently to herself as the warmth flooded her body and she watched in astonishment as her solid self began to fade away.

'El? Are you in there? Open up? It's me - *Prof!*'

Elena bit her lip. Just a few more seconds.

'If you're not coming out then I'm coming in,' he said in a singsong sort of way as if she might be playing games with him.

Elena screamed silently. There was still the faintest outline of her body - like a strange mirage.

'Okay,' Prof yelled from outside and, sure enough, the door opened and he was there, staring right at her - *through* her.

The mask had worked its magic but she didn't know what to do next.

'Elena? Are you in here?' Prof's expression was one of extreme puzzlement, like the one he wore when doing The Times crossword. 'I know you're in here,' he said but he didn't sound at all sure of himself as he approached the cubicle door. 'El?'

Of course, there was nobody there and he frowned at his mistake as he stood right next to her. Elena didn't dare breathe in case he heard her, and she didn't dare move in case he became aware of her presence. They stood, inches apart, only a tiny channel of air separating them. She could see the pores of his skin and the tiniest of shaving cuts. She could smell the deep sandalwood of his aftershave and, if she stretched out a finger, she'd feel the wild scratchiness of his tweed jacket.

Her dearest Prof had come all this way to see her but he didn't know where she was staying. How did he propose to find her, she wondered? Was he just going to wander around Venice in the hope of running into her? But wasn't that exactly what had happened?

Elena wondered what had made him stay at the Danieli. She knew he had plenty of money tucked away but to spend so much in the hope of finding her was rather silly. And what was he to think now? Would he believe the evidence of his own eyes? Or would he think he'd merely imagined seeing her?

Elena watched as he sighed and shook his head just as a woman entered the room, unleashing a torrent of Italian which, luckily, he couldn't understand but which made Elena smile in intense relief as he backed out of the toilets and disappeared down the hall.

CHAPTER 26

Rosanna was ready to pounce on Elena as soon as she got back to the apartment.

'You've missed him,' she said.

'Who?'

'Mark! Who else? You knew he was going to be coming over this evening. Where have you been all this time?'

'He could at least have waited for me,' Elena said, tired and confused.

'He did - for nearly two hours! But the poor guy got the feeling you were avoiding him.'

'Well, did he say where he was staying?'

Rosanna shook her head. 'No.'

'Then how am I meant to meet up with him?'

'I guess he'll come here again.'

Elena sighed. She had three fiancés in Venice who might turn up, unannounced, at any time. This was absolute madness.

'I'm going to bed,' Rosanna announced. 'I've had enough of today.'

Elena mirrored her sister's yawn and suddenly realised how tired she was. It had been the longest, strangest of days. She felt inside her coat for the mask and brought it out for one last look. Stefano had told her to have fun with it and she'd certainly done that today, but it was also becoming obvious that the mask was a necessary tool for coping with the over-zealous men in her life.

The Umbrian hills rolled gently into the midday heat haze in pale shades of emerald and amber. The only road visible was a tiny track up to the farmhouse which had been bleached a pale peach by hundreds of years of sunshine.

Shutters were flung wide open into a garden which rambled over rough ground. Great terracotta pots, stuffed full of herbs, jostled for space on a tiny but perfect terrace complete with wooden chairs and a table on which dishes for lunch were laid. It all looked so glorious, so picture-perfect. Until …

A dark-haired girl's head popped out of an upstairs window.

'MAMA!' she shouted. 'Mirella's pulling my hair! *MAMA!*'

'Now, you just stop that, Mirella! Leave Leda alone,' Rosanna called.

'It wasn't me, Mama. It was Chiara!' Mirella cried.

'Chiara! Get down here.'

A few minutes later, a tiny doll-like girl appeared on the terrace.

'What do you have to say for yourself, Chiara?'

'It wasn't my fault. Fabio started it.'

'Where's Fabio?'

'He's hiding. He's had a fight with Fabrizio.'

Rosanna rolled her eyes. Those twins would be the death of her. As if she didn't have enough to cope with with the three girls, and another baby due in the autumn.

'Go and get them both - NOW!'

Her head felt ready to split down the middle with pain. She sat down for a moment, her swollen hand resting on her engorged belly. Judging by the size of her, she wouldn't be surprised if it was twins again. That would be all she needed.

She looked down into the valley and wished she could take off and fly right into it…

'Rosanna?' a male voice called.

'I'm out here.'

'What are you doing?' Corrado asked, walking out onto the terrace in a foul mood.

'I'm trying to get away from everyone.'

'What?'

'I'm just having five minutes' peace and quiet.'

'Well, you've had all you're having. Now, get back in the kitchen or lunch will be ruined.'

Wearily, and without a helping hand from her husband, Rosanna got up and shuffled back into the kitchen.

'Just look at the state of the place!' Corrado complained.

Rosanna looked around the room in despair. There was an avalanche of dishes in the sink and the work surfaces were covered in cooking experiments that had gone wrong.

'It looks like Pompeii after the eruption of Vesuvius! And just look at that crostata! It looks like diarrhoea,' Corrado snarled. 'It's not like how Mama used to make it.'

Rosanna didn't dare say that it was like that because nobody ever leant a hand - that it was like that because she and she alone had to run the house and look after everybody.

'My house never looked like this, did it?' Irma complained, hobbling into the kitchen and staring accusingly at her with raisin eyes.

'No, it certainly didn't, Mama. But this one doesn't care as much as you!'

'Doesn't care?' Rosanna said, aghast, finding a little courage at last. 'Doesn't CARE? I'll have you know, your bloody mother only had one child to look after - not five, with another on the way, and a husband who does nothing but grow a few vegetables and complain of backache, and a mother-in-law with a whip for a tongue!'

'What did you say?' Corrado demanded.

'What did she say?' Irma screeched.

A sudden sound of crying came from upstairs followed by the thunder of footsteps on the stairs as five children burst into the kitchen - each one crying as if they'd lost a limb.

'Now look what you've done!' Irma shouted. 'Stupid, selfish girl! And what do you think you're doing wearing such a dress for cooking? Scarlet! Pah! It's the colour of a whore!' Irma's eyes glinted with malice.

The first photo frame hit Rosanna square on the nose. She was too stunned to react. Suddenly, Irma was throwing one after the other until Rosanna was suffocating beneath a mountain of silver. The onslaught didn't stop. Still, there were more, flying through the air, affording her a brief glimpse of Corrado at varying stages of childhood before they hit Rosanna in the face. Where were all these photo frames coming from? There seemed to be an endless supply. She was drowning.

'MAMA!' the children wailed.

'Help me!' Rosanna wailed back.

'Rosanna!'

'Help me!'

'Rosaaaaaaaaaaaaana!'

'Here I am! I'm here!'

'I know you are! Wake up!' Elena called.

And she did.

'Elena?'

'Rosanna! Are you okay?'

She sat up and rubbed her eyes. Elena had put a bedside lamp on and Rosanna slowly allowed her eyes to adjust to the light. 'I think so.'

'You were waving your arms around like a windmill.'

'I was suffocating.'

'Were you?'

'In photo frames.'

'What?'

Rosanna cradled her head in her hands in despair. 'It was horrible! It was like tea today but much, *much* worse.'

'Irma? You're dreaming about Irma Taccani?'

Rosanna nodded. 'I was trapped in this isolated farm house with Corrado and Irma and hundreds of kids. And I was fat and pregnant! It was horrible!'

'God! You've really got to do something about this, haven't you?'

Rosanna closed her eyes and let out the deepest, most grievous of sighs. 'I suppose so.'

'There's no supposing about it,' Elena said, swinging her legs out of bed and grabbing her dressing gown from a nearby chair. She winced as she saw the time on the alarm clock. It was only three in the morning. 'How about some hot milk?'

'*Merda!*'

'Hot chocolate?'

Rosanna nodded. 'That might be nice.'

Elena went downstairs, turning on lights and finding herself more awake than she thought she could be at that time of the morning. Rosanna followed her and curled up on a sofa, hugging a cushion to her as if it were a life belt.

'I don't think I want to marry Corrado,' she said a few minutes later when they sat warming their middle-of-the-night hands around their mugs of hot chocolate.

'I know you don't,' Elena agreed. 'You'd have to be certifiable to choose Irma Taccani as your mother-in-law.'

Rosanna sighed. 'That phrase *mother-in-law* shakes me to the core. The word *mother* is scary enough on its own without linking it to the word *law*.'

'Well, I'm glad we've finally established that.'

'But what do I do now?' Rosanna asked.

Elena had never seen her sister looking so fragile and she put her arm around her shoulders and kissed her on her cheek. 'You have to tell Corrado.'

The wide eyes closed in realisation. *Mio Dio*! Do I?'

'How else can you end all this?'

'It's just-'

'What?'

'So scary!'

'Tell me about it. Remember, I've got to break off two - I mean - one of my engagements,' Elena stumbled but Rosanna didn't seem to hear her blunder; she was too bound up in her own problems. 'At least you're not engaged.'

'But Irma will flail me. I know she will! She'll probably break into the apartment when I'm asleep and drag me out and drown me in the lagoon!'

'Rosanna! She'll do no such thing!' Elena sighed, trying not to look over her shoulder into the dark shadows of the apartment. 'She has nothing to do with this. It's between you and Corrado, okay?'

'I know I shouldn't let her get to me but I can't tell you how much that woman terrifies me,' she confessed.

Elena bit her lip. That Irma Taccani, like the overbearing woman in the Danieli, needed taking down a peg or two.

'Don't you worry about Irma,' Elena said, giving Rosanna's shoulder a squeeze. 'I have a feeling she won't be causing you any more problems.'

CHAPTER 27

Elena woke early despite the disturbed night's sleep. She got out of bed and looked across at Rosanna who was still fast asleep. Her skin was pale and she looked as if she wouldn't wake up for at least another few hours so Elena left the room quietly and sneaked downstairs for breakfast. There was something she had to do.

Picking up Rosanna's address book, Elena found Corrado's address and jotted it down on a piece of paper which she put in her inside pocket - along with the mask. She scribbled a quick note for Rosanna.

Hope you had a good lie-in. Have gone out. Don't wait for me for lunch. If anyone turns up, tell them I'm due back at any moment! Love, Elena x.

After the quickest of breakfasts, Elena left, closing the door quietly behind her. She knew roughly where the apartment was and it didn't prove hard to find. It was strange to think that Rosanna had been there, in that very spot, less than twenty-four hours ago, feeling anxious and alone. Elena felt her blood boil at the thought of how her sister had been treated and, with a particularly angry finger, she pressed the buzzer of the Taccani flat. No answer. She pressed it again. And again. Then she remembered Rosanna complaining that Irma had been rude to her over the intercom and then refused to open the flat door. Was she in or just ignoring the buzzer?

Elena tried a different buzzer.

'Hello?'

'Hello,' Elena said politely. 'I have a delivery of flowers.'

Without even asking whom the delivery was for, Elena was buzzed in. She climbed the stairs and stood outside flat number five before knocking loudly on the door. Again, she waited, her ear pressed up against the door. She could definitely hear somebody in there and, from the lightness of step, it was a woman.

Elena decided to put the mask on. There was only one other flat on that floor so she'd have to take a chance on being seen. The transition from solid to invisible took an impressive ten seconds. It was getting quicker each time she wore the mask.

Standing in the draughty corridor, Elena contemplated what to do next. There was no way that Irma was going to answer the door, that was for sure, so Elena had to rely on her instincts which was why she'd got there early in the morning. And she was right.

She didn't have to wait long before the door opened and Irma Taccani, all four foot eleven of her, emerged. With a large basket over her arm, and a deep scowl etched across her forehead, Irma looked ready to do battle with the world.

Elena followed her down the stairs and out into the dazzling morning sunshine. She guessed where she was going: to the fish market by the Rialto. It was the perfect place to buy fresh produce and Rosanna was a big fan of their fruit and vegetables, coming back with large bags stuffed full of rocket and tomatoes the size of apples which glowed like rare rubies.

Crossing the Rialto, Irma Taccani turned right and Elena followed. One of the joys of being invisible meant that she didn't have to keep her distance but, in the jostle of people, Elena suddenly realised what it truly meant to be invisible. She hadn't really stopped to think about it before. But she was beginning to find out that, just because she had the ability to disappear, it didn't mean that she disappeared altogether - she still took up space and that, for Elena, was a real problem as she'd always bruised easily and people just kept knocking into her as if she wasn't there, which, of course, she wasn't. It wasn't as if it was their fault; they weren't doing it on purpose but Elena had the feeling that she'd end up completely black and blue when she finally took the mask off.

Following somebody you don't particularly like was rather tedious, Elena decided. She'd have to spice things up a bit. The problem was, there wasn't really much she could do at the fish market, was there? She looked around her. It was an extraordinary place: a rosy red-bricked building with tall stone columns decorated with fantastic fish heads rising into fine arches, huge lanterns hanging from the beamed roof, and the early morning sunshine casting a red glow onto the stalls through the bright canopies. The stalls were simple structures with lights hanging overhead so that the fish glowed and glistened as if still underwater. Most of the fish rested on beds of ice and there were buckets under the stalls to catch the melt water.

There was an incredible swordfish on one of the stalls but the back of his body had been amputated and he looked lost and forlorn.

He didn't belong there, and Elena felt guilty for looking at something which had about as much business being on a table as she had being at the bottom of the ocean.

She watched as one stall holder watered his produce with a small orange watering can. The floor was also wet, shining like polished marble. Elena, who'd never really liked fish, felt almost sad as she saw the heaped bodies of prawns, their tiny black eyes seeming to accuse the shoppers who passed them by. *See what you've done*, they seemed to say.

And then she saw the crabs: their spiky limbs tangled together as if they were fighting for space. Elena looked up to see where Irma Taccani was. She was just inches away from Elena, and Elena found her invisible hand reaching out and picking up one of the crabs. Without being seen, she dropped it into Irma's shopping basket.

'*Mio Dio!*' Irma Taccani exclaimed a few seconds later, pulling the crab out of her basket and dropping it onto the table in front of her. The man behind the stall stared at her and then started laughing.

'What are you laughing at, you lumbering idiot! You put that in there for a joke? Some joke! Am I laughing?'

'I didn't go near your basket. And you be careful who you call an idiot, you old crab!'

'How dare you!'

'You think yourself lucky that I don't charge you for that!'

'You wouldn't catch me paying for anything from you!' she spat, her tiny eyes flaming with anger and humiliation as she stormed out of the fish market as fast as her little legs would carry her. Her mouth was working overtime as she spat out oaths and curses over the incident in the fish market and Elena did her best not to laugh out loud.

Reaching the flat once more, Elena followed Irma up the stairs, making sure her own footsteps were silent. Irma's progress was slow and, for the briefest of moments, Elena felt sorry for her, but she soon roused herself by remembering how mean she had been to Rosanna.

Standing a few feet behind her, Elena watched as Irma retrieved her key from her bag. Like in the Danieli, it was all about timing. The key was in the lock and the handle was being turned. The door was open. NOW!

'Irma!' Elena called softly from behind her shoulder before

walking lightly down the hallway a little.

'Who's there?' Irma asked, craning her head back a little but not letting go of the door handle. There wasn't enough space for Elena to get through.

'Irma!' Elena called again.

Irma's tiny eyes narrowed until they'd almost completely disappeared. 'Who is it? Is that you, Dora?' she asked, walking towards the stairs and peering down.

Elena took her chance and ran lightly into the apartment. She was in! Almost

immediately, she was struck by the neatness of everything. There wasn't a cushion that was out of the place, the curtains were drawn just so and a large collection of silver photo frames shone brightly on a sideboard. Elena took a step closer to look at them and noticed that they were all of Corrado. These must have been the photo frames from Rosanna's nightmare, Elena thought, and she had a sudden urge to throw them all out of the window into the nearby canal.

The flat door slammed and Irma Taccani came in muttering under her breath. Elena watched as she walked through to the kitchen and started to put her shopping away, wondering, exactly, what she was going to do with her. She amused herself, for the time being, with unstraightening the curtains and squashing the cushions into unpleasant shapes but that wouldn't amount to a satisfying revenge even though it was funny to see Irma's puzzled expression as she walked back through to the living room.

The answer came when Irma took a duster to a picture on the wall. It was one of the few pictures in the flat that wasn't of Corrado. It was of the Virgin Mary. That was it, Elena smiled.

'Irma Taccani!' Elena suddenly bellowed, surprising herself by the strength of her own voice.

Irma dropped her duster and span around to face the empty space that Elena was occupying.

'Who is it?' Irma asked, obviously terrified. It was, Elena thought, probably the first time in her life that this woman *had* been terrified.

'Who do you *think* I am?' Elena boomed.

'Mary, mother of God!' Irma squealed, looking at the picture she'd been dusting.

'That's right,' Elena said, trying very hard not to scream with laughter.

Irma crossed herself and sank to her knees. 'How have I displeased you?' she asked, eyes closed as if in prayer.

Elena paused for a moment, marvelling at how easy it had been to have this dragon of a woman sink to her knees before her.

'I've been watching you lately and I am not pleased with what I see.'

Irma's eyes sprang open as if in shock. 'What have I done? Tell me what I have done and I will make amends.'

'You're damned right you will!' Elena boomed, and then wondered if the Virgin Mary would really use the word *damned*, but it was too late and Irma hadn't seemed to notice. 'You are a mean and crabby old woman, Irma Taccani,' Elena continued, not worrying too much about the vocabulary she now attributed to the Virgin Mary. 'And you've been mean and crabby to those around you.'

'Crabby?'

'Why do you sound surprised by that word?'

Irma shook her head as if in confusion. 'The market - the crab!'

'What are you talking about?'

'N-nothing,' she stammered. 'But I don't understand what you mean! My darling Corrado! He means more to me than life itself. I cannot think what I've done to hurt him.'

'I am not talking about Corrado, you silly woman,' Elena continued, getting into her stride as the godly messenger.

'Then who? I hardly see anyone else.'

'No,' Elena said, 'you don't have many friends, do you, Irma Taccani?'

Irma shook her head. 'My boy! He's all I need.'

'But he is an adult now. He will soon make a family for himself.'

Irma nodded, and silence ruled for a moment. 'I think I see now,' she said at last.

'What is it you see?'

'I think I might have been unpleasant to his girlfriend.'

'Think? THINK?' Elena shouted.

'Forgive me! Forgive me!' Irma babbled wildly.

'You were most unpleasant to her. *Most* unpleasant!'

'But she-'

'What? What did she do to you? There is no excuse for the way you behaved. None at all.'

Irma shook her head. 'Forgive me! Tell me what I should do.'

Elena thought for a moment, dragging her mind back to the days of confession. 'Five *Our Fathers* and Eighty-eight *Hail Marys*,' she said, her voice serious.

'Eighty-eight?'

'You have a problem with that, Irma Taccani?'

'Oh, no! But why eighty-eight?'

'You dare to question me?'

'No! Oh, no!'

'Then I will leave you to begin,' Elena said, making sure Irma's eyes were closed in prayer before she quietly let herself out. Before she left, she turned around to see a shaking Irma Taccani clinging on to her rosary and saying the first of eighty-eight *Hail Marys*.

CHAPTER 28

Elena and Rosanna weren't the only ones to have had a disturbed night's sleep. Mark had tossed and turned and, after realising that he wasn't going to find any sanctuary in sleep, had got up at seven o'clock and left his hotel. He'd walked three miles before breakfast which surprised him because he wasn't used to walking further than to his local supermarket.

Venice was the best city to get lost in, he decided. He wasn't quite sure where he went on his early morning exploration although he had recognised San Marco. It was ghostly quiet when he walked through it and it was easy to imagine it was like that all the time. He wandered in and out of the arches of the Doge's Palace, feeling as if he was inside some gargantuan wedding cake, and then spent a few, quiet moments looking out across the bright water of the lagoon. He'd never seen so much water in his life. Being a city boy, water had been something to drink or bathe in - never something simply to look at.

Walking, he'd found, was very therapeutic. With each step he took, he felt a little less anxious and a little less stressed. He let his feet take charge and had found himself at the Rialto where he grabbed something to eat. By now, the city had been awake for some time and the vaporetti were packed with people off to work. Mark wondered what it would be like to get a boat to work. Looking at the queues and the people squashed together, he surmised that it was really no different from catching the bus or the Tube. The novelty of water-based transport would soon wear off, he thought cynically, crossing over the Rialto Bridge and turning right.

He soon found out why there were so many people around as he came across a market. Wandering around the stalls, he bought a couple of large red apples before heading to look around the fish market. The smell of salt-water tickled his nose and made his stomach rumble even though he'd just eaten. He'd never shopped at a proper market before; he was a supermarket kind of guy and his trips involved nothing more time-consuming than grabbing a basket and dashing madly, grabbing as many microwavable goods as he could.

So it was quite pleasant to have the time to just wander around, smelling the smells and seeing the sights, and it culminated in him seeing the most extraordinary thing.

He'd just passed a stall on which was a very impressive display of fish when a crab seemed to have flown into an unsuspecting shopper's basket. Mark's eyes had almost been out on springs; it was the strangest thing he'd ever seen and, for a minute, he wondered if he was still half-asleep. Had the crab still been alive? He hadn't thought so, and he couldn't help grinning as he watched the old woman's response. She gave a load of abuse to the stall-holder whom she clearly blamed for the incident but Mark had seen that he'd had nothing to do with it; the crab had simple flown into the woman's basket. There was no other explanation for it. Maybe it was a species of crab peculiar to the Veneto region?

Mark looked around for someone to share the joke with but there was nobody. All he could think about was how much Elena would have laughed if she'd seen it and he knew that it wasn't half as funny seeing it alone as it would have been if they'd experienced it together. It wasn't that he felt half a person without her - he didn't buy in to all that rubbish - it was just that life wasn't as much fun without someone who was on your side, someone you could say, *Hey! You're never going to believe what happened to me today!* Or to assure you that you were right and that it was the world that had lost its marbles - not you. Everybody needed that other person to sound-off to and, for Mark, only Elena would ever do.

He'd been bitterly disappointed when she hadn't turned up at the apartment, and there wasn't any consolation in the fact that Rosanna had been equally annoyed. She'd paced up and down, periodically cursing in Italian and flinging crockery around in the kitchen. He'd sat for an unbearably long time, having no idea what to say to Rosanna or what to do if Elena didn't turn up. He kept giving her the benefit of the doubt. *She'll be here in another ten minutes'*, he'd think. *If she's not here by then, I'm going.* But, as soon as the ten minutes had elapsed, he'd wait another ten minutes.

Finally, he'd lost patience and, with an apologetic and apoplectic Rosanna following him down the steps to the front door, he'd left.

'I don't know what to say,' she'd called after him. 'I'll give her a piece of my mind when she gets back.'

Mark had given a brief smile and headed down the dark calle on his own. At the time, there'd been a part of him that had never wanted to see Elena again. What was he meant to think when she'd not shown up? Didn't it prove that she no longer cared about him?

Leaving the market, he felt angry, confused and very alone.

Rosanna picked up the note and read it. She pursed her lips, feeling deprived of picking a fight with Elena. She'd woken up in a bad mood after her nightmare of turning into a fat Italian mama surrounded by squawking kids, and the only vent for her emotions was her sister and, as she wasn't there, Rosanna felt at a loss.

She fed cat-child before pushing it outside with an angry toe. Just where had Elena gone to so early in the morning? Rosanna could only hope that it was to sort things out with either Reuben or Mark - if not both. But then, Elena didn't know where Mark was staying, did she?

'She must be with Reuben,' Rosanna said aloud, stopping in front of a mirror. She gazed at her reflection. Her eyes looked wild from her disturbed sleep, even though she'd slept in late. At least she didn't have any bookings that day. But there was one thing she couldn't avoid. She had a date with Corrado. Before she'd escaped from tea with his mother, Corrado had made her promise to meet him at a restaurant on the Lido where they could talk properly. Corrado had never used the phrase *"talk properly"* before and it set all sorts of alarm bells ringing in Rosanna's mind.

'It's the house in Umbria!' she whispered. 'The house and the kids. And *Irma!*'

She span around from the mirror, her eyes as wide as a cartoon character's. She knew what was coming - it was her nightmare vision of the future. She had to put a stop to it before things got out of hand; she had to tell Corrado that it was over.

CHAPTER 29

After the strange Elena-mirage, Prof had spent the whole morning trying out his patchy Italian on unsuspecting shopkeepers and café owners, proffering a small photo of Elena which he kept in his wallet. He was met with nothing more than shrugs and shaking heads. It wasn't as easy as he'd thought it would be. He'd naively thought Venice would be rather like a friendly village where everybody would know each other, but it was no different from any other city.

To make himself feel slightly better, he visited the Peggy Guggenheim Collection where he marvelled at the modern art even though he hadn't been able to understand a single brushstroke, and squinted at some rather phallic blue glass which he knew Elena would have had him blushing and laughing at had she been with him. It all left him feeling rather hungry so he found a very nice restaurant overlooking a pretty square.

Choosing a table outside because the weather was really very mild and the sunshine was most pleasant on a tweed jacket, he ordered himself lunch with a glass of house white. A chap could very easily get used to this, he thought, stretching his legs out under the table. He looked out at the houses across the quiet square: they were painted in shades of fondant pink and mellow red which had the most pleasing effect on the eye. He smiled, turning back to take a sip of the wine that had arrived.

It was then that he noticed a young woman sitting at a table opposite his. He hadn't seen her when he'd first sat down and he couldn't understand why. She had a mass of auburn curls which caught the spring light and danced in the breeze as if they were a part of it. Her skin was pale and she had a smattering of freckles over her nose as if a child had flicked a paintbrush at her. Prof couldn't help but smile. He'd always been rather susceptible to a pretty face and this one was Pre-Raphaelite pretty. He watched her for a moment and tried to see what she was doing. She'd finished her lunch and was writing in a lined pad with a bright silver pen.

As if he'd called out her name, the woman looked up and caught him staring at her. Prof immediately felt himself blushing and felt ashamed that he'd intruded into her private space but the woman returned his smile, quite unselfconsciously.

'You're English, aren't you?' she asked him suddenly.

He nodded, surprised by her boldness. Anyway, how could she tell he was English? Had his Italian accent been that bad when he'd ordered his meal or was there something unmistakably English in his tweed jacket and bow tie?

'Yes,' he said. 'You?'

'Of course!' she replied in an accent as sharp as cut glass. 'Although my name isn't terribly English - Anastasia Dupres.'

Prof smiled at her very confident but seemingly natural way of introducing herself.

'I'm Sigmund,' he said shyly.

'Pardon?' she said, leaning forward in her seat. 'I'm afraid we won't be able to hold a satisfactory conversation if you sit all the way over there.'

'Oh!' Prof said, looking confused.

'I meant, would you like to join me?'

Prof felt another blush spreading over his face but found himself nodding and standing up, walking towards her table and sitting down.

'Now, darling,' she said, as if she'd known him for aeons, 'what did you say your name was?'

'Sigmund.'

'Sigmund?'

Prof nodded, waiting for the laughter which inevitably followed whenever he introduced himself. 'Yes. Sigmund Mortimer,' he said, extending a hand to shake hers.

'I don't think I've ever met anyone called Sigmund before,' she said with a gorgeous, open smile whilst shaking his hand firmly. It was the best reaction he'd ever had to his name. 'You're the first,' she added flirtatiously.

Prof wasn't sure how to respond to that and became even more flustered when the waiter came out and scowled at him. 'Oh, I've moved,' he explained unnecessarily.

'It's so nice to have somebody to talk to,' she said. 'Travelling alone can be so dreadfully dull.'

Prof nodded. 'Yes.'

'And I do an awful lot of that with my job,' she added.

Prof noticed how she effortlessly fed him conversation starters. It was a rather enjoyable experience and he allowed himself the pleasure of going with the flow.

'Don't you want to know what I do?' she said.

'Oh! Sorry!' Prof said, realising that he'd missed his cue because he'd been watching the way the sunlight shone through her hair, turning it a wondrous ruby red. 'Of course! What do you do?'

Anastasia laughed. 'I'm a travel writer. I'm doing an article for *Vive!* at the moment.'

'Really?'

She nodded. 'I know it's not the best of papers to write for but they pay well and the exposure will do me good,' she said, uncrossing and crossing her legs to the side of the table, giving Prof a quick glimpse of her shapely legs.

Prof picked up his glass of wine and took a generous mouthful, feeling very hot all of a sudden.

'Do you read *Vive!*?' she asked.

'No,' he said. 'Hardy and Dickens mostly.'

'Really!' She laughed again, a wonderfully light laugh which reminded him of champagne bubbles. 'You know, when you first came and sat down, I had a feeling you were a teacher.'

Prof smiled. 'Was it that obvious?'

'Yes but in a good way. I bet you're a wonderful teacher,' she said. 'You look kind, approachable-'

'Lenient!' Prof interrupted.

'Are you?'

'Well, I do have one or two students who can run rings around me,' he said, thinking of Elena and her ever-extending deadlines.

'I bet you do,' Anastasia said, her eyebrows rising naughtily. 'I wasn't so lucky at my old school. We had nothing but nasty nuns. I never had anyone as nice as you.'

'Well,' Prof said, not quite knowing how to respond.

There was a moment's silence when he was very aware that her eyes were glued to him. It had been a long time since he'd felt so completely at the centre of somebody's attention. He'd never quite had that feeling with Elena. She always seemed as though she was only partially with him - as if part of her was somewhere else. It was like the emotional equivalent of looking over somebody's shoulder at a party in the hope of finding a more interesting person to talk to.

'So,' she said, 'what is Sigmund doing in Venice?'

'I'm engaged,' he said.

'Oh!' Anastasia said, her eyes widening in what looked like surprise.

Prof felt a little abashed. Perhaps he should have mentioned it before. 'I'm actually here to see my fiancée,' he explained further.

'Where is she?' Anastasia asked, looking around as if she might fear her arrival at any moment.

Prof gave a little smile. 'I'm not really sure.'

'You're not sure? You mean, you've lost her?'

'No. Not exactly. It's more like I haven't actually found her.'

Anastasia frowned. 'This is confusing!' she said. 'Do tell me more!'

As the waiter arrived with Prof's meal, Anastasia ordered a bottle of wine for them.

'I followed her out here, you see,' Prof began, loading his fork with spaghetti. 'She's here to see her sister and has absolutely no idea that I'm here.'

'You mean she came out here on her own and left you behind?'

'Yes.' Prof said. 'YES!' he nodded. 'Well, I wasn't going to have that!' he said, suddenly getting excited.

'Good for you, kitten!'

'So, here I am.'

'But you don't know where she is!'

'That's it!' he said.

'I see,' she said. 'Well, no, actually - I don't! How could your fiancée up and leave without telling you where she was going?'

Prof swallowed a mouthful of spaghetti and then shrugged. 'Because I let her, I suppose.'

'Oh!' Anastasia said thoughtfully. 'Then she's one of these pupils of yours who runs rings around you?'

'Yes,' he said dolefully. 'She always gets away with merry hell.'

'And you didn't think to ask where she'd be staying?'

'No.'

'But she didn't even leave a phone number for you to contact her at?' Anastasia asked.

'No.'

'Has she a mobile?'

'No,' he said, twisting his fork into another mound of spaghetti.

'Sweetie!' Anastasia said breathily. 'It sounds to me like she doesn't want you to be able to contact her. Have you thought of that?'

There was a moment's pause; it was Prof's turn to frown.

'You hadn't, had you?' she said, her frown mirroring his perfectly.

Prof's spaghetti untwisted from his fork and fell in golden coils on his plate. 'No,' he said at last.

Anastasia gave him a sympathetic smile. 'Sweet man,' she said, and laid a hand over his and gave it a gentle squeeze.

There was no stopping Elena as she left Irma Taccani's apartment. She'd been at it all morning: knocking people's hats off, tapping people's shoulders and even going as far as nipping a very cute gondolier's bottom as he touted for custom by the side of a canal. He'd looked so shocked that she was quite lucky he hadn't actually fallen into the murky green water and taken her with him.

By lunchtime, she was quite exhausted and found a quiet calle in which to take the mask off, slipping into her old self with the tiniest of tingles. Was this what Superman and Wonder Woman felt like when they turned into super-humans, Elena wondered, and then felt guilty. What she'd been doing had been far from super-human. She'd done nothing but cause havoc for her own amusement. Apart from dealing with Irma Taccani: that had been a truly inspired piece of divine justice. Elena wished she could share the joke with Rosanna but realised that that wouldn't be possible.

Following the calle round, Elena came out into a quiet square she hadn't seen before. That was all part of the joy of Venice: there was always something new to discover. The lunchtime light shone full-blast, lighting up the houses which seemed to guard the little square and giving everything a golden glow.

There was a restaurant on the far side and Elena thought she'd treat herself to something. Walking across the square, she heard the pleasant sound of laughter coming from one of the tables and noticed a beautiful red-haired woman. She looked so happy, sitting in the sunlight, a glass of wine in her hand and the light breeze lifting her hair away from her face that Elena didn't notice her companion at first. She completely overlooked the tweed jacket, the glint of the sun on the round glasses and the unmistakable bow tie.

It was her dear old Prof - with another woman.

CHAPTER 30

'Mark!' Rosanna cried, opening the door. 'What are you doing here?'

Mark gave Rosanna a puzzled look. 'What do you mean?'

'I wasn't expecting you,' she said, and then sighed. 'I'm sorry. That sounded so rude of me. Please, come in.'

Mark followed her up the steps, knowing what he would find at the top of them - or rather, what he wouldn't find.

'I take it Elena isn't in again,' he said and the hopelessness of his tone made Rosanna's heart ache.

'No, she isn't,' she said. 'But you know you didn't leave your address last night?'

'I do know. I didn't feel like leaving it,' he said sounding, at once, both sulky and regretful. 'Here,' he added, taking a notebook and pen from his pocket and writing it down. 'If she wants to get in touch, she has no excuse now.'

'Mark-'

'Yes?'

Rosanna could see the pain deep in his eyes as well as hear it in his voice and, at that moment, she wanted to tell him absolutely everything there was to know about her sister. She wanted it to be as clear to him as it was to her; she wanted him to understand.

'Mark, I-'

'What?'

She paused and, in that brief moment, she lost her nerve. 'Would you like something to drink?' she asked.

'A large glass of arsenic would go down a treat,' he said, following her through to the kitchen. 'You're not working today?'

She shook her head. 'No, thank God! Are you missing your work?' she asked, quite glad to enter the realms of small talk.

'Are you joking?' he said, giving a little laugh. 'As soon as I go back, I'll be counting the days until the next holiday.'

'So, what have you been doing today?' She turned to face him and saw a pair of melancholy eyes staring into space.

'I've been pounding the streets of Venice.'

Rosanna nodded, sympathising immediately with the trials of a fellow pounder. 'I know how that is,' she said.

'You do?'

She gave him the faintest of smiles. 'Oh, yes!' She poured hot water into the mugs of coffee and they walked through to the living room where they sat on one of the huge sofas. There was a few moments of silence when they both deliberated over who should be the first to intrude on the other's privacy.

'I don't know what to do,' Mark said finally and his voice sounded brittle and broken.

Rosanna looked across at him and was sure she could see tears threatening to fill his eyes. 'You have to talk to Elena.'

'I KNOW! But how am I meant to talk to her when she avoids me as if I had some kind of contagious disease?'

'No,' Rosanna said. 'I mean you have to *really* talk to her.'

'What do you mean?'

'You've never done that, have you? I don't mean that as a fault in you; I know what she's like, believe me! I know she hides away and keeps things deep inside her. But you have to get past that. You have to *talk* to her!'

'That's why I came out here,' Mark said quietly. 'I knew something was wrong. What is it, Rosanna?'

Rosanna sighed. 'I can't tell you that, Mark. You must ask Elena.'

'Is it something I've done?'

Rosanna shook her head gently. 'No. It's nothing you've done.'

'Because I've been wracking my brains and going mental over the last few days.'

'Don't give up on her, Mark,' Rosanna found herself saying. She wondered where the words had come from and why she'd said them. She realised the implications - she was saying that she hoped Mark would win through - over Reuben. She looked at Mark as he sat next to her. He looked drained of colour and so unsure of himself - like a little schoolboy who is stuck on a sum but is too afraid to ask the teacher for help.

'I won't give up,' he said, giving Rosanna a weak smile and, at that moment, she felt sure that he wouldn't. He might not have been as roguishly handsome as Reuben nor have his arrogance or confidence but there was something else of the hero about Mark. He had a depth to him that made Rosanna feel as if he'd always be there to take care of things. There was a kindness in his eyes and a gentleness in his expression that touched her heart and made her feel sure of him.

'And you're sure you can't tell me what's really going on here?' he asked again.

Rosanna shook her head. 'You wouldn't really want me to, would you?'

Mark sighed and shook his head. 'I guess not.'

Rosanna looked nervously at her watch. Why did Elena's fiancés always turn up when she had to be getting ready to go out? She had a few hours yet but she needed to be alone in order to psych herself up for the evening ahead and, as much as she hated the idea of Mark leaving the apartment without seeing Elena again, she knew she was going to have to persuade him to go pretty soon.

'Look,' he said, 'I don't want to get in the way here. It seems I do nothing but pester you. You've been so kind, Rosanna.' He stood up from the sofa and Rosanna immediately felt guilty at having wished he would leave.

'Anytime,' she said, standing up.

He then did something most unexpected: he leant forward and hugged her and there was a warmth in his embrace and she felt stunned and flattered all at once.

'Thanks,' he whispered to her and, before she could say anything, he left.

'Elena!' Stefano said in surprise as she entered the mask shop. 'What brings you back so soon?'

'Is there somewhere I can sit down?' Elena asked, suddenly feeling drained of all energy.

'Wait one moment,' Stefano said, disappearing through the door at the back of the shop - the door through which customers were not permitted to pass. Elena looked around. Once again, the shop was empty. She'd only ever seen one customer other than herself. How on earth did Stefano and his wife make a living, she wondered?

'Here,' he said, coming back with a small wooden chair. 'Can I get you a drink?'

'A water would be lovely, thank you.'

Once more, Stefano disappeared into the back leaving Elena alone with the hundreds of faces hanging from the red walls.

'What are you lot looking at?' she said, taking her bad mood out on the innocent watchers. There was a particularly petulant-looking plague-doctor mask - its long nose looking very haughty.

'Oh, shut up!' Elena snapped.

'Pardon?' Stefano said, coming through with a glass of water.

'Nothing,' Elena said, feeling very foolish.

'Talking to the masks, eh?' Stefano chuckled. 'I know all about that! They've been my companions for years, some of these fellows.'

Elena looked around the walls with renewed interest. 'Really?

'Oh, yes. Some of them are permanent fixtures, you see. Work colleagues, you could say. They will never leave this shop.'

'Which ones?' Elena asked.

'The one you were talking to.'

'How do you know which ones-' Elena paused. 'You just know, don't you?'

Stefano nodded. 'And he does have the cheekiest of expressions, doesn't he? It's as if he can read minds, that one.'

Elena's eyebrows rose. 'Can he?' she asked.

'What?'

'Read minds!'

'Of course not! What made you think that?'

'Because -'

'- of the mask I gave you?' he finished for her.

'Well - yes!'

'They're not all magical, you know.'

Elena shook her head. 'I don't understand how some are magical whilst others aren't.'

'How come some people are ignorant pigs whilst others are angels?'

Elena laughed.

'Things just are. I don't control them,' he said with a shrug.

'But you knew about the mask you gave me.'

Without a word, Stefano turned sharply on his heels and disappeared through the little door. Elena sat forward on her chair, her eyes on the door, waiting for him to return. But he didn't. The masks hanging on the wall next to her seemed to titter and snigger. *You shouldn't have said that!* they seemed to say. *You naughty girl! You've done it now!*

'Why?' she asked. 'What's he going to do?' Elena whispered to them as if they could hear her. She felt nervous. Perhaps she should leave Viviana's. Just go whilst Stefano was in the back room. What was he doing back there? Had she offended him? Was he going to demand that she gave him the mask back? Her hand flew inside her jacket pocket to check that it was still there. It was.

'Stefano?' she called quietly.

At last, he came back into the shop.

'What were you doing out there?' she asked, her nerves betraying her.

'I had to go to the toilet! Who are you? My mama?'

Elena couldn't help but smile as she watched him bend over his worktable behind her.

'What are you making?'

'I'm never quite sure,' he admitted. 'The masks kind of evolve.'

Elena narrowed her eyes as if she didn't quite believe him. She remembered art lessons at school were teachers drummed it into you that you must plan, plan, plan. Art didn't *evolve* - it was researched, mapped out and edited before the thing took on any real life of its own.

'Why did you come here today?' Stefano asked her.

Elena sighed. She wasn't sure she wanted to talk about it any more. After the incident with Prof, she'd felt so angry and confused and, at first, was going to march right up to him and punch him on the nose before demanding to know what he was doing. But she'd merely stood and watched for a few minutes as he'd chatted easily to the woman with the red curls, and she'd felt all her anger draining out of her body. It had been the strangest of sensations. Now, she wasn't quite sure how she felt about it.

'I was going to yell at you.'

'Really?'

Elena nodded. 'It's the mask. I think it's doing strange things to me. I can't explain it. It's as though I'm becoming somebody else.'

'That's the true magic of masks. You should watch a person when they first put one on - it's as if they were taking a drug or drinking that one drink that will take them over the edge into their other, truer selves. Masks can give you a confidence, an arrogance, a distance from yourself. They can make you feel invincible, invulnerable and -'

'Invisible!' Elena interrupted his little speech.

'Well, yours can.'

Elena frowned. 'I was invisible today.'

'Good!' Stefano said, nodding his approval. 'I told you to have some fun with it.'

'No!' Elena cried. 'I mean, I was invisible when I took the mask off!'

'Eh?'

'I saw somebody I know but he didn't see me.'

Stefano's white eyebrows narrowed. 'And you didn't speak to him?'

'I didn't know what to say so I came here.'

'I can't give you a mask for that, I'm afraid.'

Elena sighed. What had she expected from Stefano? It had seemed quite natural for her to head for the little mask shop when she'd found herself in trouble but she knew in her heart that he couldn't really solve her problem.

Watching Stefano wielding the most delicate of paintbrushes, something occurred to Elena and she reached for the mask in her pocket once more.

'Stefano,' she began, holding the mask up to the window so that it shimmered and shined like a little sun. 'You realise that you could make an absolute fortune from this mask, don't you?'

Stefano looked up from the mask he was working on, frowned and shook his head. 'What do I want with a fortune?' he scoffed. 'I am happy. This is enough,' he said, gesturing around the shop.

Elena stared at him in disbelief. 'But you'd never have to work again. You could retire and live anywhere you chose! Just think - you and Viviana could buy a villa on the Amalfi coast or-'

'No, no, no! I don't think so.'

Elena's forehead creased in bemusement. She couldn't quite believe him but, as she continued to watch him as he worked, she realised that some people actually enjoyed their work - loved it even. Stefano's work was his life: it was the air he breathed and the energy that coursed through his veins.

'But think what this could mean to the world!' Elena said, trying another line of reasoning.

'Pah! The world! What world is there outside of my shop? What could compete with the day to day existence of creating beautiful things which people treasure?' he said, gesturing to his friends on the wall behind him where rows of exquisite faces seemed to wink back at him. 'What could compare with choosing the paints, the ribbons, the sequins and feathers; of blending knowledge and imagination to create something unique? Eh? I don't want anything else,' he said simply, putting his paintbrush down and looking at her directly. 'I gave the mask to you, Elena. It is yours to do with as you wish but I wouldn't advise giving it to anybody else.'

'I wasn't going to,' she said hastily.

'I'm glad to hear it.'

Elena looked down at the golden mask, feeling rather honoured. 'Why did you choose me, then?'

'I told you before - the mask chose you,' he said quietly as he continued to work.

'Are all the masks magical? For the right person, I mean?'

Stefano shook his head. 'So many questions!'

'But do you know the answers?'

He looked up at her and their eyes locked. 'I don't think I have the answers you want,' Stefano said at last, breaking the spell with a blink and returning to his work.

Elena smiled. 'I'd better be going,' she said, putting the mask inside her coat pocket once more.

'Good luck,' he said as Elena made to leave the shop.

'Thanks,' she replied before realising that she hadn't even told him that she needed any.

CHAPTER 31

Elena couldn't remember the last time she'd sat in a church. She had a feeling it had been the time Rosanna had visited one February and dragged her out on a Sunday morning, before her eyes were open, to sit in an Arctic-cold church.

She'd been so nervous at entering this one with the mask in her pocket that she'd taken it very slowly so she could turn and run if any bolts of lightning were thrown her way.

Now, sitting on a hard wooden pew and staring at the altar, Elena felt a little more at ease. Some time ago, and she couldn't quite pinpoint when, she'd moved away from religion. It hadn't been a case of getting out of bed one morning and saying, that's it: I'm not religious any more - it had slowly crept up on her. But sitting in the church now, it would be easy to believe again. The very air seemed thick with Divinity. Perhaps it was the whiteness of the walls or the brightness of the candles, but there was an undeniable sense of peace.

On one of the walls nearby, there was a beautiful painting of the Virgin Mary set behind a little altar of its own. When Elena first noticed it, she felt herself blushing, hoping Mary wouldn't turn her eyes towards her and punish her for her cruel revenge on Irma Taccani who was probably still working her way through her *Hail Marys*.

The Virgin's dress was a startling lapis lazuli and it was that which had first caught Elena's eye. She was holding the infant, Jesus, whose alabaster skin seemed to glow with holiness, but it was Mary who was the focus of the painting: she wore an expression of indescribable peace. Elena gazed at it and wondered what it must be like to feel that calm. She hadn't felt calm like that for a long time - if ever. It was something which eluded Elena but this picture breathed peace: from Mary's serene face and the gentleness with which she held her baby, to the pastoral landscape seen through the arched window behind her. Elena could feel her vision dissolve as she looked at it, allowing her eyes to be led out into the distant hills. It reminded her of somewhere: a somewhere she hadn't seen for a long time; a somewhere far removed from the bustle of the world around her now.

'Positano,' she whispered. Positano. It was more than a place: it was a state of being and, as Elena thought about it, she could almost feel her feet beginning to itch. She could go there - to their mother's. She bit her lip trying to suppress her excitement. Of course, she knew it was running away again and that Rosanna would be furious but, if she acted quickly, she could be packed and out of the apartment before Rosanna knew about it. Didn't she have a date on the Lido that night? Elena looked at her watch. She could pack what she needed whilst Rosanna was out and leave first thing in the morning before her sister was even up.

Elena looked at the landscape in the picture and felt a sense of great calm washing over her. It was as if she was there already.

Rosanna was always surprised by her reaction to the Lido. It was just so noisy. The absence of cars and buses on Venice really made its mark and, whenever she visited the Lido or the mainland, she'd invariably get a headache. The main street was a migraine-generator and Rosanna could smell the pollution in the air. How could anyone live there? she wondered, squinting her eyes against the onslaught of traffic and trying her best not to breathe. She really did think of herself as a true Venetian now. To her, there was no other place she could contemplate living and that was one of the deciding factors in breaking up with Corrado. His dream of a little place in the Umbrian hills made Rosanna's spine constrict with fear. Goosebumps of revulsion would break out over her body at the thought of leaving her beloved city.

Corrado was waiting for her at the restaurant when she arrived, his hair newly-washed and his face clean-shaven. He looked sweet. He was wearing a new pair of jeans she hadn't seen before and a white shirt which, no doubt, had been pressed by his mother. He'd obviously made a huge effort for their date which made things far worse. He hadn't picked up on what she was feeling at all, had he? He still thought of their relationship as something that was moving forwards.

Rosanna took a deep breath before walking over to his table.

'Corrado,' she said when he didn't look up from the menu.

'Rosanna! You look lovely,' he said to her softly as he got up and kissed her cheek before pulling her chair out for her.

'Thank you,' she said. 'You look nice too.'

He shrugged. 'Mother picked out the shirt for me,' he said and Rosanna felt herself wince. They hadn't spent a full minute in each other's company and yet Irma Taccani had already made her presence felt.

'I've just got to -' Rosanna leapt out of her chair and pointed to the back of the restaurant and headed quickly to the ladies' before she had a chance to mouth off about Corrado's mother.

Inside the ladies', she gazed at herself long and hard in the mirror. She looked tired - as if she could quite happily fall asleep for a year. In fact, she had an overwhelming desire to go straight back to Sandro's apartment right there and then and just hide herself under the bed covers. For a brief moment, she looked around, wondering if there was a back way out of the restaurant - a window in the toilets or something, but she shook her head. She was being ridiculous. She had to stay and sort this out. Wasn't that what she was always telling Elena to do?

Washing her hands slowly to give herself a few seconds to compose herself, Rosanna psyched herself up for the evening ahead. She'd never broken up with anyone before - not like this, anyway. Previous relationships had either never taken off in the first place or had drifted, quite naturally, into non-existence without the need for a showdown. And what was the correct way to go about it? Should she wait until the main course or was it more polite to have finished dessert first?

As she dried her hands, Rosanna felt a deep frown embed itself across her forehead which she knew would not shift itself for at least a week now. She felt so wretched, and the beginnings of a headache were tap dancing at her temples.

Taking a deep breath, she opened the door, realising that she couldn't spend the entire evening in the toilets. Corrado looked up and smiled as she crossed the restaurant.

'I thought you'd fallen in,' he said as she sat down.

'I wasn't that long,' she snapped, in no mood to laugh.

'I've ordered starters,' he said.

'How do you know what I want?'

Corrado frowned. 'I guessed, based on the fact that you normally have the soup.'

Rosanna frowned back. 'Well, I might not have wanted soup tonight.'

'You want me to order something else for you?'

'No! Soup is fine,' Rosanna sighed, hoping it would come in a bowl big enough to drown herself in.

There was a moment's silence.

'I *had* been looking forward to this evening,' Corrado said, his voice shot through with hurt and, immediately, Rosanna felt riddled with guilt again. Why was she being so nasty? Couldn't they just enjoy their last meal together? After all, they'd been together for two years and they'd been good years too.

'I'm sorry,' Rosanna said at last, and then immediately regretted apologising. If she started apologising, she'd get all emotional and that wouldn't do. She had to remain strong and detached.

'You're not sorry at all, are you?' Corrado said, surprising her by his intuitiveness. It was a quality she'd never credited him with before.

'Corrado,' she began and then stopped, not quite knowing what to say next.

'What?'

'I –'

Again, there was a pause which seemed to swallow huge chunks of time before one of them dared to speak.

'You want to break up with me, don't you?'

Rosanna's eyes widened in genuine shock.

'When does this date back too, then?' Corrado asked calmly.

'What do you mean?'

'I thought you were happy. I thought *we* were happy? And you can't have been if you've been planning this.'

'I haven't been *planning* this!'

'No?'

'No!'

'But you knew you were going to tell me tonight?'

Rosanna nodded. 'Yes.'

'*Merda*! Rosanna! You could have told me over the phone and saved me the expense of a meal!'

Rosanna stared at him as if she hadn't heard him right. 'Is that all you can think about? Is that all you have to say?'

'God! You know I don't earn enough for this kind of place. Especially if we're not even going to bother enjoying the food!'

Rosanna stood up, scraping the chair back noisily and causing half the restaurant to turn and stare at them. 'I didn't want it to be like this, Corrado. We've had some good times together and I wanted us to be friends.'

'Oh! Spare me the 'friends' speech!'

'I'm only trying-'

'Don't!'

There was a prickle of ugly silence as they stared at each other. It was just the kind of uncomfortable moment that Rosanna had been so desperate to avoid but now she guessed it was unavoidable.

'I'm going to go now,' she said in a very small voice. Corrado said nothing and so she turned to leave the restaurant just as the waiter arrived with two bowls of soup. Rosanna just had time to see that Corrado had, at least, got her choice of starter absolutely right.

CHAPTER 32

'It's so easy to get overweight in Italy, don't you think?' Anastasia asked Prof in a restaurant on the mainland.

Prof nodded, his mouth otherwise occupied with yet another glorious concoction.

'I'm lucky,' Anastasia continued. 'I mean, I get paid to review this sort of thing as part of the travelling scene so my weight is an occupational hazard I'm quite happy to put up with.'

Prof's eyebrows rose. 'There's nothing wrong with your figure, I can assure you,' he said.

'Thank you, darling!' she said. 'You are a sweetie.'

Prof smiled. So many compliments had been fired at him that day that he felt he couldn't possibly take any more. 'Please!' he said, raising his hands as if he could deflect further praise.

Anastasia just laughed. 'You are funny!' she smiled, shaking her head so that her red curls bounced off her cheeks. 'So,' she added, 'tell me more about these students of yours.'

'What would you like to know?'

'Everything! Have you ever had a difficult student? I imagine teaching to be one of the hardest jobs in the world.'

'Well, when they come to university, most of them have gone through that difficult phase already and are actually happy to buckle down and work.'

'So, you haven't any juicy tales of student rebellion?' Anastasia asked, taking a sip of wine, her eyes sparkling in the dim light of the restaurant.

Prof looked thoughtful. 'There was one time,' he began.

'Go on,' Anastasia said.

Prof grinned. If she sat any further forward on her seat, she'd be in his lap, he thought. 'We were about half-way through our study of Charles Dickens,' he said, 'and I'd noticed that one of my students hadn't been to any of the classes. I'd asked around and none of her friends seemed to know anything about it. As I was about to hand out the coursework assignments, I thought I'd better get things sorted out and so I left a note in her pigeon hole to arrange a meeting.

'She came to my room at the designated time and I looked for any tell-tale signs of illness or work-overload but nothing seemed to be the matter. She'd never been the most out-spoken of students but it did seem odd that she should miss so many classes so I asked her why she had.'

'And what did she say?' Anastasia asked with the eagerness of a journalist scenting a story.

'She said she didn't *do* Dickens.'

'Didn't do Dickens?' Anastasia repeated.

'That's right!' Prof said. 'I was somewhat dumbfounded and I waited for her to explain.'

'And - did she?' Anastasia asked when Prof paused for a moment.

'Oh, yes! When I gave her another copy of the coursework I wanted her to do, she handed it right back and, when I asked her why, she told me that Dickens had killed her father.'

Anastasia's eyes stretched in surprise. 'How extraordinary.'

'And,' Prof said, 'unfortunately, true. Her father had worked as a salesman and was obsessed with audio books. Apparently, he listened to them all the time and, well, he was listening to one when he hit a patch of ice travelling through Northumberland and came off the road down a ravine. The police reported that *Oliver Twist* was still playing when they arrived on the scene.'

Anastasia's mouth opened a fraction. 'That's so sad!' she said.

'Isn't it?'

'And what did you say to her after she told you that?'

'What could I say? I gave her an alternative essay to do. *Bugger the Dickens*, I told her!'

'Oh! You dear man!'

'Other than that, I've had a long career with very little of interest happening to me. No major disruptions from students or fellow members of staff. In fact, put like that, I sound quite boring.'

Anastasia stretched a hand across the table and placed it on his. 'You're not boring,' she said and her dark eyes sparkled at him. 'You're wonderful. Simply wonderful!'

*

Rosanna had had some headaches in her time but none quite like this one. What had started out as an anaemic tap dance had now transmogrified into an army of hammers in her head. With each step, her head reverberated with pain so that even the short walk down to the vaporetto was an unbearable torture.

She wished she could magic herself back to the apartment. No. She wished that she'd never come out in the first place. What on earth had made her think Corrado could behave in an adult way? He'd never needed to be an adult - not whilst he still lived under the same roof as his harpy of a mother.

She struggled on down to the vaporetto, the cool air doing nothing to ease her throbbing head. For a moment, she wondered if she'd actually be able reach home at all. She felt ready to collapse at any moment. *Don't be silly*, she whispered to herself. *You'll be home in less than an hour.*

'Are you all right?' a voice suddenly asked. Rosanna could hardly see who it was through a veil of tears which she'd been trying not to spill.

'What?' she asked.

'I said are you okay?'

The voice sounded familiar. Rosanna wiped her eyes, resolving not to be such a baby and, looking up, saw a dark figure standing next to her. It was Reuben.

'You're not all right, are you?' he said. 'What a bloody stupid question to ask.'

Rosanna felt her new resolve crumble in an instant and new tears sprung up in her brown eyes.

Reuben instinctively placed an arm around her shoulder. 'Look,' he said, 'come with me. You're not in any state to go anywhere on your own. You're heading back to Venice, yes?'

Rosanna nodded.

'Come back to my room and we can have something to drink and I'll take you back to your apartment after that, okay?'

'Yes!' she cried, her vision blurring through more tears.

When the vaporetto arrived, Reuben helped Rosanna to a seat indoors and she closed her eyes as they sped over the lagoon back towards Venice. The rocking motion made her feel even more queasy but, luckily, it was a short crossing.

'Come on,' he said a few minutes later. 'We're here.'

Feeling shaky and dazed, Rosanna allowed herself to be led out. 'How far is it?' she asked.

'Not far. I'm at the Danieli. It's not far,' he assured her, and it wasn't.

'Here,' he said at last, guiding her into a room just a short time later.

'I'm so sorry, Reuben. I don't want to bother you but I really don't feel so good,' Rosanna whispered, her hands seemingly trying to squeeze the pain out of her head.

'Can I get you anything? Aspirin? Paracetamol?'

'Please!' she said.

Reuben rooted around in a toiletries bag and produced a packet of aspirin. 'Two?'

Rosanna nodded lightly, feeling that two packets wouldn't shift this particular headache. 'Have you some water?'

'Of course,' he said, taking a new bottle from his bedside table.

Rosanna undid it, took the pills and had a good drink. 'Would you mind if I had a sleep?' she asked. 'If I could just close my eyes for a while -'

'Of course!' Reuben said.

'I'm so sorry,' Reuben,' she said again.

'It's okay - *really*,' he said, motioning to the bed. 'I'll give you some peace.'

'Oh! Please don't let me disturb-'

'It's okay,' he interrupted, 'I usually go down to the bar at this time of night - it's great for catching up on my sketches. Please, make yourself comfortable. I'll see you later, okay?'

Rosanna heard the door close behind him and allowed her head to sink into the pillow on his bed.

'This is amazing!' Anastasia cooed as Prof escorted her through to the lobby bar.

'It is rather special, isn't it?'

'Special! I feel like a movie star!' she said.

Prof looked around the bar and immediately saw his English acquaintance, Reuben, sitting in the corner with his sketchbook out. For a moment, he wasn't sure how to approach things. He'd told Reuben that he was engaged, hadn't he? And now he'd brought back a woman to his hotel who wasn't his fiancée. Not that there was anything going on between them, he assured himself. They were merely passing time in one another's company - enjoying the occasional meal and drink together. He had no intention of it going any further than that. He was engaged, after all.

'Are we going to get a drink?' Anastasia asked.

'Yes. Of course,' Prof answered, hoping that Reuben would be too wrapped up in his art to come over and force an introduction.

Reuben liked his position at the back of the bar. He might just as well have been invisible, he thought, for the little attention he attracted. That was how he liked it, of course, but he had caught Sigmund's eye as he'd walked into the bar with a gorgeous red-head he'd naturally assumed was his fiancée. He caught her vibrant elegance with a few quick lines on the page, and then he stopped. It was hard to concentrate when there was a beautiful woman asleep in your bed upstairs. He'd wanted to stay and watch as she'd curled up on the bed, her dark curls spilling out over the pillow and her large, brown eyes closing against the world. Her olive skin looked drained of colour and he'd wanted to make sure she was all right.

He whistled, long and low, between clenched teeth. That's not what he'd wanted at all, was it? He'd wanted to undress her and leap onto the bed with her - *that's* what he'd wanted!

His pencil pressed darkly into his sketchbook as he drew angrily, wondering what she'd been doing on the Lido. She'd been wearing a dress the colour of dark amethysts. Had she been on a date? He didn't even know if she had a boyfriend or not. Perhaps that was why she was so upset - she'd argued with somebody. From what he'd seen of Rosanna, he knew she had a temper.

Reuben put his pencil down and looked at his watch. He'd been in the bar for over an hour now and really couldn't afford to sit there ordering drinks all evening. In fact, he was planning on booking out of the Danieli in the morning as it was far too luxurious for his wallet.

Getting up, he left the bar and wandered outside the hotel where he stood and gazed out over the dark lagoon. There was a bitter chill in the breeze now which reminded him that summer was still a long way off.

Reuben's mind ticked over the past few days. It had been extraordinary and not at all what he'd expected from a trip to Venice. He'd come in order to sort things out with Elena but he didn't feel as if they'd got anywhere. And then, he'd met Rosanna. What exactly was going on there? He walked along the waterfront, his hands deep in his jacket pockets. He was engaged to Elena but he was falling in love with Rosanna.

'Hell fire' he exclaimed into the night air, turning round and marching back towards the Danieli. He was going to tell her. There was no other way around this: he was, for once in his life, going to give in to honesty - whatever the consequences.

CHAPTER 33

Elena waited and waited for Rosanna to come back before finally going to bed. She was all packed for the next morning and was quite relieved to avoid having to lie to her sister about what she'd be doing the next day. She'd already written her note of apology, explaining how she couldn't really have a trip to Italy without visiting their mother. Rosanna would understand - maybe not immediately, but eventually.

She looked up into the dark beams above the bed and wondered what Rosanna was up to. Her evening with Corrado was certainly dragging on. Perhaps she'd had second thoughts about splitting up with him. Perhaps he'd proposed and Rosanna had been swept away by the moment and had banished any thoughts of becoming a big fat Italian mama in Umbria. Maybe the prospect of having Irma Taccani as a mother-in-law paled into insignificance when compared to the bleak prospect of being alone.

Elena turned over and beat her fists into the pillow to plump it into shape. She sincerely hoped that Rosanna hadn't given in after all they'd talked about and yet what else could have possibly happened for her to be so long in coming home? She knew, from experience, that breaking up with someone was one of the hardest things to do but it was very often one the quickest.

Reuben stood outside his hotel room and ran a nervous hand through his hair. He was shaking - actually shaking! And his breathing sounded like an asthmatic dragon. This was ridiculous! He'd never felt like this before in his entire life. He'd had more control over himself when he'd experienced his first nude model at age fourteen. He'd had more composure when he'd sold his first painting at what he'd believed to be a ridiculously inflated figure. So what was so scary about a sleeping beauty?

He knocked lightly on the door before walking in.

'Rosanna?' he called quietly so as not to disturb her if she was still asleep. There was no answer. He walked across the room and saw her asleep on the bed and his mouth dropped open in wonder.

As he watched her laying her, her chest softly rising and falling, he didn't quite know what to do so he did what he did best: he sketched. Sheet after sheet of the sleeping woman in front of him. A full body. A face. A close-up of her mouth and nose. A study of her eyelashes and the way they swept her skin. Her hands, the nails long and elegant. Everything about her was beautiful.

Time flew by and, before he knew it, he'd run out of paper. He looked at his watch and discovered that it was after eleven. He'd had no idea it was so late. What were they to do now? Should he let Rosanna go on sleeping whilst he made himself comfortable elsewhere or would she be annoyed with him when she woke up? Should he wake her now and see her safely back to the apartment?

'Reuben?' a low voice caught his attention and he looked up to see Rosanna sitting up, her mass of dark curls spilling over her shoulders in a dangerously beautiful tumble.

'How are you feeling?' he asked, putting his sketchbook to one side and leaning forward slightly.

She gave a weak smile. 'A bit better, thank you. What time is it?' she asked, looking around the room for a clock.

'It's late,' he said.

She frowned. 'How late?'

'Gone eleven.'

Rosanna cursed. 'Is it *really*? You should have woken me! Why didn't you wake me?'

'Because you were asleep!' Reuben said, his voice rising to meet Rosanna's.

'Now what am I meant to do?' she asked, swinging her legs off the bed and flinging angry feet into her shoes.

'I'll walk you home, of course,' Reuben said, standing up and reaching out for his coat.

Rosanna muttered something under her breath.

'Pardon?'

'You don't realise how far it is, do you?' she asked.

'I thought Venice could be crossed in less than an hour?'

'Not in these shoes!' she said, and then stopped.

'What?' Reuben asked, following her gaze.

'What's that?' she asked, looking at his sketchbook. 'Is that me?'

Reuben grimaced as she picked up the book and flicked through it.

'These are of me? Whilst I was sleeping? You were drawing me whilst I was asleep?'

Reuben wasn't sure what to say. 'Forgive me,' he said at last. 'I couldn't help it.'

Rosanna was flicking through the pages. 'You've got me exactly,' she said. 'You're good,' she said. 'Much better than Sandro. He always makes me look so heavy and I'm not that heavy, am I?'

'No!' Reuben gasped.

'I don't mean to be vain, but I think I can say - with some honesty - that I'm not fat.'

'You're certainly not,' Reuben assured her. 'And you're not vain, either.'

Rosanna gave a little smile. Her fingers continued to turn the pages until, after a few more, she stopped. A deep, beautiful frown landed on her forehead and Reuben instantly knew what she'd found – the sketches he'd drawn of her after he'd first met her – the ones he'd imagined. Rosanna – naked.

There was a painfully elongated silence when no words seemed adequate and then, neither was sure who made the first move: they just kind of lunged at each other, mouths clashing together as if that first kiss couldn't possibly wait a second longer. Hot mouths met and tongues chased each other as hands grabbed and pulled. It was fast and furious, it was indescribably wonderful. And it was over as quickly as it began.

'Shit!' Reuben said.

'*Merda!*' Rosanna said at the same time. 'What was that?'

'Man!' Reuben stood up and walked away from the bed as if from the scene of a crime.

'I can't believe that just happened,' Rosanna said. 'You're my sister's fiancé!'

'I know!'

'I've never done anything like this before,' Rosanna admitted.

'Neither have I,' Reuben said.

'*Merda!*' Rosanna cursed again. 'What an evening I'm having!' She hid her head in her hands as if her headache was coming back for a repeat performance.

'Rosanna-'

'I've got to go,' she said, standing up quickly.

'I'm coming with you.'

'No – don't!'

'I'm not letting you walk across Venice in the dark.'

'Don't be ridiculous! I'm not helpless, you know.'

'Well, you didn't say no to my help a few hours ago,' Reuben fired back.

Rosanna glared at him. 'No,' she said slowly, 'I didn't and, as a gentleman, I didn't think you'd mention it either.'

Reuben looked down at his shoes. 'I'm sorry,' he said. 'I didn't mean that. I only want to do what's right.'

'Then you shouldn't have kissed me!'

'You didn't exactly push me away, did you?'

Rosanna threw her hands up in the air and muttered something in Italian.

'What?'

'Nothing! I'm going.'

'You're not going anywhere without me.'

'Suit yourself. Just don't think you're coming anywhere near the apartment or my sister. I need to get my head round this,' Rosanna said, heading towards the door. 'I mean, what is all this about? What the hell are those pictures about?'

'I thought you liked them,' Reuben said.

Rosanna looked confused. 'I - do. But - I don't think you should be drawing pictures of me.'

'Would it help if I told you I couldn't stop myself? Would it help if I told you that I haven't been able to think of anything else but you since I met you?'

'But you're with my sister!'

'Why do you keep saying that? I KNOW! Do you think I don't know that?'

Rosanna was wearing a pained expression now and, for a moment, they just stared at each other. 'What are we going to do?' she asked at last.

Elena heard the door open and breathed a sigh of relief. Rosanna was back. But she wasn't alone - there was a man with her. Elena frowned in the darkness. How could Rosanna have let things turn out this way? She was meant to break up with Corrado, not spend the whole evening with him and invite him in for the night as well. Elena had a good mind to go down there right at that moment and give Corrado a piece of her mind.

Her fingers itched for the mask. She would put the mask on and scare the living daylights out of Corrado just as she had with his mother. By the time she finished with him, he wouldn't want to come near Rosanna again.

Her hand crawled across the bedside table to where she'd placed the mask. She took the lid off the box and put it on without the need of a light. It was a strange experience turning invisible in the dark. She felt the tingle that was becoming as familiar as a heartbeat but it was odd to lift the bedding to see nothing there.

Swinging her see-through legs out of bed, she walked across the floorboards of the bedroom. The voices downstairs were a little louder now – Corrado was obviously invited in for a coffee and maybe something else. Well, Elena thought, she wasn't going to allow that. She tiptoed out of the bedroom, her bare feet sneaking down the wooden steps into the living room below. She was determined to put a stop to this ridiculous relationship once and for all. It was up to her to make Rosanna see the truth. She would thank her in the long run, she was sure of that.

But, as she reached the bottom of the steps, she froze. The voice of Corrado had morphed into that of Reuben, and he was speaking in hushed tones to Rosanna.

'I think we should tell her straight away. Why wait?'

'Stop it! Just let me think for a moment.'

'That's why you agreed for me to come with you, isn't it?'

'No! No, it isn't. Stop twisting what I said.'

Reuben sighed and Elena strained to hear what they said next.

'I don't think I can go on without telling Elena – that's all I'm saying.'

Elena stood stock still even though she didn't need to; they couldn't see her even if she'd decided to do a handstand and walk forward with her feet in the air. She noticed that they were sitting a little closer than seemed absolutely necessary. In fact, they were sharing that sacred space that was usually only shared by lovers.

She didn't need to think of what to do next. Shaking fingers reached up and untied the mask and it slipped away with the merest of tingles.

'What have you got to tell me, Reuben?' she asked.

Reuben and Rosanna's heads span around in unison.

'Where the HELL did you come from?' Reuben asked.

'What do you have to tell me?' Elena asked again.

Reuben got to his feet. Suddenly, he didn't look so confident. It was as if he'd quite forgotten what he'd been so desperate to say.

'What are you doing here, anyway?'

'Elena,' Rosanna said, getting up from the sofa. 'There's something we've got to talk about.'

'I know that!' Elena shouted. 'Just bloody get on with it!'

There was complete silence as they all stared at one another. Elena's eyes narrowed as she watched Reuben and Rosanna exchange glances.

'What's going on?' she said in a voice so low it was barely a whisper. It was as if she already knew exactly what was going on. She could read their faces and really didn't need to hear what they had to say to her. 'I don't believe you,' was all she said before turning away from them and running up the stairs to the bedroom.

'Elena!'

Elena slammed the bedroom door shut behind her. Her heart was thudding wildly - like the time she'd first tried on the mask. She was still clutching it in her hand and, for a moment, thought about putting it on but she could hear Rosanna coming up the stairs after her.

'Elena? Can I come in?'

Elena couldn't speak. She stood, frozen, in the middle of the room.

'I'm coming in,' Rosanna said, knowing there wasn't a lock on the door and, suddenly, the two sisters were facing each other.

'Reuben's gone,' Rosanna said.

'Didn't he have anything to say to me?'

'Not whilst you're in this mood.'

'And what sort of mood would you expect me to be in when I've just found out that my sister and my fiancé are having an affair?'

'We're *not* having an affair! I never said that, did I?'

'Don't play games with me, Rosanna! I saw the way you were looking at each other - it's obvious.'

Rosanna sat down heavily upon the bed, her face framed with

pain. For a moment, neither sister spoke. It was as if they were waiting for something to come and take them away so they wouldn't have to face the next few moments.

Rosanna looked up. Elena was still standing in the middle of the room clutching the mask between shaking fingers.

'Why are you holding that stupid mask? You're really freaking me out, Elena!'

'*I'm* freaking *you* out?' Elena yelled. Suddenly, it was attack time again. 'You're the one who's run off with my fiancé!'

'And you're the one with *two* fiancés!' Rosanna spat back.

'That doesn't mean you have the right to come and choose one of them for yourself!'

'You make it sound like I wanted this to happen.'

'Well, didn't you?'

'No! I didn't plan any of this-'

'It just happened! Is that it?' Elena asked sarcastically.

Rosanna sighed heavily and she held her hands up in the air in a gesture of pure hopelessness. 'I don't know what the hell happened! How can I explain?'

'And you weren't going to, were you? If I hadn't come downstairs and heard you, you weren't going to tell me.'

'I wanted to get things sorted out first. Look, Elena, this has only just happened. I wasn't sure-'

'I don't think I can talk about this just now,' Elena said, her calm, quiet voice cutting across her sister's hysterical one.

'Then when will we talk about it?'

'When I get back,' Elena said.

Rosanna frowned. 'What do you mean? Where are you going?'

'I'm going to see Mama.'

'What?'

'That's all I can do right now,' Elena said, walking across the room and taking out her suitcase.

'You were going anyway, weren't you?' Rosanna said. 'You've already packed. You were running away again, weren't you?'

'I'm not running away.'

'Yes you are! You're always running away from something! That's why Reuben came out here to see you - because you were running away from him. And Mark too.'

'Don't you *dare* start lecturing me in things you know nothing about!'

'What do you mean, *things I know nothing about?* I'm your sister, for God's sake! If *I* don't know what goes on in that head of yours, *nobody* does!'

Again, their eyes locked in battle.

'I'll sleep downstairs tonight,' Elena said, a tiny quiver in her voice the only betrayal of her otherwise rigidly calm demeanour. 'And I'll be leaving first thing in the morning.'

'I think you should stay,' Rosanna said but Elena was already out of the door, her suitcase in one hand and the mask in the other.

CHAPTER 34

Reuben crossed the Piazza San Marco and stopped in the smaller, more intimate Piazzetta. The bright pink lamps were lit and the arches of the Doge's Palace took on a hauntingly beautiful quality. The Campanile towered behind him, shooting up into the inky night. It was all exactly the same as when he'd walked across it less than an hour ago with Rosanna, yet so much had happened. Elena knew; he'd betrayed her. And yet the world was still a beautiful place. How wrong that seemed, and how awful it was that he wished Rosanna was with him now. How was it possible to fall in love so quickly? Had he ever really been in love with Elena? What had it been other than love? He'd proposed to her, for goodness' sake, and yet he'd been able to cast her aside so brutally within a few days.

He could still see the hurt haunting her eyes as she'd stared at him in Sandro's apartment. He'd stood, torn and useless, between the two sisters, no longer knowing where his allegiance lay. So, he'd left - like a coward who can do nothing else.

He wondered what was happening there now. The vain and base part of him wished he could have stayed to see the two sisters fighting over him. He'd never had the pleasure of being desired by two women before. Staring out over the lagoon, he tried to imagine the scene.

'He was mine first!' Elena would shout.

'That doesn't mean you love him more!' Rosanna would retort.

'How do you know how much I love him?'

'Because no heart is bigger than mine when it comes to Reuben! Nobody could possibly love him more than me! I would drown in the lagoon for him!'

'And *I* would drown *you* in the lagoon for him!'

They would then lunge towards each other, nails and hair flying…

Reuben shook his head, feeling ashamed, if somewhat turned on, at having envisaged such a scene and proceeded to punish himself by envisaging quite a different one:

'You can have him, you slut!' Elena shouted.

'You must be joking! I don't want your soiled goods!'

'I was going to break up with him anyway. He's no good to me any more.'

'Well, throw him in the lagoon because I don't want him either,' Rosanna spat.

'I've got a better idea - we'll *both* thrown him into the lagoon - with his paint box tied round his neck to make sure he sinks!'

'You're on!'

Reuben shivered. That scene was probably closer to the truth, he thought, his features glum. He should never have left the apartment; he couldn't bear not knowing what was happening there.

The truth was, nothing half as dramatic as Reuben had imagined was taking place in the apartment. It was stonily silent. After their initial fight, Elena had gone downstairs to bed and Rosanna had shut her upstairs bedroom door. Each remained in their self-imposed isolation as if an ocean divided them rather than a flight of stairs.

Neither could sleep. Elena couldn't get comfortable in the single bed in the spare room and kept tossing and turning as if the mattress were harbouring a hundred hibernating hedgehogs. Finally, she got up and switched on a bedside lamp. It was a strange room with a low, slanted ceiling. It was also home to stacks of Sandro's canvasses and Elena found herself looking through them. There were several of Rosanna, and Elena's eyes narrowed at her new enemy. Luckily, there were no palette knives lying around or goodness knows what might have become of Sandro's paintings.

Elena groaned. Why hadn't Rosanna been happy with her own artist, Sandro? Why did she have to go and steal *her* artist? For one dreadful moment, Elena wondered if Rosanna was finally getting her own back for the time when she had poached one of her boyfriends. It had been so many years ago that she'd almost forgotten about it. But, no, it wasn't as simple as revenge, was it? She'd seen the way Rosanna and Reuben had looked at each other. Rosanna wasn't using Reuben to settle some long-standing score. That would have been easy to sort out. Love, on the other hand, couldn't be sorted out, could it? You had to just let it be.

Elena had to face the fact that she'd lost Reuben, and she was in the process of losing Prof as well by the look of things. He'd seemed so at ease when she'd seen him with the red-haired woman. How had he met her, she wondered as she returned to the uncomfortable bed? Perhaps she'd come with him to Venice? Yes! After Elena had hung up on him the other night, he'd gone out and found himself a new woman to bring to Venice in order to get his own back on her. Or, worse: he'd found out about her and Reuben. He'd sussed her out - invisibility mask and everything - and decided that she wasn't worth the bother.

Elena tugged angrily at the lumpy duvet and sighed in despair. Everyone was getting their own back on her, weren't they? Only Mark was hanging on in there for her but she wasn't at all sure she wanted him to. In fact, she'd done a good job of wrecking things with him already. He was probably back in London already, crossing her name out of his little black book and deleting her from his mobile phone. Or was he still in Venice? She'd have time to find out before she left for Positano in the morning. She could settle things then - make a clean break. Reuben and Prof might well have given up on her but she wasn't going to let that happen a third time. As she gave her pillow one last thump before closing her eyes, she made a decision: *she'd* be the one to finish things with Mark.

Prof lay awake in bed staring at the dark ceiling. He'd crossed the Piazzetta two hours before Reuben but hadn't been thinking about the beautiful architecture; he'd been thinking about the beautiful Anastasia. They'd taken forever to say goodnight to each other outside her hotel.

'Did I tell you about the time I visited Verona?' Anastasia had asked.

'I must just tell you about this fabulous restaurant in Primrose Hill,' Prof had said.

It was as if they were delaying saying goodnight for as long as possible.

'Seeing as we're both on our own here,' Prof had finally said, 'how about lunch tomorrow?'

'It can get so lonely sometimes, and I detest eating alone - it's so depressing!' Anastasia had said.

When she'd turned to go, Prof had felt a strange emptiness like a child being left at the school gate for the first time. He'd wanted to call after her and find some other useless piece of trivia to discuss but she'd disappeared.

He'd never had that with Elena, he'd thought. She'd always just left. A quick glance at the clock and off she'd trot. He'd always felt that he was a bit of an inconvenience to her - that she had somewhere else to be or someone else to see. With Anastasia, he'd felt as if he was the complete centre of her attention.

Walking down the Riva towards the Danieli, Prof wondered what was happening to him. He'd come out to Venice with the distinct idea of setting a date for his wedding. He'd flown out a man in love - impatient to get his life moving in the right direction at last. So what had changed?

Anastasia.

Surely he wasn't as fickle as that? He shook his head, his feet marching right by his hotel and on down the Riva until he reached the spot overlooking the famous Bridge of Sighs which was very appropriate, he'd thought, letting a long sigh out into the still night air.

The easy companionship of Anastasia had made him see Elena in a different light. He had only been with Anastasia for half a day and yet he knew so much about her.

'Here's my mobile number,' she'd said after lunch, handing him her business card.

He'd got absolutely no idea what Elena's number was. She'd even told him that she didn't have a mobile phone but he'd once heard it beep during a seminar.

'I'm the youngest of three girls,' Anastasia had said by the time dessert was presented to them.

He didn't even know what Elena's sister was called. No, when it came down to it, Prof knew very little about Elena Montella.

But, lying in bed at the Danieli now, he felt in a bit of a quandary. He was an engaged man who had fallen under the spell of another woman. He'd never been in that sort of a situation before. Life had always been so simple for him: he'd been a bachelor with the occasional girlfriend. Now, he had two beautiful women and one important decision to make.

CHAPTER 35

After the most appalling night's sleep, Elena got up and threw herself under a warm shower in an attempt to revive herself. The apartment was quiet and she did her best not to make too much noise. She couldn't tell if Rosanna was awake or not. If she was, she was using her sense and allowing Elena to get out of the way before venturing downstairs.

She felt quite numbed by the events of the night before. They seemed almost like a nightmare: horribly frightening at the time but hard to comprehend in the light of day. Had it really happened? Had she witnessed Reuben and Rosanna together, eyes locked like honeymooners? As she walked through to the living room, she threw a glance over to the sofa where they'd been sitting as if it was to blame somehow.

She decided not to risk breakfast in the apartment; she could get something to eat en route but she poured herself an apricot juice and downed it quickly. The sooner she was out of Sandro's, the better.

Picking up the suitcase which she'd packed the night before, she crept down the stairs and left, closing the door quietly behind her. It was only a ten-minute walk to Mark's hotel and, as she'd only packed a few things for her trip to Positano, she didn't mind dragging her suitcase through the streets.

The early morning air was cool and she inhaled a few deep lungfuls in an attempt at self-medication but nothing was going to ease the dull leaden feeling lodged inside her heart. She felt lost and alone in a city that didn't care about her. It had lured her in with its pretty pink palazzos and its gentle serenity but it had chewed her up and spat her out. It was definitely time to leave.

She bit her lip. She'd make things quick with Mark and get away from Venice as soon as she could

'You're running away again, Elena,' a voice in her head told her – Rosanna's voice. They might not have actually been on speaking terms but it didn't stop Elena from hearing her.

'Shut up, Rosanna!' she said.

It wasn't her fault that her fiancés were behaving badly. She couldn't be held responsible for Reuben falling in love with her sister or for Prof meeting somebody else so why should she be expected to stay and fight? They obviously weren't worth fighting for, were they?

As she entered a small campo, she checked the piece of paper on which Mark had jotted the address of his hotel. She looked around. It had to be here somewhere. And then she saw it - hiding in the shadows of a small calle across the other side of the square. It wasn't the Danieli, that was for sure. It was more like a poor relative – a cousin twice removed, perhaps.

Elena opened the door and asked the receptionist to ring Mark's room. It was still early so he was probably in bed. He'd never been an early riser. Turning to face the door, Elena tried to compose herself for the scene ahead. She closed her eyes for a moment.

So, Rosanna thought she was running away, did she? That she wasn't up to facing a situation? Well, what was she doing now, then?

'Elena?'

Elena span around and saw Mark. He looked bleary-eyed but his smile showed that he was pleased to see her.

'Hello, Mark.'

'I had a feeling you'd come today.'

'Did you?'

He nodded. 'I don't know why. Did you want to go somewhere and get some breakfast? I can go and get dressed properly-'

'No,' she interrupted.

'Oh,' he said. 'Shall we meet later, then?'

For a moment, she didn't know what to say. There was such expectancy in his voice and in his eyes.

'Mark-'

'What?' It was his turn to interrupt and, from the tone of his voice, he'd guessed what she'd come to say – just as Elena had guessed what Reuben had wanted to say to her the night before.

'I'm going away for a while.'

He frowned. 'But you've done that already by coming here.'

'I'm going to visit Mama.'

It was then that Mark noticed the suitcase. 'And I don't suppose there's any point in me trying to persuade you to stay?'

'Not really.'

'And you're not here to invite me to go with you, are you?'

She shook her head. 'No.'

'So, why did you come to tell me?'

Elena paused and took a deep breath. 'I've come to say goodbye.'

Mark stared at her silently. 'Why does that sound so final to me?' he asked, his eyes narrowing as he took a step closer to her. 'Why do I get the feeling that you're breaking up with me?'

Elena couldn't bear to look at him and so cast her eyes down to the floor.

'Elena? Talk to me. Is it because of our fight the other day? Is it my fault?'

She shook her head. 'No,' she said.

'Then what's going on? I thought we were engaged?'

She could feel her fingers bunching themselves into confused fists. She couldn't very well explain to him that she'd become engaged to another two men, could she? She couldn't tell him that an engagement looked slightly different to her than it did to him.

'I don't think things are working out,' she managed at last.

'Since when? They were fine a few days ago when we were back in London. Are you telling me something's happened between then and now? God, Elena! I can't understand you! I'm doing my best to make sense of all this but you keep dropping these bombs and I'm beginning to think that I don't really know you at all.'

'That's exactly why I think we should break up,' she said, her voice tremulous. 'I don't think we can ever understand each other.'

'But you're not giving things a chance! Each time I try to get close to you, you leg it in the opposite direction! I've followed you out here to Venice to try and talk to you and now you say you're off again. Where are you going this time? How long can you keep on running?'

Elena could feel tears vibrating in her eyes. It was time to leave. Things were getting out of control.

'Don't shout at me,' she said.

'I'm NOT shouting!' Mark shouted and then became aware of the receptionist's presence and immediately felt self-conscious. 'I'm not shouting,' he repeated. 'I might be raising my voice slightly but that's only because I want to be heard,' he said, giving her a tiny smile which was so like the first smile he'd given her that she couldn't help but smile back.

'Come on, Elena. You can't leave things like this. I won't let you.'

A strange silence hung between them and Elena wished she could turn to the mask for help. This was one time she truly wished she could just disappear.

'I've got to go.'

'No you haven't.'

'I've made up my mind,' she said.

'Then *un*make it.'

She shook her head. 'It won't work, Mark. I know it won't.' She stopped, waiting for him to contradict her but he didn't say a word. They stared at each other. He looked scruffy with his uncombed hair and his unshaven face. His blue shirt was crumpled and he'd done his buttons up all wrong. For a split second, she almost reached forward to correct them but her hand delved into her pocket instead and she took out the ring he'd bought her, handing it across to him.

'Won't you say goodbye?' she asked but he didn't say a word nor did he make a move to receive his ring.

'Please take the ring,' she said.

Mark stood perfectly still, as if paralysed, so Elena took a step forward and slipped it into the pocket of the crumpled shirt with the buttons done up the wrong way, picked up her suitcase and left the hotel.

She half-thought that he might follow her outside – perhaps run after her and ask her, once more, not to go. But he didn't. He'd finally given up on her. So why did she feel so desolate? Wasn't that what she'd wanted? Wasn't that what she'd asked of him?

As she entered the campo, a single tear fell down her cheek. Quickly, she brushed it away with the back of her hand. She wasn't allowed to do that; crying was for cowards and she wasn't a coward – she was strong.

Rosanna had lain in bed listening to Elena moving around the apartment, wondering when she would leave and when it would be safe to venture downstairs. She had to get out to an appointment on the Lido with a retired art teacher who liked his models on time and naked within two minutes of arriving.

She'd tiptoed to the ensuite bathroom and stared at the mirror above the sink. Her face had been unnaturally pale and her eyes had looked hollow and lifeless. Not that the retired teacher would notice. He always left her face blank. The only thing he ever noticed was her torso.

Only when Rosanna had heard Elena leaving the apartment did

she venture downstairs, treading with cautious feet as if Elena might come back at any moment. Thankfully, she didn't. But she had left a note - obviously before the revelation of the night before.

Gone to visit Mama. Forgive me for not telling you earlier! Love, Elena x

Forgive *her*? Rosanna could easily forgive Elena but could Elena ever forgive her?

It was a breezy boat ride out to the Lido. The water looked greyer than usual and the view back to the Riva was dull. Even a jewel like Venice couldn't sparkle when you were in a bad mood, Rosanna thought. The most beautiful of cities could fail to inspire you when your life was falling apart.

Rosanna caught sight of the fondant pink façade of the Danieli and wondered what Reuben was doing. Probably looking for a cheaper hotel, she thought, remembering what he'd said the night before.

She tried to fix her mind on the morning ahead but it kept diving back to the previous night and his dark eyes staring into hers and the touch of his hands on the back of her neck. And his kiss. She blushed as she remembered - ashamed at having received it and yet longing for another.

She remembered the sketches in his book. He'd imagined her naked over and over again. The thought sent a warm shiver through her body. He'd been fairly accurate too! Had he really imagined it all or had he used Elena's body? She didn't want to think about that - it raised too many prickly issues. Like the fact that she'd stolen her sister's fiancé. It was unforgivable. Elena was right to leave. What other option was there? But would she be coming back? Was she just having a cooling off period? And what did the future hold? If Reuben and Rosanna were going to make a go of things, Elena would have to come round eventually, wouldn't she? Or maybe she wouldn't.

Rosanna closed her eyes and groaned. She didn't want to be the cause of a big family bust-up but what was she going to do? She was falling in love with Reuben but it was looking as if she'd have to choose between going out with him or having a sister. It just didn't seem fair. She hadn't felt this way about somebody for years. Why did Fate have to choose her sister's fiancé for her to fall in love with? Why couldn't life be easy? Why couldn't she have loved Corrado and adored his mother?

She gazed up into the pearly grey sky, half-imagining that somebody was watching her from above - somebody who was having a laugh at her expense.

CHAPTER 36

Reuben was out of the Danieli first thing in the morning and had booked himself into another hotel less than a fifth of the price. Of course, it didn't have a view of the lagoon but at least he wouldn't feel guilty any more. Anyway, he thought, there was no telling how long he might be staying in Venice now and it would be exorbitant to pay out more than he really needed to.

Leaving his things in his new, more modest room and finding a small internet café, he emailed a few contacts at home letting them know that he wouldn't be back for a few days. As he sent his messages, he wondered what the future held in store. He was serious about Rosanna, and the ferocity of his feelings surprised him. He found himself contemplating the possibility of selling up in London and moving out to Venice to be with her. Would that work? He certainly got the impression that she wouldn't want to leave Italy and he had come to see the magic of Venice in the short time he'd been there. Could he base himself there? He didn't see why not. The place was idyllic for an artist.

He thought of Sandro Constantini and how annoyed he'd be when he got back to discover that his favourite model had been poached by another, more superior artist. Reuben grinned to himself. Of course, Sandro Constantini was Italy's main export in the art world and Reuben would certainly have a rival but he'd never feared competition – it was healthy enough - and it would be fun to try to overtake Signore Constantini in the fame-stakes.

The prices of property in Venice had to be considered, though. Reuben's place in London wasn't the largest in the world nor was it in one of the most fashionable locations. In fact, it was more derisible than desirable. He wondered if Rosanna had any money put by. He didn't expect she earned much as a model. So, he thought, they wouldn't be buying a palazzo on the Grand Canal in the near future. In his mind's eye, he conjured up a spacious room with one of those smoky-white glass chandeliers, and golden mirrors reflecting the opalescent Venetian light. A marble floor, polished like a mirror, led to a picture-perfect balcony and, turning to the left, the unrivalled view of the white dome of Santa Maria della Salute. Turning back into the room, Rosanna was lying, naked and lovely, on an antique chaise longue, her dark eyes beckoning to him.

Reuben jolted as a finger tapped his shoulder like an angry woodpecker. He turned to see a ginger-haired man with thick glasses and a backpack the size of Gibraltar nodding to the computer Reuben was sat at.

'Keep your hair on!' Reuben said. 'I was just logging off.'

As he left the internet café and walked across a small campo, he couldn't quite believe the recent chain of events. Since the day before, he'd broken up with his fiancée, declared his love to Rosanna and mentally moved home from London to Venice. Life, he thought, could really be rather exciting.

Rosanna was back at the apartment by lunchtime. She'd been right about the retired teacher on the Lido; he hadn't noticed the vacant look of her eyes nor the skin like curdled milk. She'd stripped and sat and he'd painted and paid.

She threw herself under a hot shower which was what she usually did after a sitting. It was as if she was washing away the gaze of the artist and restoring her body to herself. It also gave her time to think. Water, to Rosanna, was a provoker of thoughts. Whether it was a rainy day, a boat ride on the lagoon, staring into the jade depths of a canal or luxuriating in a steamy shower, each sent her mind into an inner labyrinth of reflection.

She was just towelling herself dry when she heard the front door.

'*Merda!*' she cursed. People always seemed to time their visits for the moment you stepped out of the shower or placed a plate of hot food on the table.

Padding through the apartment with bare feet, she ran down the stairs and opened the front door.

'Reuben!' she said, genuinely shocked to see him.

'Rosanna!' he said, genuinely shocked to see her too - in a bathrobe.

'I was in the shower,' she said, quite unnecessarily. 'Come in before I freeze to death.'

'Is Elena in?'

'Of course she isn't! What do you think? Do you think we've been having a nice cosy chat?'

'I don't know!' he answered tersely.

'We rowed and she's gone to Mama's.'

'Where's that?'

'Positano.'

'Oh.'

'Yes. And I don't think she'll be coming back.'

Reuben looked somewhat relieved by this last comment.

'I've got to put some clothes on,' Rosanna said, dripping on the floorboards in a perfect echo of the first time they'd met.

'Rosanna?' he called from downstairs as she was shoving her head through a light cotton jumper.

'What?'

'How long are you going to be?'

'I'm getting dressed!' she shouted back, tutting at his impatience. What was it with artists? They expected you to dress and undress in the most unreasonable of time spans.

She reached in to the chest of drawers and stepped into a pair of jeans before returning back downstairs. Reuben was pacing up and down the apartment like a caged panther and Rosanna felt desperate for him at that moment. He might have seemed like the strong, invincible type but he was really just a little boy.

'I don't know what to do!' he said.

'How about we sit down?' Rosanna said, giving him a small smile.

He nodded and they sat down.

'I feel terrible about all this,' he said, sitting forward a little so that his back made a long slope away from Rosanna.

'And *you* didn't see Elena last night.'

Reuben winced. 'Was she angry?'

'What do you think? Of course she was bloody angry! We both betrayed her - together! How horribly clichéd is that?'

'God!' Reuben groaned. 'I was feeling all right this morning. In fact, I was walking around as if I'd just won the lottery or something. And then I thought - really thought about what I'd done to Elena.'

Rosanna narrowed her eyes at his tone of voice. 'You mean you want this to stop here?'

Reuben turned to face her. 'No!' he cried, taking her hands in his. It was the first physical contact they'd had since the evening at the

Danieli and Rosanna's body heated up as if she'd spontaneously combusted.

'Because I'll understand if that's what you want.'

'Will you?' Reuben asked, genuine puzzlement in his face.

'NO!' Rosanna shouted suddenly. 'Of course I won't! I'll hate you if you do that to me!'

'But I wasn't going to - I mean, I'm not planning to!'

They sat staring at one another for a moment, Reuben's fingers stroking Rosanna's. And then they kissed.

'I'm falling in love with you,' he whispered when they finally moved apart.

'I should hope so,' Rosanna whispered back with the tiniest of smiles. 'I may have sacrificed my sister for you.'

'Do you really think you have?'

Rosanna sighed. She felt as if she were about to cry which would have been dreadful and probably enough to scare Reuben off for good. 'I don't think she'll want to talk to me for a long time.'

'I don't think she'll want to talk to me - *ever!*'

'Then we've got a problem, haven't we? If we want to be together.'

Reuben nodded. 'But I don't think we're going to sort it out today.'

Rosanna leant back against the sofa. Reuben was right: there was absolutely nothing they could do about it now. This problem was not the kind to be solved in twenty-four hours. They'd be lucky if it was sorted in twenty-four years.

There was a knock at the door.

'Are you expecting someone?' Reuben asked.

'No.'

'It wouldn't be Elena, would it?'

Rosanna shook her head. 'She'll be in Positano by now.'

'Are you going to answer it?'

'I think I should,' Rosanna said. She was the sort who never liked not answering the door or the telephone because it would bug her for hours afterwards in case she'd missed a life-changing call.

'Mark?' she gasped a moment later.

'I'm sorry. I should have called,' he said, looking flustered.

'What are you doing here?' Rosanna asked, looking over her shoulder.

'Can't you guess?'

Rosanna nodded slowly. 'She's not here, I'm afraid.'

'I know,' he said. 'Can I come in?'

Rosanna frowned. 'I-'

'Rosanna? Who's that?' Reuben's voice called from the top of the stairs.

'Oh, I'm sorry. I didn't know anyone was here,' said Mark.

'I'm just coming,' Rosanna called back up to Reuben, turning back to face Mark. 'I'm sorry,' she began. 'Can you call back later?' she asked, half-pushing the door closed, but it was too late: Reuben was standing beside her.

'Hello,' Mark said, nodding to Reuben. 'I'm Mark.'

'Mark?' Reuben said, the word exiting his mouth like a bullet. 'The teacher?'

Rosanna rolled her eyes as if she could already see the scene ahead, and the realisation that there was nothing she could do to stop it.

'Yes, I'm Mark. Have we met?'

'No,' Reuben said tersely. 'But I think you know my fiancé.'

'Yeah?'

'Rosanna's sister, Elena,' Reuben said with a dark scowl.'

'What do you mean?'

'Why the hell are you here?' Reuben demanded.

'Reuben-' Rosanna started.

'What business is it of yours?' Mark asked defensively.

'Because I want to know if you've been seeing Elena behind my back.'

'Of course I bloody have. I'm engaged to her!'

'What? What the hell are you talking about?'

'Elena is my fiancé. Or, rather, she was until she returned my ring this morning.'

'Oh, Mark!' Rosanna cried.

'But she's engaged to *me*!' Reuben shouted.

'Aren't you forgetting something?' Rosanna interrupted.

'What?' Reuben barked at her

'You broke up with Elena to be with *me!*'

'You're engaged to Elena?' Mark said, his forehead set in a series of serious wrinkles.

'*Was* engaged to Elena!' Rosanna corrected.

'When, for God's sake?'

'Yesterday!' Reuben said.

'I don't understand.'

Rosanna flung her hands up to the heavens. 'I *knew* this would happen! And I knew Elena wouldn't be around to sort it out when it did!'

Rosanna pushed Reuben up the stairs and Mark followed behind.

'Rosanna!' Mark shouted. 'Are you going to tell me what the hell is going on or not?'

'YES!' Rosanna yelled back. 'Look. Just come in and sit down - both of you!' she said, seeing Reuben turning to face her with a dark scowl.

'You knew about Mark and you didn't tell me?' Reuben said.

'It wasn't like you think.'

'Then what was it like?' Reuben asked.

'Sit down - both of you!' Rosanna told them, her voice holding the authority of a headmistress. 'This hasn't been much fun for me either, you know. I told her to sort things out.'

'I can't believe this,' Mark said. 'Was she really engaged to us both at the same time?'

Reuben looked over at Mark and, for the first time, their eyes met in what could have been interpreted as shared suffering.

'I don't know how or why she did it but, yes, she was engaged to you both at once.'

Mark and Reuben glowered at Rosanna.

'Well, don't look at me as if I had something to do with it! I did my best to get her to sort things out - believe me!'

'But now she's not engaged to either of us!' Mark pointed out.

Rosanna sighed and shook her head.

'But you two are together now - have I got that right?' Mark asked.

Rosanna looked across at Reuben to help her out.

'I broke up with Elena last night,' he confessed.

'You did?' Mark asked Reuben incredulously.

'Well, not in so many words. Actually, I didn't need to say anything. She kind of guessed.'

'And then she broke up with me. No wonder she was behaving crazily this morning.'

Mark sank down on one of the sofas. His skin was deathly pale.

'Mark!' Rosanna said, sitting down next to him and taking his hands in hers. 'She loved you! She really did!'

'And what about me?' Reuben asked.

Rosanna turned to see the hurt in Reuben's face. 'She loved you too!'

'You can't love two people at once,' Reuben said flatly.

'You're one to talk!'

Reuben flushed scarlet. 'But would she have told me?'

'Or me?'

Rosanna bit her lip. 'Look,' she said, 'I really believe she loved you both - in her own way. I *truly* believe that! I don't know what her plans were. I'm her sister but that doesn't mean she tells me everything.'

'And you weren't going to tell either of us?' Mark asked.

'That wasn't really my place, was it?'

'I can't get my head round this,' Mark said. 'Yesterday, I was engaged. Today, I've been dumped and find out that my ex-fiancée was engaged to two men at once and that the other man dumped her before she dumped me and is now seeing her sister! Have I got that right?'

'Mark!'

'What?'

'You make this sound awful!'

'It *is* awful!'

'You make it sound like it's all my fault,' Rosanna said, a sob rising in her voice.

Reuben sat down next to her so that she was sandwiched between him and Mark.

'It isn't your fault. We know that!'

'Reuben's right, Rosanna! I'm sorry,' Mark said. 'I didn't mean to sound so angry.'

'I didn't want any of this to happen,' she said, her eyes suddenly filling with tears.

'We know,' Reuben said, putting an arm around her shoulder.

'It's just, all this has come as a bit of a shock,' Mark said.

'That's right,' Reuben added, seemingly working in tandem with Mark.

Rosanna reached into her jeans pocket, pulled out a tissue and trumpeted into it. 'This is terrible!' she said. 'I can't believe all this has happened.'

'What was that?' Reuben suddenly asked.

'What was what?' Rosanna asked, mopping her eyes with her sodden tissue.

'I thought I heard the door.'

'I didn't lock it,' Rosanna said in sudden panic.

The three of them turned around from the sofa to face the steps up from the front door and listened as heavy footsteps were heard approaching them.

'*MERDA!*' a voice filled the room as an angry, dark-haired man entered the living room. 'I go away for a couple of months and come back to an orgy in my studio!'

Sandro Constantino was back home.

CHAPTER 37

Naples. Home of the pizza, Mount Vesuvius and some of the worst drivers in Italy, Elena mused as she navigated her way from Naples airport in her hired Fiat Uno. It was a horrible journey through the long, endless tunnels until she hit the coast road to Positano. Then, the horrors of the journey melted away as the beauty of the sea assaulted her. She always forgot how beautiful it was. Clinging to the knife-edged cliffs, the houses, painted in yellows, pinks, reds and whites, looked ready to tumble into the bright sea below if the merest wisp of a breeze shook them. The houses themselves were far simpler than the ones she'd left behind in Venice. Who needed columns and arches and endless domes when one had the sea to look at? Positano's architecture was far less ostentatious. Clean, simple lines prevailed which made the town look rather Lego-like from a distance. On closer inspection, however, balconies and pots of flowers softened the lines and showed themselves to be worthy of a thousand holiday snaps and postcards.

It was a bare and bony landscape along many stretches, with vegetation losing its battle against the impenetrable rock, but Elena loved it. It was just what she needed at the moment and she was glad she'd made the decision to come.

Emiliana Montella had only been in Positano for two years. She was a bit of a nomad and had owned, since Elena and Rosanna had left home, two apartments in Rome, a villa in Calabria, and a farmhouse in Liguria before selling up and moving to Positano. Elena hadn't really been surprised. Her mother had always loved beautiful things and beautiful places, and Positano was, perhaps, one of Italy's loveliest towns.

Slowing the hire care to take a treacherous bend in the road, Elena took a quick look at the sea. The light was bewitchingly bright and forced Elena to reach for the sunglasses which she rarely wore in London. Shifting down a gear, she took another hairpin bend and found herself behind a coach of tourists no doubt on their Amalfi coast tour. It gave her time to admire the scenery herself. The roads and view were also a perfect distraction from everything she'd left behind her because there was very little room left in head for problems when she was driving on these roads and that was just how she liked it.

Sheer cliffs towered to her left whilst expensive villas sat to her right, gazing out over the sea from behind their security gates. Elena wondered what it would be like to live in a place whose gates were higher than the walls of the house. Would she be happy somewhere like that? Would she be able to close out her troubles behind such gates?

She didn't have time to ponder her question as she came into view of Mama Montella's house: a two-bedroomed, white-washed cube tucked into a cliff on the outskirts of the main town. With its sea views and small veranda, it was breathtakingly beautiful. Her mama lived alone there. Elena and Rosanna's father had died when they were small and Emiliana hadn't remarried until recently. However, things hadn't worked out and she had filed for divorce within eight months

Elena pulled into the short driveway. There was no need for gates here but Elena announced her arrival with a friendly toot of her car horn.

'*Mia bambina!*' her mama soon shouted, her short, plump arms outstretched towards Elena as she got out of her car and crossed the driveway. She was five foot nothing but was wearing three inch heels even though she was in the privacy of her own home, and her dark hair, which had been dyed for as long as Elena could remember, was piled on top of her head, adding two more inches to her.

'Mama! How are you?' she asked, kissing her mama and receiving her papery kisses on both cheeks.

'Mustn't complain,' Emiliana said which, of course, was a lie. Elena knew what was to follow. 'But I still have these terrible pains in my shoulders. My doctor assured me the climate here would improve things but – pah! What does he know?'

'You look well,' Elena said, knowing she'd be in trouble if she didn't flatter her mother within the first ten minutes of their meeting. 'Your hair looks pretty like that.'

'And you look –' Emiliana began, her eyes squinting, '- tired. And your ends are split too. Look at the state of yourself. A young woman must never let herself go.'

Elena sighed. Nobody could insult you in quite the same way as your mother.

She followed her into the house and marvelled at how clean and bright it was. Every surface glowed an astral white and there were bunches of bright flowers everywhere.

'Where on earth did you get all these flowers from, Mama?'

'They're from Giovanni. He thinks he can get round me with flowers.'

Elena smiled. Her mama had never been short of admirers and would never be wanting in the flower or jewellery department for long. However, keeping her men was another matter. She had the beauty and skill to attract but a temper and temperament which drove away.

'Your sister rang me before you got here,' Emiliana said without seeing the need of a preamble.

Elena followed as she walked through to the kitchen and put the kettle on.

'Did she?' Elena asked, trying to sound nonchalant as she looked out of the picture window in front of the sink. It looked down a steep hill straight down to the sea which dazzled with diamonds. In fact, everything about Positano was diamond-bright. Venice was a pearl, Elena thought, but Positano was a diamond. Dishes would be a pleasure to wash with a view like that, Elena mused, trying desperately hard not to think about what Rosanna might have told their mama.

'She sounded very upset,' Emiliana said.

'And I suppose you're not going to believe my version of things now.'

'It's not a case of whether I believe things or not. What I want to know is why can't my two girls get on together? What did I do to make you argue all the time? I never argued with my sister.'

Elena looked puzzled. 'You never had a sister.'

'But, if I had, I wouldn't have argued with her like you and Rosanna,' she stated. 'Anyway, what's all this arguing about?'

'Nothing! And we don't argue all the time – only when she steals my fiancé.'

'Ah! And you never stole her boyfriends, eh?'

'She wasn't actually engaged to any of them, was she?'

'Does that make a difference, then?' Emiliana asked.

Elena was silenced for a moment. 'Yes,' she said, but she wasn't at all sure now she came to think of it.

'A lover is a lover – whether he's put a ring on your finger or not.'

Elena didn't dare look round at her mama. Her tone of voice said it all. Elena had been an absolute cow to Rosanna when they'd been growing up and yet Rosanna had forgiven her for everything: all the misdemeanours and mistakes. But this was different. They were adults now and you just didn't go around stealing fiancés. It wasn't right.

'Reuben was my fiancé, Mama,' Elena sighed.

'And so was Mark, wasn't he?'

Elena flinched. So Rosanna had told their mama everything. Well, so much for sibling loyalty, she thought. Although, why was she expecting loyalty from Rosanna after what she'd done?

'You don't understand,' Elena said but she sounded feeble even to her own ears.

'You're right! I *don't* understand! How does a daughter of mine end up with two fiancés, eh? That's not the way I brought you up.'

It was true enough. Emiliana Montella might never have been short of admirers but she'd certainly never entertained more than one at a time.

Elena walked through to the living room and made towards the window which looked out over the sea but there was a rival for her attention: a little table by the window. It was round and made of a dark wood but the wood was almost invisible under numerous photo frames. For a moment, it reminded her of Irma Taccani's photographs and she immediately felt guilty as she thought of what she'd done that day. She'd bought the mask with her to Positano but, at that moment, she felt as if she never wanted to see it again. It had caused nothing but trouble.

She looked at the collection of photographs. There was a photograph of Elena in a pram the size of a juggernaut, and another of her sister's first birthday. There were school portraits of both sisters: Elena with her jutting cheekbones and Rosanna with her slightly rounder face. Both had the same dark, dark eyes and irrepressible smiles. There was a holiday photo of the two sisters on Capri. Their hair was swept back by the warm breeze that Elena could almost feel on her skin now even though she'd been just thirteen when she'd felt it. The whole table was dedicated to Elena and Rosanna and it made Elena feel so sad that they were no longer speaking to each other. She wondered what their mama would do. Would she divide the photos up, slicing through the ones of the two sisters together and place them on separate tables?

'You cannot separate yourself from your sister,' Emiliana said as she entered the room with two cups of coffee.

Elena turned around. That was the other annoying thing about mothers. Not only could they insult you like nobody else in the world, but they could also read your mind at twenty paces.

'You'll have to talk to her at some point. You can't run away from her.'

'I'm not running away,' Elena said, sitting down opposite her mama and taking a cup from her. 'I just needed some space. How was I meant to think with Rosanna and Reuben there in front of me?'

Emiliana shook her head. 'I don't know what there is to think about. They're together, no?'

'Yes,' Elena said, sounding puzzled.

'And you broke up with him?'

'Because they were together!'

'But you also had this Mark?'

'What's he got to do with anything?'

'You tell me, Elena! You're the one engaged to him.'

'We're not engaged any more.'

'Why? Is Rosanna seeing him too behind your back?'

'Don't be ridiculous!'

'I'm not being ridiculous. It seems to me that you're the one who's being ridiculous!'

Elena sighed. Why, no matter where she went or whom she confided in, did her problems seem to double in size?

'I was hoping you'd be a little more understanding,' Elena said, her tone accusing.

'I'm trying to be but I really don't understand what's been going on. Are you going to tell me how you came to be engaged to two men?'

'Three.'

'What?'

'I was engaged to three men. Well, I was. I suppose I'm still officially engaged to one of them.'

'Three? But Rosanna said two.'

'She doesn't know about the third.'

Emiliana's face scrunched up into a frown worthy of a gargoyle.

'Don't look at me like that! It isn't as bad as it sounds,' Elena assured her.

'What do you mean, *it isn't as bad as it sounds?* How can you say such a thing? You've been leading these men on, haven't you? You've been pretending to be someone you aren't. Just like when you were young.'

'Mama-'

'No, Elena! You will listen to me *this* time. You're always getting yourself into impossible situations and then running away from them. Well, you can't live your life like that. You have to think of those around you. The world isn't your personal amusement park - you have to realise that.'

Emiliana paused and Elena stared down at the floorboards, dreading another outpouring, but her mama didn't say anything. In fact, she got up and walked across to the table on which the framed photographs stood. Elena watched as her mama leant forward and picked one up, turning to present it to Elena. It was of a young man. He was very handsome, and his dark eyes smiled out of the silver confines of the frame making Elena feel as if he was in the very room with them.

'Why do you keep that photograph?'

'Because it's part of our album,' Emiliana said slowly.

'I asked you to put it away,' Elena said. Her voice was calm but there was an icy undertone to it.

'You can't put the past away into a drawer and expect it to stay there.'

'I didn't say you could.'

'But that's what you're trying to do again now, isn't it? By coming here?'

'No!' Elena said, getting up and walking towards the window. 'I came here to think things through. Why doesn't anyone think I'm capable of that? Why do you all think I'm running away?'

'Because that's what you normally do.'

Elena swallowed hard. She knew the truth when she heard it and it hurt. 'I'm trying to sort things out,' she said calmly. 'I really am.' She looked across the room at her mama and she felt like a young girl again - a girl who thinks she's clever and capable but who is drowning in her own confusion.

'Won't you help me?' she asked.

Emiliana put the photo frame back on the table, pursed her lips and nodded. 'If you really mean it.'

Elena swallowed hard and looked across at her mother. 'I mean it,' she said.

CHAPTER 38

Rosanna groaned inwardly as Sandro Constantini lunged into a tirade. As though she didn't have enough to cope with already with her sister's two ex-fiancés.

'I trusted you, Rosanna, and this is what you get up to the minute my back is turned,' he yelled, his face contorted with anger.

'But I'm not getting up to anything!' Rosanna said.

'Then who are these two men in my apartment? What will the neighbours think, eh? You'll be getting me a bad reputation and I do not need a bad reputation at this stage of my career!' he said, dramatically tossing his thick fringe out of his eyes. 'Come on, then. Who are they?'

'They're my sister's fiancés,' Rosanna explained.

'Eh? What do you mean? How can they both be her fiancés?'

'You're right – they're not. At least, not any more. She broke up with them. Or, rather, Reuben broke up with her and she broke up with Mark.'

Sandro's eyes widened in complete incomprehension. 'Well, I want them out of my apartment! And where's my *Bimba*?'

Rosanna looked around desperately for the cat-child. She hadn't seen the since she'd kicked it out that morning and hoped it hadn't got itself lost. She might be able to get away with being caught with two men in the apartment but, if anything had happened to the cat-child, she'd have to get herself a lawyer.

'Didn't you hear me?' Sandro said. 'Out! Out!' he cried dramatically and Rosanna chased the two of them down the stairs.

'Rosanna!' Sandro yelled from the kitchen. 'Have they gone yet?'

'They're leaving right now,' she yelled back.

'I hope they took their shoes off before coming in,' Sandro added.

Reuben and Mark looked at one another and started laughing.

'*Please!*' Rosanna said. 'You've got to go.'

'Rosanna,' Reuben began.

'What?'

'Come and see me as soon as you can,' he said.

'I will.'

'Soon!' he repeated leaning forward to give her a kiss. 'Here's where I'm staying now,' he said, pressing a card into her hand.

'Okay,' she said. 'I'm sorry about Sandro. He's just tired from travelling.'

Reuben shook his head. 'He's an asshole.'

She shook her head and gave him a small smile. 'But he's a very kind asshole,' she said.

She opened the door for him and watched as he left and then, she turned to Mark.

'What will you do?' she asked.

He shrugged his shoulders. 'There's not much for me to stay here for now, is there? I guess I'll be heading home sooner than I thought.'

Rosanna frowned. 'Are you sure you won't stay? I'm sure Elena will be back soon.'

'Are you?'

Rosanna bit her lip. 'No.'

'I don't think I'll ever see her again.'

'Don't say that!'

'That's how she left me feeling.'

Rosanna felt as if her heart was bleeding inside her. 'Mark! Won't you go to her?'

He sighed a long, hopeless sigh. 'She doesn't want me there. She didn't even want me here, Rosanna.'

'She *did!* I'm sure she did! She just didn't know it!'

He shook his head.

'You have to try again! Won't you? Please, Mark-'

'I'm tired, Rosanna! I'm so bloody tired of all this.'

Rosanna looked at him and could see that he was telling her the truth - he looked absolutely exhausted. Elena had done her very best to drain him of all life.

Rosanna took his hands in hers. 'You're a fool if you believe she doesn't love you.'

They looked at each other and he shook his head. 'I was a fool to believe that she did.'

*

Prof and Anastasia had, once again, met for lunch. Prof realised that it was turning into a bit of a routine, albeit a very nice one, but he wasn't meant to be getting into routines with other women when he was engaged to Elena, was he?

The conversation hadn't flown as easily today and Prof thought he knew why: he was feeling guilty. It almost felt as if Elena was with him, sitting beside him with an expression of horror - wondering what he was doing with another woman. He wanted to explain things: it wasn't what it looked like. But that was such a cliché. Anyway, what exactly *was* this thing with Anastasia? He was still in love with Elena.

He fidgeted in his chair and looked at his watch surreptitiously under the table.

'It's nearly two o'clock,' Anastasia said.

'Sorry,' he said, his face flushing. 'I should think about going.'

'Where?'

He felt cornered. He didn't actually have an answer for her and she seemed to know that.

'It's my last day tomorrow,' she told him, her large eyes peeping up through her thick red fringe.

'Is it?'

She nodded. 'Then it's back home. Back to the four walls and cooking for myself again.'

There was a pause. Prof felt that the very air about him was full of reproach and he swore he could feel his skin prickling with the discomfort of deceit.

'So,' Anastasia began.

'So?' Prof echoed. Their voices seemed to say this was the end of their non-affair. What had started out as being such fun had crumbled away as they both faced the reality of their situations.

'Look,' she said, her hand reaching out across the table to touch his ever so lightly. 'I know things are difficult for you at the moment and I don't want to get in the way of you making a decision, but I do want you to know that I'm here. Or rather, I'll be there - if you want me to be there. You've got my number?'

Prof nodded. He had. She'd given it to him the night before and he'd taken it, carefully placing it in his travel copy of *The Selected Works of Byron*.

'And you'll call me if you need to talk?'

'I will,' he said, daring to look across at her. She smiled at him.

'Things will work themselves out - one way or another,' she said.

'Of course they will,' he said, wondering why it took a relative stranger to tell a professor such a thing.

They called over to a waiter for the bill and Anastasia picked it up.

'No, no,' Prof said. 'Let me.'

Anastasia seemed a little reluctant but Prof took the bill from her. 'It's the least I can do to thank you for your time.'

She smiled. 'You know, I didn't really believe in English gentlemen until I met you,' she said.

As they left the restaurant, they sighed in unison and then laughed.

'Have you time for a walk?' she asked.

Prof nodded. He looked absent-minded, as though he didn't really care too much what they did next and so they walked in silence, gazing half-heartedly in the shops stuffed to bursting point with bright glass. There were photo frames, vases, wineglasses, necklaces, bracelets and earrings.

Anastasia wrinkled her nose in distaste. She'd never worn costume jewellery. Something she did have a weakness for, though, was jewellery boxes and, when she saw a display of beautiful wooden-inlaid boxes in rich reds, blues and chestnuts, she grabbed Prof's arm and was in the shop.

'What do you think?' she asked, picking up a small, oblong box which played *O Sole Mio*. It was Prof's turn to wrinkle his nose.

'A bit cheesy?'

He nodded. 'Just a bit.'

She picked up another: an octagonal box in a dusky red with a pattern of flowers on the top. She opened it up and the bright notes of Beethoven's *Für Elise* flew out into the shop from the red velvet interior.

'Oh, yes!' Anastasia grinned. She turned to see what Prof thought but he'd left the shop. She frowned just as a sales assistant walked over to give her his music box spiel.

'I'll take it,' she said, producing a credit card before the assistant had time to open his mouth.

'I lost you,' she said a moment later outside the shop, her new acquisition well-wrapped up in a carrier bag.

'Sorry,' he said.

They walked out and found themselves in San Marco. The tables outside *Quadri's* and *Florian's* packed with tourists, the Easter sunshine prising jackets and jumpers from them. The Campanile soared high into the sky, its vivid green spire tipped with a golden angel and, standing opposite, the wedding-cake dreaminess of the Doges' Palace. It was only a short walk from here to the Danieli, and Prof was itching to get back to his room but he wasn't quite sure how to go about it.

'I really didn't expect to meet someone like you out here,' Prof admitted at last in a voice barely above a whisper.

'I didn't expect to be met,' Anastasia replied.

Prof looked down at his shiny shoes and wondered how, exactly, they were to say goodbye. They'd passed the boundary of handshakes and yet weren't familiar enough for an embrace. But Anastasia solved the problem by leaning forward and kissing him daintily on the cheek.

'Goodbye, darling,' she said. 'Don't you go forgetting me, will you?'

Before Prof had a chance to tell her that he could sooner forget himself, she'd turned and walked away into a crowd of tourists and was gone.

Prof gazed up into a sky dotted with tiny white clouds, the haunting notes of *Für Elise* playing in his mind. It had been part of a programme he'd taken Elena to hear on their first date together, and the unexpected reminder in the shop had shaken him. It was as if somebody was reminding him that he wasn't meant to be there with Anastasia.

'Remember this?' Emiliana asked, walking through to the living room with an old, stuffed bear in her arms.

'Fernando? Where on earth has he been?'

Emiliana shook her head. 'Rosanna gave him to me after my divorce.'

Elena stretched her hands out to greet the ancient bear. 'Dear Fernando! I'd forgotten all about him!'

Fernando, the custard-coloured bear, who'd been around for as long as Elena could remember, was "a sharing bear". He didn't belong to anyone in particular - rather he was given to the member of the Montella family who was in need of him most at the time. He'd been given to Elena and Rosanna when they'd split up from boyfriends or been dumped over the years; when they'd been unsuccessful in interviews; when Rosanna had failed her driving test for the first, second and third time; and every other family incident which required a custard-coloured cuddle.

'You know why I'm giving him to you now?'

Elena frowned. 'Because I've just split up with two fiancés?'

'No. Because I think you should give him to Rosanna.'

'Rosanna!'

'She sounded very upset when she rang.'

'*She's* upset? *Mon dio!* That really is the limit! I'm made out to be the villain here. I don't believe it!'

Her mama shook her head silently. 'Take Fernando. You know it's the right thing to do.'

'I'm not using Fernando as a peace offering. It would be more appropriate for me to give her a cobra.'

Emiliana glowered at her daughter. 'Can you hear what you're saying?'

'At least I'm being honest! I really think it's me who needs Fernando - not Rosanna!'

Emiliana threw her hands in the air in desperation - a gesture which immediately reminded Elena of her sister. Her mama was right - there would never be any running away from her family; there was nowhere to hide from your relatives because they were a part of you. Still, that didn't mean you had to forgive them in a hurry.

'I'm not ready to speak to her yet,' Elena said after a few moments of silence.

'But you will talk to her?'

Elena sighed. 'Not yet.'

'You need to sort this out. You can't let it fester away-'

'I know, Mama! Just let me get my head round things, please!'

The two women looked at each other across the small living room. 'I hate to see my two daughters fighting. You've no idea what that does to a mother!'

'Don't start!'

'Well, you'd better put a stop to all this nonsense soon.'

Elena got up. 'Mama! This isn't my fault!'

Her mama glared at her.

'Well,' Elena began, 'maybe it is – a bit. But don't heap *all* the blame on me.'

'I'm not apportioning blame. That's not my job.'

Elena sighed. It seemed that that was exactly what her mother was doing.

CHAPTER 39

'So, how did your trip go?' Rosanna asked Sandro the next morning. Her question was more out of politeness than real interest, and she was still rather angry at him for his rude eviction of Mark and Reuben.

'It went very well,' he said. 'In fact, so well that I may have to leave Venice.'

'Leave Venice?' Rosanna asked, shocked. Sandro was as much a part of Venice as the water and he'd lived there most of his life. How on earth could he think about leaving? And there was something else which shocked Rosanna: how such a move would affect her. If Sandro left that would mean she'd have to leave too.

'It's really very inconvenient,' Sandro explained, his face scarred with a scowl. 'I mean, my whole life is here but, I'm told, I have to be in New York if I really want to make things happen. That's the place to be for me now.'

'Oh,' Rosanna said, stunned. Already, she was planning ahead. There'd be no more freeloading off Sandro Constantini. No more lucrative modelling assignments from the only real artist she sat for. That was bad news.

'But how can you think of leaving Venice?' she asked in a plea for him to think about all he'd be giving up. 'How can you contemplate living in a place without water? And living in a place with high-rise buildings! How will you *breathe* in such a place?'

'Venice isn't the only place in the world with water, Rosanna! New York's surrounded by water and, as to open spaces, there's always Central Park,' Sandro said in defence of his new home.

'But how will you cope without this place?' Rosanna said, sounding more and more like an anxious mother who doesn't want her only child to leave home.

'I'll have to find another place,' he shrugged, taking in the studio with a quick glance. 'The change will be good for me and, more importantly, good for my art. I feel ready for a new beginning. An artist shouldn't ever become settled or too complacent or they stagnate.'

So, Rosanna thought, that's what it all came down to – Sandro Constantini's art. She was fighting a losing battle there, wasn't she? She was up against an artist's ego and bank balance.

'I don't think your *Bimba* will like it,' she said at last, pulling out her trump card.

Sandro's face froze and he gave a weary sigh. 'I've been thinking about her,' he said. 'New York is no place for a cat.'

'No!' Rosanna agreed, thinking that the animal she had hitherto hated might now turn out to be her saviour.

'I'll have to give her away, I suppose,' he said, his mouth puckering up into a blossom-like kiss – the sort he usually reserved only for his precious *Bimba*.

'Give her away!' Rosanna was aghast at such a declaration. The cat was his child. Was he really willing to make this sacrifice for his career? She wondered.

'I have to make this sacrifice for my career,' he said.

'Gosh!' Rosanna said. 'I don't know what to say.'

'I could think of nothing else on the plane back. My mind was a maelstrom!' he said, ever the drama queen. 'I love this place, of course.'

'You'll never find another like it,' Rosanna interrupted.

'I know. You don't need to tell me that.'

I do, she thought. Before you sell it. 'So, you're really prepared to give it up?'

Sandro threw his head back and gazed up at the criss-cross of dark beams. It was a space like no other. Would he be able to find such a space in New York? Was there such a space anywhere in the world to rival this one?

'I don't think I can really sell it,' he said at last.

Rosanna breathed a sigh of relief. Thank goodness for that, she thought.

'I will, perhaps, rent it out.'

Even worse. There was no way that Rosanna could afford to rent something like Sandro's.

'Do you have anyone in mind?' she asked, realising that she'd soon be packing her bags and heading back to the mainland.

'It would be a good idea if I could find another artist,' he said thoughtfully.

'An artist?'

He nodded. 'It makes sense. It's such an excellent space.'

'Yes!' Rosanna said, getting excited. 'And I might just know somebody who'd be interested.'

'Really?'

Rosanna nodded. She wasn't sure what kind of money Reuben made or even if he'd be interested in moving to Venice but it was worth a try.

'Because, if you know of someone, perhaps my dear *Bimba* wouldn't have to move after all!' he said, getting excited.

Rosanna frowned. That wasn't quite what she had in mind.

'There would be a discount, of course, if you could find somebody to look after the cat!'

Rosanna smiled. Things might just work out in her favour after all.

CHAPTER 40

Elena's first morning in Positano was spent taking a coastal path around the cliffs. The sea was a thousand shades of blue and the spring sunshine had forced her to roll up the sleeves of her jumper.

She walked with quick, definite strides, as if she knew where she was going. She didn't, of course. She was just following the set route in the hope of finding a little bit of peace and space.

She stopped and sat down on a low, sun-warmed stone wall and let her gaze fall down the sheer slope to the sea. Her mama had woken her early with a cup of coffee and the subtle words, 'Wake up! You've got a lot of thinking to do!'

'Thanks, Mama,' she's muttered back, pulling the sheets around her face in an attempt to escape back into sleep. It didn't work, of course. If Elena had needed any reminding as to where Rosanna got her plate-clattering-in-the-sink skills from, she'd had it that morning. Her mama had moved through the house with the force of a tornado, only she managed to make more noise.

'Ah! You're up at last,' she'd said when Elena had surfaced, as if that hadn't been her intention all along. 'I've got to go out,' she'd added.

Elena nodded, thinking that she might be able to sneak back into bed.

'I'll drop you in town,' her mama said. 'Come on! I'm leaving in ten minutes.'

Elena didn't bother arguing. Her mama had told her to go for a walk to, 'get your head cleared out', and so here she was. But just how did you clear your head out? She'd crammed so much into hers recently that she didn't know where to begin.

For a moment, she thought about the golden mask. She'd brought it with her and it was safely stashed in the boot of her hire car in case her mama had a surreptitious rifle through her luggage.

Hadn't Stefano told her that the mask would help her with her decisions? It couldn't help her here in Positano, could it? Maybe the mask only worked in Venice.

All of a sudden, everything became clear. She had to go back to Venice. As surely as she'd had to leave, she had to return. She'd had to get away in order to do that, she could see that now, and she would return with a clear head – and a plan.

Although Elena would never admit it, her mama had been right all along. There was no getting away from facing up to her responsibilities.

With this new resolution, Elena got up and route-marched back along the coastal path. She was going back tonight and she was taking Fernando the bear with her.

On Sandro's arrival back, Rosanna had been relegated to the spare bedroom. Life in the luxurious double bed upstairs was over. It was a good job, she thought, that Elena had left when she had otherwise she'd have had to explain that to Sandro as well as the two male visitors. Luckily, Sandro hadn't asked any more questions about Reuben and Mark, and Rosanna had been careful not to mention them, even though she had plans for Reuben.

'This artist of yours,' Sandro said over a cup of coffee on his first morning back, 'do I know his work?'

Rosanna bit her lip. 'His name is Reuben Lord and he's English.'

'Never heard of him,' Sandro said dismissively. 'He can't be that good if I've never heard of him.'

'He's very good,' she said. 'Just waiting for his big break, that's all. Just like you had to wait for yours – remember?'

Sandro nodded thoughtfully. 'It was always coming, of course, but it took its time all the same,' he said.

Rosanna curled her fingers up into a tight ball. He really could be the most conceited of people sometimes.

'And Reuben's will come too and just imagine how wonderful it would be if you had some sort of knowledge of that. He could be your protégé!'

Sandro's eyebrows rose. 'Yes!' he said, a finger raised to his mouth. 'You might have something there. I'd have to see his work, of course, before I committed myself.'

'Of course,' Rosanna said, humouring him.

'I wouldn't want to put in a good word for him in the circles I now move in if his work was inferior.'

'And I'm sure he'd look after your *Bimba*,' Rosanna said, crawling into his favour on Reuben's behalf.

'He's kind, then?'

Rosanna nodded. 'Oh, yes,' she said, not bothering to tell Sandro how Reuben had recently dumped Elena for her without so much as a text message.

'And he's in Venice now?'

'Yes.'

Sandro frowned as a thought raced through his mind. 'He isn't one of those men who was here in my studio when I came home, is he?'

Rosanna paused as she tried to think of a way around this.

'Because I didn't like those guys,' he elaborated. 'They looked like freeloaders.'

'You think everyone looks like a freeloader.'

'Everybody *is* a freeloader!'

Rosanna glared at him. 'Are you including me in your sweeping statement?'

Sandro glared back at her and then started to giggle like a girl. 'My dear Rosanna! You are a delightful exception.'

Rosanna continued to glare at him, not sure what he meant by that comment but relieved that it had got them away from Sandro's cross-questioning as to who Reuben was.

'So,' Rosanna began, 'do you want me to talk to my friend about your apartment or not?'

Sandro sighed. 'Yes, yes! If he's a friend of yours, that's good enough for me.'

'And it will be a special rate rent?'

'If he agrees to look after my *Bimba*.'

'He will.'

'And he won't be able to move any of the canvases I leave here. It will still be my apartment.'

'Of course, Sandro. He'll have every respect for your work,' Rosanna said, thinking that it would all probably be moved down to the basement at the earliest opportunity.

'Then we might well have an agreeable arrangement.'

Rosanna smiled to herself. She couldn't wait to tell Reuben.

*

Emiliana was delighted with Elena's decision.

'You won't regret it!' she told her earnestly. 'You and Rosanna have many things to sort out but it will all work out in the end, believe me.'

The more her mama went, the more Elena became nervous.

'Families must stick together,' she went on. 'Through the good times *and* the bad.'

Why was it, Elena wondered, that you were always fed clichés at such times? It was one of the few times in her life when she needed to hear something good and honest and original. Prof would have those sort of comforting words for her, she felt sure of that. Yes, her dear Prof would be just the right sort of person to talk to if only he wasn't bound up in all this business too.

'Mama,' Elena said, 'I'm going to make a call.'

Her mama said something about keeping it short as she wasn't made of Euros.

'I'll be using my mobile.'

'I didn't know you had a mobile.'

'No. I just got it,' Elena lied.

She walked through to her bedroom and fished in her suitcase for the phone she kept hidden. Was she really going to do this? She supposed she had to. She had to make a start on sorting out the huge mess she'd got herself into.

She rang the number and waited.

'Hello?'

'Prof?'

'Elena? Is that you?'

'Of course it is! Who else calls you Prof?' she said, immediately feeling at ease for hearing his kind voice.

'Where are you?'

'I'm in-' she hesitated. 'I'm in Positano,' she finished.

'I thought you were in Venice.'

'I was. And I will be again this evening.'

'I thought I saw you the other day – at the Danieli here. Were you here?'

Elena gasped. She really wanted to sort things out but she wasn't ready to confess everything yet.

'No,' she lied, her face screwing up at her horrible lie. 'But I saw you,' she said.

'You did? Well, why didn't you say something?'

'You were with somebody.'

There was a moment's silence.

'Elena,' Prof began, 'it's not what you're thinking.'

Elena grimaced. She'd rung her dear Prof to get away from clichés. 'I wasn't thinking anything.'

'I just met this woman and we had lunch.'

'Oh.'

'A few times, actually. She's very nice. You'd like her.'

Elena frowned. Prof would make a terrible adulterer.

'Sorry,' he said, 'that didn't come out quite how I meant it.'

'It's all right,' she said.

'No. It isn't,' he said. 'I feel terrible about it.'

'Why?'

'Because every minute I was with her, I should have been with you.'

Elena paused. She wasn't sure what to say. And what exactly was *he* saying? He was feeling guilty but did that mean he still loved her? And did she love him?

'Prof,' she began hesitantly.

'Yes?'

'How do you feel about me?'

'What do you mean?'

She took a deep breath. She wasn't being very fair, was she? She knew how she felt about him. She wasn't in love with him. She didn't think she ever had been.

'Elena?'

'I'm still here.'

'You sound strange,' he said. 'What's wrong? Why are you asking me how I feel about you? You know how I feel.'

'Yes,' she said in a whisper. 'But I'm not sure how I feel about you any more.'

'Is this because of Anastasia?'

'Who?'

'The woman I was with because she wasn't anything to do with us-'

'I know,' she assured him. 'And it's got nothing to do with her. This is just about me. I've not been fair to you, Prof. I've been selfish and mean and you deserve better than that.'

'Elena, are you breaking up with me?'

She closed her eyes and took a deep breath. 'Yes,' she said. 'I'm sorry. I'm really sorry. I'll return your ring.'

'Sod the ring! I don't want the ring – I want *you*!'

'Do you? Do you really?'

'Yes! Of course I do. I don't go around proposing to anybody, you know. It took me forty-nine years to pluck up the courage to ask you.'

'But I'm all wrong for you.'

'Why do you say that? Is it the age thing?'

'No.'

'Then what?'

'I just don't think we're suited – not really.'

'But we get on so well.'

Elena sighed.

'Look,' he said, 'I don't want to break up with you on the phone. This is horrible.'

'I know it is and I'm so sorry but I had to tell you. I've not been very honest with you lately – with anyone, in fact,' she said. That was the closest she was going to get to the truth.

There was a pause and a crackle of static on the phone.

'Are you still there?' she asked.

'I'm still here. I'll always be here for you, Elena.'

Elena felt tears spring to her eyes. 'No,' she said, 'don't be. I don't deserve you.' And then she hung up.

CHAPTER 41

The Alilaguna from the airport was packed with holidaymakers keen for their first glimpse of Venice. Elena could safely say that she was the only person on board who was dreading reaching her destination. The flight back had been delayed by an hour and she'd been sat in front of a baby who'd howled for the entire journey. Now, she felt hot and irritable.

When they reached the Fondamenta Nove, it was nearly lunchtime. Elena dragged her suitcase off the boat and followed the waterfront round over the Ponte Panada and dipped into a calle. Making sure it was all quiet, she reached into her coat pocket for the mask and put it on, keeping hold of her suitcase. She loved the fact that the mask not only turned her invisible but anything she was holding too so that her suitcase disappeared which was a blessing really because a suitcase going for a walk on its own would have looked a bit peculiar.

It took only about eight seconds for the mask to work its magic this time which was just as well because a couple of teenagers turned into the calle kicking a football. They didn't seem to notice when it bounced off her invisible suitcase.

Elena took the familiar route from the waterfront to the apartment, wondering if Rosanna would be in and how she was going to get in herself if there was anybody around. She took the key out of her handbag and boldly inserted it into the keyhole, turning the handle and letting herself in. That was the easy bit. If she closed the door behind her, it would make a clang worthy of a medieval castle and she had to be sure nobody was in before she did that.

Standing absolutely still, she craned her neck up the flight of stone steps into the living room. She couldn't tell if the place was empty or not: it was so huge that there might very well be a party going on in the spare room at the back and she wouldn't be able to hear. She waited. At last, she felt sure she heard a voice: a man's voice. What could she do? She could simply leave the door open: it was a quiet area and everyone knew everybody else, but that would probably get

Rosanna into trouble. Yet she had to get in. She couldn't afford hotel prices and didn't want to have to go as far as the mainland. And she needed to see Rosanna – that was what she'd planned.

Leaving the door very slightly ajar, she walked slowly up the steps into the apartment. The voice was becoming louder now but it wasn't one she recognised which meant it wasn't Mark or Reuben. Who could it be? Not Corrado, surely?

Then she had her answer: in the kitchen, a tall, thin man with foppish hair was stooped down stroking cat-child. Sandro.

Whilst he was making a fuss of the cat, Elena took the opportunity to sneak through to the spare bedroom at the back of the apartment. Three stone steps led down into it and she carried her suitcase down them carefully, trying not to knock or scrape anything.

Pushing the bedroom door open, she crossed the room and shoved her suitcase under the bed. It was then that she noticed a nightgown on the other single bed in the room. It was Rosanna's nightgown. Of course! If Sandro was back, Rosanna would be relegated to the spare bedroom which meant that Elena couldn't possibly sleep in there.

Or could she? A sudden thought occurred to her. What would happen if she wore the mask at night? She wouldn't be able to sleep under the covers because she'd still take up space and that would show but what if she slept on the bed itself? Rosanna wouldn't be any the wiser, would she? Elena didn't snore or anything. She might just get away with it but perhaps she'd be best to check before she put the mask to the test. She'd never worn it longer than a few minutes and didn't know what it was capable of.

Entering the living room, she saw that Sandro was now standing in front of one of his easels wearing the discontented look artists often wore. The canvas he was looking at was one of a street scene – obviously New York, and he didn't look happy with it. As he walked back to examine it, an idle finger found its way up his right nostril where it scratched, twirled and scraped. Elena grinned to herself. It was still a great novelty for her to witness what she shouldn't be witnessing but she didn't hang around. She was a woman on a mission.

Leaving the door slightly ajar, she ran out of the small calle and on into the heart of Venice. After her journey by car, plane and Alilaguna, it was good to stride out through the streets again.

Cannaregio always felt safe and Elena soon took her mask off and lost herself in the Easter crowds heading towards the Accademia Bridge. She smiled as she saw the monstrous Easter eggs filling the shop windows, and dark chocolate bells bejewelled with bright flowers.

The streets of Dorsoduro were teeming with tourists too who blocked bridges in their attempts to get the perfect photograph. Workers, too, caused chaos as they tried to manoeuvre goods over endless steps in metal trolleys, reminding Elena that everything in Venice had to be shipped in.

Thankfully, it became quieter when she turned into the little calle that led to Viviana's. When she'd first arrived in Venice, she'd got the feeling that it wasn't just a labyrinth but a labyrinth that changed every day, so she'd been surprised by the speed at which she'd learnt to navigate the backstreets.

She felt a sudden sense of calm as she neared the shop – as if she'd been going there for years - feeling as if Stefano and Viviana were part of her family rather than people she'd only met a few days ago.

She saw that there were a few new masks in the window: a couple of the traditional bautas and a new jester with pretty silver bells and, inside the shop, there was a huge wooden chest full of bright faces. The original gold mask was still in the window too, its skin gleaming and its hollow eyes seeming to take in the whole of Elena in a simple glance, and Elena couldn't help but wonder what would happen if she put that mask on. Were all the masks in the shop passports to adventure? Stefano seemed so sure that he'd given Elena the right mask for her but her curiosity was getting the better of her and she pushed open the door and heard the merry tinkle of the shop bell.

Once again, there was nobody around and the curious silence of the shop enveloped her. Elena turned to look into the window, her heart hammering inside her chest as she leant forward to pick up the golden mask which had enticed her into the shop in the first place.

'I wouldn't do that if I were you,' Stefano said, making Elena jump.

'Stefano?' she said. 'I didn't hear you.'

'I'm never far away,' he said.

'No,' Elena said, and it was true. She didn't know for sure what he got up to in his secret room at the back of the shop. Most of the other mask shops had counters and work benches in the shop itself but not Stefano. Some of the tools of his work were on display along with the occasional mask but, for the most part, he kept his trade under wraps – away from the glare of inquisitive eyes.

'Why did you want to try it on?' he asked.

'I – I don't know.'

'You must know.'

Elena's glance fell to the floor. She felt so silly having been caught like that. What did she think she was doing? Wasn't one mask enough?

'I'm sorry,' she said at last.

Stefano nodded. 'They're addictive, aren't they? I should know.'

Elena stared at him and saw a strange light dancing in his eyes. There were hidden worlds there, she thought: secrets and surprises and mysteries and magic. He knew things that would never pass into the realm of ordinary people. Elena had had a glimpse of it with her mask but how much more was there to find out? Perhaps she'd never know.

'Be content,' he said. 'You have the right mask for you.'

'I know,' Elena said, feeling spoilt and ungrateful. 'And it's the mask I've come to ask you about. I need it to help me with something.'

'Good,' Stefano said. 'I'm pleased it's of use.'

'Oh, it is,' Elena said. 'I mean, I hope it will be. The thing is, I need to wear it all night and I was wondering if that was possible.'

There was a pause when Stefano's white eyebrows lowered over his dark eyes and his face was stiff with concentration.

'You need to wear the mask *all* night?' he said with a look of extreme concern.

'Yes,' Elena said. 'Is it okay if I do?'

'It should be okay,' he said thoughtfully.

'You're sure?'

He nodded. 'There's only one way to find out,' he said, and he gave a little chuckle. Elena wasn't at all sure she felt comforted by him.

Rosanna had called Reuben's hotel to arrange to meet at a café in a nearby campiello. She wasn't going to turn up at his hotel, that was for sure. Things were moving far too quickly with Reuben and she wanted them to slow down. That's what she told herself as she left to meet him. But she knew it didn't make any sense because she was about to try and persuade him to leave his life behind in London, move to Venice and rent Sandro's apartment. If that wasn't forward, she didn't know what was. For one thing, they hardly knew each other, and there was still the problem of Elena to sort out.

'I think you should go and see her,' Rosanna blurted as soon as they met.

'What?' Reuben said, his dark eyes narrowing. 'Why? She broke up with me.'

'But that doesn't change the fact that we're together now. Even if you two had broken up anyway.' Rosanna sighed. She'd been so excited by the idea of Reuben renting Sandro's apartment but, before they talked about it, they had to discuss Elena. 'This problem isn't going to go away, you know. It isn't just going to get better because of the passing of time. If anything, it will get worse. These things have a habit of festering and getting out of all proportion.'

'I know,' Reuben agreed. 'But I can't see what to do about it. She ran away from us, remember? I don't think she wants us to go after her.'

Rosanna shook her head. Reuben sounded just like Mark but Rosanna wasn't so sure about his belief in what Elena wanted.

'I think I should go.'

Reuben shook his head. 'I don't think that's a very good idea.'

But Rosanna didn't appear to be listening to him and got her mobile from her bag and rang her mama's number.

'Mama? I think it might be a good idea if I visited.' There was a pause. 'What? Back here? Are you sure? I've not heard from her. What time?' There was another pause. 'Do you know where she's staying? Oh.'

'What is it?' Reuben asked but Rosanna waved her hand at him.

'No. I'll stay here. Perhaps she's waiting for me at Sandro's. Okay. I'll call soon and let you know what's happening.'

Rosanna switched her phone off and looked across the table at Reuben. 'Elena's left Mama's and is back in Venice.'

'When? Where?'

'I've absolutely no idea. But that's a good sign, isn't it? I mean, she wouldn't have come back unless she was ready to talk, would she?'

Reuben shook his head. 'It might mean she's come back to kill you.'

Rosanna's eyes widened in horror. 'I don't know why you think it's funny.'

'I don't!'

'Because, if she wants to kill me, she'll probably want to kill you too!'

After leaving Vivianas's, Elena took a vaporetto to San Marco from where she walked down the Riva degli Schiavoni. The further she went, the quieter it became - the majority of tourists not venturing much further than the Bridge of Sighs. The pavement broadened out into the lagoon and the sunshine made the distant view back to the Doges' Palace and the campanile hazy and dreamlike. Boats danced across the water and a few gulls mirrored their movement in the lilac sky above.

Elena found a white stone seat to sit on. There was no point in going back to the apartment just yet to sit perfectly still and invisible. She wasn't sure where Rosanna was or when she'd be back but she wasn't going to hang around waiting for her. But what *was* she going to do when Rosanna did get back? She'd seemed so sure of herself in Positano but now butterflies fluttered with worry in her stomach. She felt so nervous. She really wanted to sort things out; it was the only way they could all move forward but what if everything went horribly wrong? She knew she'd acted irresponsibly and been unfair to Reuben - to all her fiancés - but she was determined to make amends, she just wasn't quite sure how.

Watching the world go by was one of the loveliest pastimes in Venice but two hours was more than enough and Elena got up with a numb bottom. She managed to get back into the apartment easily. Sandro had gone out and Rosanna was still out too. Probably with Reuben, she thought. The traitors. She groaned; she still felt so angry and betrayed by both of them and yet felt guilty and appalled at hating them both for it.

She crossed the living room and headed down the steps which led to the spare room at the back of the apartment. There were two double beds there and Rosanna had taken the one on the right. Elena had already hidden her suitcase under the one on the left and observed that there was a good ten feet between the beds so that should prevent them from knocking into each other unintentionally in the night, and at least there wasn't a chance that Reuben would be calling at the apartment now that Sandro was back.

She lay down on the bed, mask-less for the time being, and stared up at the white ceiling. Three large beams crossed the sloping ceiling and you had to be careful getting in and out of bed lest you knocked your head against one. Elena shut her eyes. It was a very comfortable bed and it was easy, after her day's travel, to fall into a deep sleep. She didn't hear Sandro coming back in, moving canvasses around. Nor did she hear Rosanna returning home and clattering dishes in the sink. It wasn't until cat-child leapt up on the bed and placed a purring face next to her ear, that she awoke.

'Oh my lord!' she said, hearing Sandro and her sister talking in the next room. Leaping off the bed, Elena grabbed the mask and put it on as she hurriedly made the bed. She'd been asleep for hours and it was dark outside. She might have been caught there. How would she have explained herself?

Once invisible, she crept to the bedroom door which had been ajar all the time, cat-child following her and rubbing herself against Elena's invisible leg. Elena tried to shoo her away but she remained, resolutely, by her side, making Elena wondered if she were, indeed, invisible to the cat.

Sandro sounded excitable and Rosanna's voice was angry.

'How many times do I have to tell you? I closed the door after me!'

'You're sure?' Sandro asked.

'It isn't an easy door to leave open, is it? You can tell when you close it because the whole street vibrates! Of course I closed it! Stop questioning me about it,' Rosanna yelled. 'You probably left it open yourself.'

'I did no such thing!' he exclaimed like a wronged child. 'I only hope it's not been permanently open since I've been away.'

'Of course it hasn't! I've looked after your place as if it were my own.' Rosanna sighed. 'Look, have you checked that nothing's missing?'

'That's just what I've been doing.'

Rosanna looked around the studio and saw that there were canvasses everywhere.

'I don't think anyone is going to walk through Venice with a canvas the size you paint them.'

'They might have moored a boat at the canal at the end of the calle.'

'It's not very likely, is it?' Rosanna said.

'They're very precious to me. They're the most valuable things I have.'

'And that's why I always make sure the door is closed behind me.'

Elena cringed in the shadows of her invisibility. She'd known this would happen and she'd known Rosanna would get all heated up about it too.

'Something strange is going on,' Sandro said, looking around. For a moment, he stared right into Elena's eyes. 'I can't quite put my finger on it but there's something not quite right here.'

'What do you mean? Everything seems perfectly normal.'

Sandro shook his head. 'No. I can feel a change,' he said.

Elena watched in horror as he walked straight towards her. Could he see her? Would he let on if he could?

'*Bimba!*' he cooed, bending down to pick up the cat that was still comfortably winding its way around Elena's legs. 'What are you doing, you silly *Bimba?*'

He picked the cat up and took it back to a sofa where he flopped down and placed it on his lap.

'I think the open door was a sign,' he said.

'You think everything's a sign.'

'I think it's a premonition of my leaving Venice. Don't you?'

'No,' Rosanna said. 'I think it was an unfortunate accident and that you should probably get your lock seen to.'

'The door was open - representing my leaving - the start of a new life,' Sandro said, suddenly looking animated.

'Don't be silly.'

For a moment, he looked crestfallen. 'Well, that's what I think,' he said.

'I'm going for a shower,' Rosanna said. 'And then I'm going to bed. I'll see you in the morning.'

Sandro nodded. Elena watched as Rosanna walked right by her without any recognition whatsoever. It was the oddest feeling - as if she'd died and been forgotten already.

Suddenly, Elena's stomach gave a volcanic rumble. Rosanna froze on her way to the bathroom, turning around with a look of surprise on her face. Elena bit her lip, wrapping her arms around her tummy in an attempt to stop it. Luckily, it did stop and Rosanna shook her head and disappeared into the bathroom.

Elena's heart was pumping wildly. This business of being invisible was proving more risky than she'd first thought. Now, she was having grave doubts about being able to sneak into the kitchen and pinch some food in order to quieten her disorderly stomach. Sandro had left the cat-child licking its limbs on the sofa and was examining some canvasses at the far end of the studio so Elena was able to sneak through and find a bar of chocolate. Not very substantial but at least it wouldn't make suspicious dishes.

She walked silently through to the living room and back to the spare bedroom. If Rosanna was going straight to bed, Elena thought she'd better be heading that way too because she wouldn't want to be stumbling about in the dark, trying not to wake her up.

Entering the bedroom, she walked carefully towards her bed, aware that she couldn't put the lights on and that there were low beams everywhere. Finding her bed, she sat on the edge, trying not to wrinkle the bedspread. She'd have to wait for Rosanna to get settled before she could think about making herself comfortable.

Luckily, she didn't have to wait long. Rosanna came through, snapping on the light switch. She was wearing the dusky pink nightgown Elena had seen on the bed earlier, her hair newly washed and blow-dried. She turned down her bedding and then knelt on the floor, her hands pressed together in prayer. Blimey, Elena thought, did she still really do that? Elena strained to hear what she said but it was all whispered. At one point, she thought she heard her name but she couldn't be sure.

Making the sign of the cross, Rosanna got up and turned out the light. Elena stretched out on her bed, adjusting the mask so that it felt comfortable and, soon, the two sisters had fallen asleep together.

CHAPTER 42

When Elena had hung up on Prof, he'd felt stunned, betrayed and relieved all at the same time. He couldn't quite believe it had happened and yet there'd been a little part of him which had expected it. His colleagues had warned him of the perils of passion with pupils, and even his mother had been a little concerned about the age difference. But Prof felt that this break hadn't been anything to do with their ages. There'd been something Elena wasn't telling him and, in his heart of hearts, he'd supposed she was never quite the one for him.

He'd been swept away by it all, of course. Which man of his age wouldn't have been flattered by the attentions of a beautiful young woman? And he'd been willing to make changes for her: to give up his bachelordom and share his life with somebody. But that wasn't going to happen now.

For a moment, he felt a hollowness like he'd never experienced before. He closed his eyes. He'd lost Elena and there was no getting her back. There was nothing he could do. His time in Venice had been wasted.

'*Don't you go forgetting me, will you?*'

Prof's eyes opened with a start. He felt sure he'd heard Anastasia's voice as though she was in the room with him. It was as if she'd heard him thinking that his time in Venice had been wasted.

'It hasn't, has it?' he said to himself. 'God!' He shook his head. This was confusing. He felt like he was betraying Elena by thinking about Anastasia so soon after their engagement had been broken off but he couldn't stop himself.

He got up and began to pace the room. His plane tickets were booked for tomorrow. He'd be home by the afternoon. He picked up his *Selected Works of Byron* and flicked through the pages. There was her number. He felt a small smile tickling the corners of his mouth. Anastasia didn't really expect to hear from him, did she? Well, he thought, he might just prove her wrong.

*

The two young girls were playing outside in a sunny courtyard. They were laughing and smiling, their dark hair flying about their faces as they ran after each other.

'Catch!' the taller of the two girls shouted, throwing a custard-coloured teddy bear at her small sister. She caught it with ease and threw it back again.

'Throw it again!' the younger sister begged.

'No. I want to play with it now.'

'But I do too!' the younger sister said. '*Please!*'

'No. I was playing with it first. Go and find your own toy.'

'That's not fair!' the young sister shouted, stamping her feet and crossing her arms over her chest. 'Give it to me!' she said, making a lunge towards the teddy.

'Stop it!' the older girl yelled.

Two pairs of hands clutched at the teddy bear, pulling the bright yellow fur in both directions at once.

'You're hurting him! Stop it!' the older sister cried.

'I'm not the one who's hurting him. *You* are.'

Both girls tugged harder, their cries and screams escalating until the inevitable happened - one of the teddy bear's arms tore clean off. They stared at the poor wounded bear: the older girl holding the main body and the younger holding the amputated limb.

'Look what you've done!' the older girl cried.

'I didn't do it!' the younger girl said, her lip trembling. Then, without warning, she let out a scream.

'What? What is it?' the older girl asked. But she had her answer as soon as she looked at the bear clutched in her hands. Its face was no longer that of a teddy bear: it was a man's...

Elena bolted up from the bed and knocked her head, hard, against one of the low beams. She let out a cry and instantly wished she hadn't because Rosanna woke up with a start.

'Who's there?' she called into the darkness.

Elena sat rigid, nursing her sore head in her hands. She had no idea what time it but it was still dark and, luckily, she was still invisible so she hoped that Rosanna would right-off her cry as part of a nightmare and go back to sleep without investigating too closely. But she didn't. Of course she didn't.

'Is anyone there?' she whispered across the room.

Elena so wanted to say, 'No, there isn't. Go back to sleep.'

'Who is it? Sandro?' Rosanna asked, switching on her bedside lamp and swinging her legs out of bed. Her face was rosy with sleep but her eyes were wide and wild. She was frightened.

Elena kept absolutely still, hardly daring to breathe as Rosanna walked across the floor towards her. But there was nothing to see. Elena had made sure that her suitcase was well hidden from view and had quickly straightened the bedding underneath her and plumped up the pillow before Rosanna had turned the light on. There should appear to be absolutely nothing out of place.

Rosanna continued to move forward, her eyes searching every corner of the room in perplexity. It was obvious that she wasn't going to let this get the better of her.

'*Bimba?*' she said and Elena winced, hoping she wouldn't go poking around under the bed in search for the cat and then find her suitcase.

Finally, Rosanna gave a weary sigh and crawled back into bed, switching the lamp off and throwing them back into darkness. Elena breathed a sigh of relief and edged her way down the bed again, resting her head on her pillow. She shook her head as she recalled the nightmare from which she'd awoken. It didn't take an expert in Freud to work out what it meant.

She was just on the edge of sleep when she heard a strange sound coming from Rosanna's bed. She was crying. Elena opened her eyes but it was pitch dark in the room and she couldn't see a thing. Even so, Rosanna's crying sent a shiver through her body.

Elena woke up and saw that Rosanna was still asleep, her black hair spilled over her pillow and her mouth parted slightly. She looked like a little girl and Elena felt a stab of pain that they had fought so. She could see so clearly now that it wasn't worth it. What had she been so angry about? So she'd lost Reuben. She'd never really loved him in the first place, had she? Not from the way she'd treated him. That wasn't love, was it? And she'd risked the happiness of her sister and their friendship. Surely the whole trip to Venice had been about sorting herself out. She'd known that that would mean sorting her love life out. She'd known, for some time, that things weren't really working out with the men in her life. They were all wonderful, of course but, by being involved with all of them, she'd diluted the special qualities of each one. In short, she didn't deserve them.

It all seemed so simple now and yet she'd been so angry that Reuben had fallen for Rosanna when, in reality, it was perfectly natural: Rosanna was like Elena and yet different. Where Reuben and Elena had failed perhaps Reuben and *Rosanna* would succeed.

Making sure the mask was still firmly in place, Elena got off the bed and straightened it so that it looked unslept on. Then, leaving Rosanna sleeping, she ventured through to the kitchen. Sandro was either still in bed or out and Elena used the chance to peek into the fridge to see if there were any opportunities for breakfast. She didn't want to make a noise or lots of dishes and the one pot of strawberry yoghurt on the middle shelf seemed to have her name on it. It would mean only rinsing a teaspoon afterwards.

She took it through to the living room and sat on the sofa and then wondered how, exactly, she was going to eat it whilst wearing the mask. If she moved it slightly so that she had access to her mouth, would she remain invisible? In truth, she was desperate to take it off. It made her feel hot and her hair felt stuck to her skull. She wondered if she should take a chance. Yes. She would.

'That's better,' she smiled to herself as she slipped the mask off and ruffled a hand through her hair. Opening the yoghurt, she sat back on the sofa and breathed a sigh of contentment. She'd never been a big yoghurt eater but the strawberry stung her tongue with freshness and made her feel all pink inside.

'*Bimba?*' Rosanna's voice suddenly piped from the spare bedroom and Elena heard her footsteps approaching. 'Are you there?'

Elena quickly dived behind the sofa, yoghurt pot in hand, just as Rosanna entered the living room. But there was a problem: she'd left the mask on the sofa.

She could feel her heart hammering inside her chest. Rosanna was only a few feet away. What if she saw the mask? She had only to look in the direction of the sofa and it would be sure to catch her eye: the bright golden face gleaming against the cream sofa.

Elena wondered if she could risk stretching a hand towards the mask and pulling it towards her. Rosanna was standing in the middle of the room now, examining her nails. Would she notice Elena's hand whilst she was examining her own? Elena decided to take a chance and reached out.

'Ah!' Rosanna's voice suddenly called. 'There you are!'

Elena snatched her hand back and froze. Had Rosanna seen her? Or was she talking to that silly cat-child? She waited.

'It's no use hiding,' Rosanna said and Elena grimaced. She'd been found out. She'd have to explain things now. This wasn't what she'd planned at all. It was all going horribly wrong.

She would have to stand up and face her sister.

'I can't give you your breakfast if you hide under that chair, can I?' Rosanna said and Elena's eyes widened. She wasn't under a chair - she was behind a sofa. Rosanna *was* talking to cat-child after all. She breathed a sigh of relief until she realised that the chair cat-child was under was terribly close to the sofa which she was behind and that Rosanna might still spot her.

'Has Sandro forgotten to feed you again, eh?' Rosanna said and Elena smiled. Rosanna's voice was calm and friendly. She might pretend to hate the cat-child but Elena suspected that she was secretly fond of it, even though the animal made her sneeze.

Rosanna then did the thing Elena had been dreading: she knelt down to get to cat level. Elena moved round the sofa ever so slightly, trying to keep out of Rosanna's eyesight until she could get hold of the mask. Her hand stretched, once again, over the sofa and, with a sigh of relief, she held the mask in her hand once more. It was so stupid of her to have taken it off in the first place and she supposed the shock of Rosanna coming into the room served her right.

Tying it on quickly, she watched in amazement as she slowly began to vanish. Standing up and rubbing her sore knees, she looked across the room to where Rosanna was making a fuss of the cat-child.

'You might just have saved me from eviction,' Rosanna was saying. Elena wondered what she meant. Had Rosanna argued with Sandro? Had she been threatened with eviction since Sandro had found the front door open? Elena immediately felt guilty.

She was just about to walk, invisibly, back into the kitchen when she stubbed her toe on the corner of the sofa and the spoon she'd been carrying flew from her hand.

It was the strangest experience because, when she'd been holding it, it had been invisible. She'd been able to feel it, of course, but it had shared her shield of invisibility. Until it had left her hand. She'd seen in metamorphose into a solid object again, just in time to hit the bare floorboards with a clink.

Rosanna instantly forgot about cat-child and glanced around to see the spoon on the floor. Elena winced and backed away quietly. It was in the middle of nowhere and obviously hadn't fallen off a table or anything. She watched Rosanna's face fall into frown-mode as she walked forward and picked it up, looking around as she did so. Where had it come from? she seemed to ask. She looked bemused, angry and scared all at the same time.

'Sandro?' she called quietly, just as she had the night before when Elena had woken her by cracking her head on the beam. There was no reply. Sandro was out. Anyway, Elena couldn't imagine that it was in his nature to throw spoons about whether it was for a joke or not.

Elena watched as Rosanna examined the spoon - holding it up to the light as if that might help her work out what had happened. She then looked around the room again, up into the beams as if it had dropped down from above. It was as if Elena could read her mind. *Something weird is going on here*, she was thinking. Maybe Sandro was right.

'Come on, *Bimba*,' she said at last, a visible shiver making her shoulders twitch. 'Let's get breakfast out of the way. I want to get out of here.'

Elena was still starving and had wanted to venture out to grab a bite to eat somewhere, and determined to follow Rosanna. At least she'd be able to close the front door properly if she followed her out of the apartment.

Getting washed and dressed as Rosanna ate breakfast, Elena was ready to leave at the same time as Rosanna. She had an inkling where she was going, of course: to see Reuben. This was the moment she'd been waiting for. This was the true test of the mask but would it show her what she wanted to see? Would it help her to make her decision?

She followed Rosanna down the stone steps on tiptoe, pausing in the hallway to give her a head start and to prevent her from hearing the door clanging shut when she left. Once outside, Elena ran to the end of the street and looked left then right. It was just as she thought: Rosanna had turned right along the calle which would lead to the Rialto. Despite the fact that it was still early in the morning, the bridge was packed with tourists, each one intent on standing perfectly still on the bridge in order to get one of the definitive Venetian shots of their partner. Elena pushed through as best as she could, wondering if Rosanna really was going to meet Reuben after all or if she was merely going to the fish market.

Following her as best as she could, Elena finally broke through the crowds and made it down the other side of the bridge where Rosanna turned right. Nobody had batted an eyelid at being knocked out of the way by an invisible girl; it was so crowded that they hadn't even noticed.

Elena followed, trying to get a little bit closer to her sister in order not to lose her as the streets were becoming increasingly narrower.

The street they were walking down soon came out into a small campo and Rosanna made towards a café at the far side of it where Reuben was sitting in the early morning sunshine. Elena felt her heart quicken as she spotted him. She hadn't seen him since the night they'd broken up and it was strange to see him again when she knew it wasn't her he was waiting for but her sister.

You've made a big mistake in coming here, a little voice told her. *You shouldn't be meddling - it's not right.* But something compelled her to walk towards the table they were sitting at.

Reuben had got up when Rosanna had arrived but they hadn't embraced. Both of them looked solemn: their faces sallow and unsmiling. Elena inched herself carefully around a table and sat down on a seat adjacent to them. The café was quiet so she didn't think anyone would disturb her.

'Did she call?' she heard Reuben ask.

'No,' Rosanna said. 'She wasn't at the apartment.'

'And you're sure she's in Venice?'

'That's what Mama said.'

Elena grimaced. Their mama must have phoned Rosanna as soon as Elena had left Positano.

'Maybe she hasn't arrived back yet?' Reuben suggested.

Rosanna shook her head. 'She'd have been back by last night at the latest. My guess is she's in some nasty hotel somewhere.'

Elena sighed in relief. At least Rosanna didn't have any idea that the supernatural being haunting Sandro's apartment was, actually, her.

'I hate this!' Rosanna suddenly said. 'I just want it all to be okay but I can't see how that's going to happen - not as long as we're together.'

'What are you saying?' Reuben asked, leaning forward to try to catch Rosanna's eyes which were lowered as she hung her head in misery.

'I'm saying that I don't think this can ever work out between us. It's not fair on anyone. It's just all wrong.'

'No! It isn't!'

'How can you say that?'

'Because I love you!'

Rosanna shook her head, her face crumpling in pain. 'No! Don't say that!'

'But it's true.' Reuben picked up her hands and held them tightly. 'This is hurting me as much as it's hurting you. I feel like a right bastard but I can't lie about my feelings for you - *that's* the only thing that would be wrong.'

Elena bit her lip. Even though she was invisible, she felt like an intruder and that she really shouldn't be listening to their conversation although this was exactly what she'd planned to do in Positano.

'You do want to be with me, don't you?' Reuben asked.

Rosanna closed her eyes for a moment. She looked as if she was trying to stop herself from crying. 'Of course I do,' she said, 'but I don't think I can be - not if it means making enemies with my sister.'

Elena sat bolt upright in her seat. Had she heard her sister correctly? Did she really mean that?

'So, you're going to break up with me if Elena isn't comfortable with this?'

Rosanna nodded. 'I can't do anything else.'

They were quiet for a moment and Elena was literally on the edge of her seat not wanting to miss a single thing.

'All we really need to do,' Reuben began, 'is talk to Elena.'

Elena looked at Reuben. His eyes were big and sincere as if he was making one last plea with Rosanna. But Rosanna shook her head, seemingly resolute. Elena was confused. How could her sister be so selfless? Reuben might not be working his magic on Rosanna but it was working on her - for one minute, she felt as if she really should take the mask off and reveal herself and try to solve the mess there and then, but that would raise too many other questions so she decided it would be best to wait.

Rosanna rose from her chair, her hands still held tightly in Reuben's.

'Don't go,' he said and Elena felt as if her heart was breaking. This man was really in love with his sister, wasn't he?

'But she might be waiting for me.'

'You think she'll be at the studio?' Reuben asked.

'I don't know,' Rosanna said. 'I hope so.'

Elena heard the words and was on her feet. She had to get back - before Rosanna. She had to be there, waiting for her sister - waiting to make things right between them all again.

'I hope so too,' Reuben said, finally letting go of Rosanna's hands. 'You'll let me know?'

Rosanna was quiet for a moment and it was obviously a moment too long for Reuben. 'You will let me know? This isn't goodbye, Rosanna.'

Rosanna heard the conviction in his voice and nodded. 'I'll let you know,' she said and she left the café.

CHAPTER 43

Elena followed Rosanna, waiting to see how she would get back to the apartment: by vaporetto, which was the long way round, or on foot. It soon became obvious that she was walking and, fuelled by her upset, she was going at quite a pace too once she was over the Rialto which meant Elena would have to run if she was to get back before her, so run she did - down calli and over bridges as if her feet had wings. She was still wearing the mask which meant that people didn't get out of her way as quickly as they might have done had they been able to see her. All she knew was that she had to be there - waiting outside the apartment with her suitcase - when Rosanna got back.

Mon dio! That meant, she'd have to get inside the apartment first, retrieve her case and get back outside again - without Sandro seeing or hearing anything suspicious if he was back.

Elena's feet picked up as much speed as she was able to in the narrow streets which constantly turned corners over canals, each bridge loaded with tourists. But she was well ahead of Rosanna now.

At last, she reached the long calle that led to the apartment. There were fewer people here and she was able to bolt down it easily, arriving at the apartment quicker than even she could have hoped for, but could she get back in?

She pulled out the spare key and unlocked the door. At least that part was fairly quiet and she was still invisible so she should be able to sneak up the stairs into the living room without too much bother. She decided to leave the door open as she hoped to be out again within a couple of minutes.

Her heart was still pounding from her run as she climbed the steps. When she reached the top, she saw Sandro standing at an easel in the corner of the room. He looked furious - as if the canvas in front of him had just sworn at him and slapped him in the face.

Elena sneaked across the room and down the three steps into the spare bedroom where she quickly retrieved her suitcase from under the bed. As she pulled it out from the covers, she watched in amazement at it began to turn invisible. All she had to do was keep hold of it. She didn't want any more antics like the teaspoon incident. She had to get out of the apartment without event.

Leaving the bedroom, she hoisted her suitcase into the air so as not to make any noise with its wheels on the wooden floorboards. It was, predictably, heavy and she winced as she crossed the room. Sandro, luckily, remained by his easel pulling all manner of ugly faces at it which made Elena grin. But she didn't have time to stand and watch him so retraced her way down the steps and out of the door again. She realised that she wouldn't be able to close it behind her without arousing suspicion so she pushed it to.

All she had to do now was to take the mask off and wait for Rosanna whilst pretending to be just arriving at the apartment. She could do that; that would be the easy part. The hard part would be what she was actually going to say to Rosanna.

She stood back a little from the front door of the apartment, nervously looking in the direction from which Rosanna would come.

Elena took the mask off, watching the miraculous morphing from invisible to visible that never failed to make her gasp in wonder. She did hope that nobody was looking out of their apartment windows at that precise moment. It was a quiet street but it would be typical that some old matriarch would be hanging out of the window with a duster in her hand just as Elena was mutating. But, as she didn't hear anyone screaming, she assumed she'd got away with it.

She put the mask away in a front opening of her suitcase. She was getting so used to its presence that it was now quite impossible to imagine life without it. Perhaps she was getting addicted to magic. In truth, she didn't know if she was allowed to keep it. Stefano had given it to her as a gift but did he expect her to give it back to him once its job was complete? She didn't even know if it was allowed to leave the island of Venice. Maybe it wouldn't work anywhere else. Maybe it was a part of the magic that was Venice.

It would be awful having to give the mask up, though. Just think of all the fun she could have with it back in London. She could wear it at the college and get her own back on all the cheeky students; she could sneak into the staff room and listen to what the other tutors gossiped about.

Remembering the college, she immediately thought of Mark. It wouldn't be easy working in the same place now that they had broken up. No wonder people recommended not becoming involved with work colleagues. It was fine when things were rosy and romantic but could make for a decidedly uncomfortable work environment when things didn't work out so well. Perhaps he'd move on. Perhaps she should move on. After all, she was the one to break up with him.

Elena felt exhausted with it all. She'd known her trip to Venice wouldn't be easy but it was rapidly turning into a tragedy of Shakespearean proportions. If only she could get things sorted out; if only she could make amends.

It was then that she heard the light click of her sister's boots. It was time.

When Rosanna turned the corner, she didn't see Elena at first. Her eyes were cast to the ground as if she'd lost something and her mouth seemed magnetically pulled towards the earth too.

'Rosanna,' Elena called quietly. She didn't know what else to say.

Rosanna looked up instantly, her dark eyes wide, but she didn't speak. For a few seconds, they just looked at each other.

Elena was the first to speak. 'We need to talk,' she said simply, her voice calm, a degree of warmth creeping in at the edges.

'Where have you been? I've been so worried,' Rosanna said, daring to edge closer but not quite ready to embrace her sister. 'Mama said-'

'I'm here now,' Elena said, not wanting to lie to Rosanna. There'd been far too many lies recently. It was now, finally, time for the truth.

Rosanna's eyes filled with tears and they were instantly mirrored by Elena. And, before they could stop to think, they were in each other's arms, crying and apologising.

'I'm so sorry!' Rosanna cried.

'No - I am! It's my fault!' Elena cried back.

'I should never have become involved with Reuben!'

'No, Rosanna! I never should have! I've not been fair to you - to *any* of you.'

'I don't know what I was thinking of.'

'I wasn't thinking at all!'

'I've told Reuben I won't see him again - not if it means a rift between us.'

'You shouldn't have done that!'

'It had to be said. Things couldn't go on like this. I've been so wretched. Can you ever forgive me?'

'But I do forgive you! That's why I've come back. It's *me* who needs forgiving. I've been so selfish. I've not thought of anyone but myself for months and then I was surprised when everything started to collapse around me. I've behaved so badly to everyone - especially to you. I lied to you and then I blamed you for Reuben's feelings towards you. I'll never forgive myself for that.'

'But you must! *I* forgive you!' Rosanna said.

'I don't deserve to be forgiven!'

'You're my sister - my big sister! I don't know what I'd do without you.'

'But you'd have a much easier life without me!'

Rosanna tightened her arms around her. 'I just want us to be okay again.'

'Me too,' Elena whispered back, feeling the breath in her body being slowly squeezed out.

Finally, Rosanna inched back a little. 'We've made such a mess of things, haven't we?' She gave the tiniest of smiles.

Elena returned the tiny smile and dared to laugh as she wiped her eyes.

'Let's go inside,' Rosanna suggested and Elena nodded, taking the handle of her suitcase.

Rosanna was just fishing for her key in her pocket when she said, 'The door's open.'

'Is it?' Elena said, realising that she hadn't quite divorced herself from lying to her sister yet.

'It's Sandro! And he had the nerve to blame me.'

Elena frowned, hoping she wasn't about to cause another scene between the two of them. Rosanna led the way back into the apartment and Elena hoisted her suitcase up the stairs she'd only just come down.

'Sandro?' Rosanna hollered.

'What?' he hollered back.

'You left the door open again.'

'What are you talking about? I did not!'

'Well, it was open,' Rosanna said, once inside the living room.

Sandro frowned deeply at her. 'I'll have to get it seen to-' he stopped, noticing Elena standing behind Rosanna. He also noticed the suitcase.

'This is my sister, Elena,' Rosanna explained. 'She's in Venice for a couple of days.'

Before she could say any more, Sandro interrupted her, 'It seems like you have a whole retinue of friends here in Venice at the moment.'

'Sandro,' Rosanna began again, her voice firm, 'I was hoping she could stay - just tonight. We really need to spend some time together. You'd be doing us a huge favour.'

There was something in her tone of voice that seemed to be working its magic on Sandro because he nodded.

'Tonight, you say?'

Rosanna nodded. 'That would be great.'

'Okay,' he said. 'As long as all those men don't start turning up again.'

Rosanna and Elena blushed in unison.

'Do you want to put your suitcase in the spare room? I'm downstairs now that the big bad boss is back,' Rosanna explained unnecessarily as Elena followed her through to the very bed she'd slept in the night before. 'There's plenty of room.'

Elena nodded. She looked across to Rosanna's bed which had been neatly made up that morning but all she could think about was the quiet crying of her sister the night before.

'Elena? What's wrong?'

Hot tears slid down her face and, for a moment, she couldn't speak. 'I'm sorry,' she managed at last.

'I know!' Rosanna assured her. 'And I'm sorry to.'

They sat down on Rosanna's bed together.

'I can't bear to think how I must have hurt you,' Elena said.

'You didn't! I've told you, it was *me* who was in the wrong. I should never have had anything to do with Reuben. It was unthinkable. I can't believe I let it happen.'

'Have you seen him?' Elena dared to ask once her tears had stopped.

Rosanna nodded. 'This morning. I broke up with him.'

'But he loves you.'

'How do you know that?'

Elena bit her lip. How was she to explain that? 'It's just a feeling I have. We weren't quite right together. But you and him - who knows? It could really work. You shouldn't throw that away.'

'You mean that, don't you?'

'Of course I do.'

'But he was your fiancé.'

'But he shouldn't have been.'

Rosanna sighed. 'This is too strange. I'm not sure I know what to do.'

'You should speak to Reuben. Tell him I'm fine with all this.'

'Are you sure?' Rosanna's forehead crinkled.

'It's about the only thing I am sure of at the moment. I really think you two should be together.'

Rosanna's eyes were sparkling with tears once more. 'Elena-'

They fell into a hug and it was then that Elena remembered something.

'Hang on,' she said, getting up off the bed and opening her suitcase. 'I've brought you Fernando.'

Rosanna's lips trembled in response and fresh tears fell from her dark eyes as she took the teddy bear in a warm embrace.

'I'd forgotten all about him,' Rosanna said.

'I thought it was about time he put in an appearance.'

'Where was he?'

'I'm not sure. Mama had him. He just seemed to be waiting for me.'

'He was always there for us, wasn't he?' Rosanna smiled, holding him up and gazing fondly at the slightly faded face of the old bear.

'Everyone should have a Fernando.'

'Thanks for bringing him, Elena.'

Elena smiled. 'Thanks for accepting him.'

There was a pause. Things still felt so strange and new between them, as if they'd been separated for a decade rather than just a couple of days.

'What are you going to do now?' Rosanna asked at last.

Elena sat down on the bed next to her and shrugged her shoulders. 'I really don't know. I thought I did but I'm not so sure now.'

'Why not?'

'I'm just so relieved that we're okay again. That's all I'd really hoped for.'

'What about Mark?' Rosanna asked in a quiet voice.

'I broke up with him,' she said. It was the first time she'd said it out loud and each word stung her like an angry wasp.

'I know.'

'You do?'

'He came over here after you left.'

'Did he?'

Rosanna nodded. 'He met Reuben.'

Elena closed her eyes. 'He knows, then?'

'I'm afraid it was unavoidable.'

'And what did he say? What did he do?'

'He said he was going home, I think.'

Elena looked hard at Rosanna. 'But he came to talk to me?'

'I told him where you'd gone and tried to persuade him to go after you.'

'But he didn't want to?'

'He followed you out here, didn't he? You can't say he didn't try.'

Rosanna was right. What did she expect if she kept running away from him? Elena thought of the wounded expression on his face when she'd handed him back his ring. She thought of how she'd hoped he would follow her out of the hotel when she'd left, but he hadn't. And yet he'd come to the apartment. It had been too late then, though; she'd already gone.

But was it too late now?

'I've messed up. I can't go back.'

'That's rubbish!' Rosanna shouted. 'You came back for me, didn't you? How hard was that?' she asked, picking up Elena's left hand and massaging it in hers.

'But you're family - you understand.'

'And Mark was your fiancé. He would understand too. If you give him a chance.' Rosanna sighed. 'But what do *you* want, Elena? You have to be honest with yourself. You can't just think you want somebody - you must *know*. Mark deserves that. He's a good man and they're damned hard to find.'

Elena nodded. She didn't need to be told that.

'You have to be honest with him - if you want things to work out, you must be absolutely honest this time.'

'I know,' Elena said.

'About *every*thing,' her sister pressed.

A dark cloud seemed to pass over Elena's face. Was she really ready for that? Was that what she really wanted?

CHAPTER 44

Reuben cried like a woman when Rosanna greeted him an hour later.

'Did she say that? Did she really say that?' he asked.

'Yes!' Rosanna said, somewhat frustratedly. 'Now stop crying, for goodness' sake - people are staring!'

They were standing in the lobby of his new, cheaper hotel, and Rosanna was right: Reuben was making a spectacle of himself. He mopped his eyes with a tissue the size of a duvet and then smiled. 'Sorry!' he said. 'I don't know what happened to me there.'

'Neither do I,' Rosanna said, her cheeks flushing. She'd never seen a man cry before and she wasn't quite sure how to handle it.

'It just doesn't sound like Elena at all.'

'You don't think so?'

'I mean - she was so upset when she found out.'

'Of course she was! You two were engaged!' Rosanna pointed out.

'So what's made her act like this all of a sudden?'

Rosanna shook her head. 'I don't think it's all of a sudden at all,' she said. 'I think this has been coming on for some time now. That's why she came to Venice - to sort herself out.'

'So I'm all sorted out now then, am I?'

'Don't pretend your pride's hurt, for God's sake! This *is* what you want, isn't it?'

Reuben grinned and Rosanna couldn't help but smile back.

'What about Mark?' Reuben asked.

'I think she's in love with him. She hasn't said as much but I really think she loves him.'

'So, I never stood a chance then?'

Rosanna thumped him in the belly.

'Sorry!' he said quickly.

'I just hope she manages to sort things out. I really like Mark.'

Reuben frowned. 'You're sure you'd not rather poach him from Elena than me?'

'That isn't funny!'

He reached out towards her and pulled her into his arms. 'Sorry,' he whispered, kissing the top of her head. 'I was only joking.'

Rosanna closed her eyes for a moment. It still felt so strange being with Reuben; things had happened so quickly. For a moment, she thought about Corrado, wondering if he'd found somebody else as quickly as she had. She hoped he had. He wasn't a bad guy, not really, and she felt sure he had the makings of a really fine partner if only he could free himself from the tentacled grip of his mama.

'Are you okay?' Reuben asked.

'Yes,' Rosanna said. 'My head's spinning with all this but I'm okay.'

'Good.'

'There's something else,' Rosanna said suddenly. 'I've got a proposition for you.'

'Oh?'

'You like Venice, don't you?'

'I love Venice!' he said. 'In fact, I was thinking about the possibility of-' he paused.

'What?' Rosanna looked up at him. 'What? Tell me!' she said when he smiled a mischievous smile at her.

'Perhaps living out here.'

Rosanna's mouth widened into the happiest of smiles. 'Well,' she began, 'I might just have just what you're looking for.'

Reuben nodded. 'I knew you did from the moment I first saw you.'

Elena could have run but she'd had quite enough of running in the past few hours. Anyway, it wasn't that far to Mark's hotel and she had a horrible feeling that he wouldn't be there and that she should delay finding out for as long as possible. Why should he be there? She'd made him no promise of coming back - quite the contrary - she'd told him not to follow her. Still, as she entered the lobby and walked up to the reception desk, there was a little spark of hope inside her. She couldn't let herself imagine, for one moment, that he'd flown back to London - back to a life that didn't include her. It was just too grim. No. She had to remain optimistic. He was *her* Mark: the one who'd stood by her; the one who'd followed her out to Venice when she knew full well that he couldn't even afford a taxi fare into London let alone a plane ticket to Italy. He *had* to be there for her now.

'Good morning,' she said to the desk clerk, dazzling him with a smile which completely masked her nerves.

'Good morning,' he replied, his voice as stony as his demeanour.

'I was wondering if I could speak to Mr Mark Theodore. He's a guest here.'

The clerk shook his head. 'I'm afraid Mr Theodore has left.'

'No.'

'Excuse me?'

'You don't understand,' Elena said.

'What don't I understand?' the stony man asked.

Elena bit her lip. 'When?' she asked at last, her voice sounding helpless and hopeless. 'When did he leave?'

'Yesterday.'

'I don't suppose he left a note for-'

'He left nothing,' the man said, casting his eyes down to an appointment book on the desk in front of him. Their conversation was over and Elena's spark of hope was extinguished. Mark had left. Rosanna had said he was going back to London and yet Elena had still wanted to believe that he'd be here for her - when she wanted him to be. It wasn't meant to work out like this: this was too messy and ugly.

She walked out of the hotel, the sunlight unable to penetrate her world. She didn't see the reflection of the bright washing in the canal of the first bridge she crossed nor did she smell the waft of coffee from a window whose emerald shutters had been flung open. Everything felt dark and dismal and she felt so unutterable alone. She shouldn't have been in Venice; its beauty brought her no solace. Venice wasn't meant for the unhappy: it was a city which assaulted the senses with vibrancy but, in her sadness, Elena had completely shut it out.

Everybody should have a place to go to in times of trouble: a haven when the world is horrible and, for Elena, that place was Viviana's. She retraced the familiar path to Dorsoduro through the streets lined with mask shops. She could talk to Stefano. He would understand.

She realised that this might actually be the last time she went to Viviana's and the thought made her extremely sad. She'd only been in Venice for a few days but Viviana's had become a sanctuary and she had no idea what she'd done before it had become a part of her life.

Following the narrow streets and walking over the bridges, she found the shop again and went inside, the familiar tinkle of the bell singing its welcome to her. Peace enveloped her in comforting arms and she immediately felt easier with the world.

She glanced up at the masks hanging from the dark beams of the shop. They had become like friends: the white and gold plague doctors with their pelican-long noses; the jolly-faced jesters with their bright bells; the elongated moons with lipstick-bright faces; the sunbeams; the harlequins; and the muted masks of the *Commedia dell'Arte*. She was going to miss them all.

'You've come to say goodbye, haven't you?' a voice asked.

Elena turned to see Stefano standing right before her. He did have the most unnerving habit of doing that.

'How do you know?'

He shook his head as if in exasperation at her question. 'You have that goodbye look about you.'

'I do?'

He nodded.

'You're right,' Elena sighed. 'And part of me wants to go, of course - there are so many things to sort out - but part of me doesn't want to leave at all.'

'That's Venice for you!'

Elena nodded, suddenly realising something. 'You've never left, have you?'

'Once, when I was young and thought I knew everything there was to know about everything when, in fact, I knew nothing at all. I missed her like crazy! Not a night went by when I wouldn't dream of Venice: her colours and textures, her reflections, her bells. I would walk over her bridges and across her squares - not going anyway, you understand - just walking. And then I'd wake up and feel the full weight of being somewhere else. No,' he said, shaking his head and smiling, 'I couldn't live anywhere else because nowhere else comes close.'

Elena felt dazzled and dazed by his words, as if she'd just heard a beautiful poem. But his words also made her feel sad because she'd never had that connection with a place before. She loved Venice, of course, but she didn't belong there. She certainly didn't love London - not the part she lived in, anyway. Part of her was Italian; part of her was English. The truth of the matter was, she was a mongrel with no home to call her own.

'But home isn't always a place,' Stefano said, interrupting her melancholic thoughts.

'What do you mean?'

He looked at her closely as if assessing whether or not she was ready for what he had to say. 'Home can be a person too.'

Elena's eyes narrowed, unsure of what he was saying.

'If you have a special person then, wherever they are, that is home. You have a special person, don't you?' His voice was like her conscience speaking to her: something she wanted to suppress but couldn't.

'I do,' she replied. 'That is, I did.'

Stefano nodded as if he already knew all about it. 'And where is he?'

'I was hoping he was still here - in Venice - but he's left.'

'But you can follow him, no?'

Elena bit her lip. Could she follow Mark back to London? He had followed her out to Venice, hadn't he? Surely she could summon up the courage to do the same for him.

'I can follow him, yes. I have to - we work at the same place. But I'm not sure he'll listen to what I have to say,' she said, her eyes welling up with sadness. 'I think I've left things too late.'

'He's not *dead*, is he?' Stefano suddenly barked, startling Elena. She'd never even heard him raise his voice before let alone bellow like that.

'I - er - don't think so!'

'And *you're* not dead, are you?'

Her face creased in bewilderment. 'No!'

'Then it *isn't* too late, *is it?*'

Elena felt herself blushing. She didn't know what to say to such an assertion. But he was right, wasn't he? There was nothing stopping her except her own fear of being rejected and that was a lousy excuse for inaction.

'What are you waiting for?' he asked, his white eyebrows almost leaping right out of his head with excitement.

What *was* she waiting for? What had made her come to Viviana's? Surely she should have gone straight to the airport after finding out Mark had left. But there was something else: the mask.

'There's just one more thing,' she added. 'Will the mask be okay leaving Venice? I mean, can I take it home?'

'Is that what you came to ask me? You've postponed telling your lover how you feel about him because of a silly mask?' Stefano tutted and shook his head. 'Of *course* you can take the mask home with you! Why shouldn't you?'

'But will it work outside Venice?'

'Will you want it to?'

'I don't know,' Elena said.

'Then it probably won't.'

'Oh.'

'Elena,' he began, 'you think about things too much.'

'Do I?'

'*Yes!* Why else are you here? You keep on coming back here asking questions, questions, questions - you're the English inquisition.'

'I'm sorry - I don't mean to bother you-'

'I didn't mean that! Of course you don't bother me. I look forward to seeing you but it's always a worry when I do because I know you have these questions and I'm never sure if I can answer them for you.'

Elena gave a hesitant smile. 'I'm a bit of a wimp, aren't I?'

'No, no!' he said, shaking his head. 'I think you just lack the confidence to be honest with yourself, that's all. You have all the answers yourself but you're reluctant to dig deep enough to find them.'

She'd never thought of it like that before. As ever, Stefano was able to part the fog that was blocking Elena's vision.

'Does that make sense?' he asked.

'Yes!' Elena nodded. 'You should have your own problem page. You'd make a terrific agony uncle.'

Stefano's faced scrunched up like a prune. 'I can't think of anything worse!'

'But you've been so wonderful with your advice. I don't know what I'd have done without you. And I don't know what I'm going to do when I leave,' she said sadly.

'You'll be fine. Absolutely fine,' he reassured her.

She smiled at him. 'Thank you,' she said and then she reached forward and hugged him.

'You'll let me know how you get on, won't you?'

She laughed. 'Of course I will!'

A few moments later, when the hug looked as if it was about to become a contender for the *Guinness Book of Records*, Stefano spoke.

'Isn't there somebody else you'd rather be hugging?'

Elena wiped a tear from her eye and nodded as she let go of Stefano.

'Then go home and hug!' he said.

This made Elena smile. Maybe she did have a home after all. But there was only one way to find out for sure, and that was to leave Venice.

CHAPTER 45

The plane was travelling at over five hundred miles per hour but it didn't seem fast enough. Elena had calculated the arrival time at Gatwick and how long it would take her to get home from there. She should be back at her flat by late afternoon and could get a taxi to Mark's. She hadn't worked out what she would do once she got there. She was half-hoping that just being there would be enough and that things would sort themselves out but, in her heart of hearts, she knew there was more to it than that. She knew, this time, that she was going to have to be absolutely honest with Mark - about her past, her misdemeanours - everything. Only then could they stand a chance of sharing a future together.

She looked out of the window into the cotton-soft world of clouds. Venice seemed a whole world away now. She thought of her parting with Rosanna. After saying goodbye to Stefano, she'd returned to the apartment and told Rosanna she had to go home straight away.

'Well, don't leave it so long before you visit next time,' Rosanna had chided.

'I won't. But don't forget you can visit me too!'

There'd been a moment's pause.

'Is Reuben staying out here?' Elena asked.

Rosanna nodded, her expression hesitant. 'Is that okay with you?'

'It's fine. I'm pleased - really pleased for both of you.'

'Sandro's actually going to let his apartment to us,' Rosanna whispered.

Elena's eyes widened. 'Really? You'll both be living here?'

'I can't believe Sandro agreed to that but he's off to America and didn't want to sell up over here.'

'That's great! Reuben will love it here.'

'I know.'

For a moment, the two sisters just looked at one another but there was no rivalry between them any more, just a deeper understanding of what made each other happy and the part each could play to make things work.

'You're doing the right thing, Elena,' Rosanna had said and they'd hugged. 'Let me know how things go, won't you?'

Elena nodded. She was feeling rather emotional with all the partings that the day was throwing at her and so made her own way to the Alilaguna. She hated protracted goodbyes. Rosanna had waved her off from the top of the stairs and, when Elena had slammed the heavy door behind her, she took a deep breath in anticipation of the journey ahead.

After travelling by vaporetto, plane and taxi, Elena reached home. Her hands were shaking as she delved into her handbag for her front door key and let herself in. Dumping her suitcase and bag, she ran to her phone, noticing that the answer machine was flashing. Had Mark called her?

She pressed play. *You have three messages.*

'Hello, Ms Montella, this is John Philips calling from Lloyds TSB. If you could give me a call -'

Elena winced, thinking that all three messages were probably from him as she was overdrawn on her account again.

'Elena? Is this thing on?'

Elena groaned as the second message played. It was her mama.

'I hate these machines. Am I speaking loudly enough?' her mama bellowed. 'Give me a call to let me know you got home safely. For all I know you might have been kidnapped by the Mafia in Naples.'

Elena rolled her eyes. She should have called her mama from Venice but just hadn't had the chance.

'I worry about you girls, you know,' her mama continued. If she carried on much longer, there wouldn't be any tape left for message three. 'I want you to promise me you'll keep in touch from now on and let me know what you're doing? Okay?'

'*Okay!*' Elena yelled back.

'Good!' her mama said, as if she'd really heard her daughter.

Elena sighed in relief as her mama finally hung up. There was one more message.

'Elena? Are you there?'

It was Mark's voice, and it sounded so sad that Elena immediately wanted to burst into tears.

'I wanted you to know that I've handed my notice in at the college so there won't be any awkwardness next term.'

Elena's eyes pricked with tears as she heard Mark sigh.

'It was the only thing to do, really,' he said, his voice quiet and subdued. 'But I wish you well. Bye.'

Elena quickly pressed the rewind button and listened to his message again in case she'd been mistaken.

'But I wish you well. Bye.'

That was all: the sum product of their time together had resulted in nothing more than a cold and colourless farewell. Elena wanted to cry out loud and stamp her feet in tantrum but, instead, she grabbed her handbag from where she'd dumped it only seconds before and left her flat, hailing the first taxi she saw. Normally, Elena wouldn't pay taxi fares - not on her college salary - but this was no time to be hanging around in the vain hope of a tube or a bus turning up. She had to speak to Mark - *subito* - as the Italians would say.

Mark's flat was three miles away and the taxi driver assured her that he *was* taking the fastest route there.

'It's left here!'

'I *know!*' the taxi driver said.

'Then first-'

'Right - *yes!* That's the way I'm going.'

Elena bit her lip, worrying in case Mark had left his flat as well as his job. But he wouldn't do that, would he? He wouldn't cut off all communication between them.

'It's this house at the end of the street.'

The driver just nodded this time and pulled over. Elena threw some money at him and jumped out of the car, dashing across the pavement and pressing the flat's buzzer.

She waited. There was no answer. She pressed it again. Still, there was no answer. She tried the communal door but it was locked so she pressed the buzzer for Mark's neighbour.

'Yes?' an elderly lady's voice enquired.

'Mrs Chambers? It's Elena - Mark's fiancé. Could you let me in? I've left my keys at home.' The truth was, Elena didn't have any keys to Mark's flat. It wasn't that Mark hadn't tried to give her a set: he had! It's just that she hardly ever visited him and didn't see the need.

'I'll give you a call before I come round,' she'd told him.

'But don't you want to surprise me occasionally? Come round on the spur of the moment?'

Elena had been puzzled by that. With three fiancés, the idea of anything being spur of the moment could be disastrous. No, she had to live by a strict timetable and that meant being independent and only having her own set of keys to worry about.

Mrs Chambers pressed the magic button which released the door and Elena bounded up the stairs, two at a time, and knocked on Mark's door.

'Mark? Are you there?'

There was no reply.

'It's Elena. I need to talk to you.'

'I don't think he's in, dear,' Mrs Chambers said, her head popping out from behind her door.

'Do you know where he is?' Elena asked, hoping that she was a nosy neighbour and might be of some help.

'I've not seen him for ages,' she said. 'I thought I heard him late last night but he was in and out before I could ask him to fix my TV. It's on the blink again.'

'So you don't know where he's gone?'

The old lady shook her head.

Where could he be? Elena wracked her brains. She had no idea where he could be and she felt appalled because it showed how little she knew him. She'd taken no time to get to know his hobbies or interests, or even whom his friends were.

No, that wasn't strictly true - there was one friend she'd heard him mention. He had a strange name - quirky-sounding - the sort of name you'd give to a pet dog. Benjie or Bonzo or something.

'*Barney!*' she suddenly shouted.

Mrs Chambers, who was still watching Elena from behind her door, flinched.

'Barney *Malone!* I bet he's at Barney's! He lives in the next street, doesn't he?'

'Does he?'

Elena nodded, a big smile crossing her face for the first time since she'd left Venice.

'I've got to go,' she said, tripping back down the stairs. Her taxi had long gone but Elena thought she could remember the way to Barney's. How had Mark described the flat? It was uglier than a 1970s public convenience and smelt far worse.

'That's the one!' Elena said to herself a few minutes later as she looked up at the grim exterior. It really was unyielding in its ugliness. There wasn't a single redeeming feature except a yellow plastic pot somebody had filled with purple primulas which stood on the doorstep.

Elena walked up to the door and looked around for the intercom. It soon became obvious that there wasn't one. *Of course!* She remembered Mark telling him about how he'd have to stand in the middle of the pavement and yell up at the top flat until he was heard. Was she capable of that?

'Barney!' she yelled, startling a couple of pigeons on a fence. 'Barneeeeee!'

It was ridiculous. She wasn't even sure which window was his.

'BarNEEEEEE!'

Nothing: no response at all. She'd only succeeded in making herself hoarse.

Then, just as she'd turned to go home, a window was opened and a tousled head popped out.

'Who is it?'

Elena spun round. 'Barney - it's Elena. I have to speak to Mark. Is he there?'

Barney squinted down at her but he didn't say anything.

'Please, Barney - let me up.' They stared at each other - their eyes waging a battle of wills.

At last, Barney nodded and Elena rushed to the door to be let in, legging it up the stairs to the top floor where a door stood ajar.

'Barney?' she called.

'In here,' a gruff voice said which gave Elena the distinct impression that she wasn't welcome.

'Can I come in?' she asked, already half way down the hall which opened into a small sitting room.

'Hello,' a voice said.

'Hello,' Elena replied, seeing a very pregnant woman sprawling on a sofa. Balancing precariously beside her was a large bowl filled with bright jelly babies which her fingers dipped into with acute regularity.

'Would you like one?' she asked Elena who must have been staring.

Elena shook her head. 'No, thank you,' she said. There was something most disconcerting about watching a pregnant woman biting the heads of jelly babies.

'Is Mark here?'

The woman didn't reply.

'Please! I need to know.'

'BARNEY!' the woman shouted, making Elena leap out of her skin. 'Get your bony ass in here. It's rude to leave guests.'

Elena heard the unmistakable shuffle of Barney and he reappeared in the doorway of the kitchen which joined the living room, his off-white housecoat saggily exposing a pale chest and skinny legs.

'What?' he asked.

'This girl walks all the way up your stinking stairs and you then ignore her!' the jelly-bean woman said.

'I didn't *invite* her here,' Barney said sulkily.

'Oh! You didn't invite her!' the woman echoed sarcastically. 'Sheesh!'

'Well, what do you want me to do, Linda?' he asked, flinging his hands in the air in a manner that was very Italian.

'Come and sit here,' Linda said, beckoning to Elena. 'Now! What's a lovely lady like you doing in a horrible place like this?'

Elena gave a tiny smile. 'I'm trying to find Mark.'

'She's trying to find Mark!' she repeated, flinging the sentence across the room at Barney.

'Well, how am I meant to know where he is?' Barney responded.

Linda seemed to swell up with indignation at this question which, in the circumstances, Elena didn't think was a good idea. 'Because you're bloody joined at the hip, you two! You're thick as thieves. Two peas in a pod! You're inseparable. You live in each others' pockets!' she yelled. 'Need any more clichés?'

Barney sighed, his shoulders drooping with the weight of being under Linda's thumb. 'I don't know where he is.'

'Pardon?' Linda said, leaning forward until Elena felt sure that she would topple off the sofa.

Elena saw the look of intense annoyance in Linda's face. 'He's here, isn't he?' Elena said, turning to face Barney. 'Barney?'

'Barney!' Linda said, her warning voice quite scary. 'Barney, please!' she added, a little softness now colouring her voice. 'Take pity on a girl in love!' She got up from the sofa with a great effort, her profile looking like the back of a whale.

'Blimey!' Elena exclaimed. 'When are you due?'

'Not for another month. Worrying, isn't it!'

'Linda, I'd be happier if you sat down and didn't get so worked up about things.'

'It's you who's getting me worked up about things! Now tell this poor girl where Mark is!'

There were a few moments in which Elena looked from Barney to Linda and back again, not quite sure who was going to win and feeling very sure that she was never actually going to find out where Mark was.

'He's-' Linda started.

'- in the bedroom,' Barney finished.

'You can go through if you like - have some privacy,' Linda said.

Elena gulped. She was right: Mark had been there all along. Had he been listening to them? Had he told Barney to tell her that he wasn't there?

'It's through there on the left. Don't trip over anything. It's Barney's land-of-the-lost-guitars room.'

Elena walked out of the room, hearing Linda yelling at Barney and making no attempt not to be heard by Elena. She really did have a voice, that woman, Elena thought, and now she came to think about it, she remembered Mark telling her that she sang in Barney's band.

Barney's music hideout was at the back of the flat and, as Elena approached, she could hear strumming from behind the closed door. She felt herself smiling. She'd never heard Mark play a guitar. He was really quite good. She stood outside the door for a moment, acutely aware that he was so close and that it was just a matter of her opening the door. But what a huge task that was Their relationship was in tatters: she'd ruined it! Single-handedly, she'd wrecked what they'd built so carefully together.

She closed her eyes. Where had all her strength gone? In the taxi from her flat, she'd felt so confident and strong but, somewhere, all her strength had ebbed away. She wasn't even sure if she could reach out and open the door into the room where Mark was.

Then why did you come all this way? a voice asked her. She couldn't tell if it was Rosanna chiding her, Stefano remonstrating with her, or her own conscience. Whoever or whatever it was, it worked because her hand closed on the handle of the door and she was in the room before anything else could change her mind.

'Hey, Barney! These strings are a bit knackered, aren't they?' Mark said without looking around.

'It's not Barney, Mark,' she said.

Mark's fingers stopped strumming and he turned from his position on an old chair by the window but he didn't smile. Had she been expecting him to smile? She wasn't sure. But the absence of such a greeting made Elena feel like turning and running away again.

'What are you doing here, Elena?'

'I've come to see you.' It was a silly thing to say but his question was a profoundly silly one too. What did he expect her to say? That she'd come to audition for Barney's band?

'I need to talk to you,' she said.

'I've already heard all you have to say to me,' Mark said and, to Elena's horror, his fingers began strumming once more.

'You haven't,' she interrupted, trying not to be deterred by his indifference. 'You haven't heard everything I have to say because I've been lying to you.'

To her great satisfaction, he stopped strumming and looked up. 'I know. I met him, remember?'

'I'm not talking about Reuben.'

'No? Don't tell me, you've had another fiancé hidden away somewhere?'

Elena winced at his accuracy but didn't rise to his bait. 'Sarcasm really doesn't become you, Mark.'

'Oh, really?' he said in a tone which could have eaten sarcasm for breakfast. He began strumming again.

Elena swallowed. Her throat felt horribly dry - like her first day of teaching. She didn't know what to do. There was no training for this; no manual to tell her how to handle this sort of situation.

'MARK!' she suddenly shouted. 'Will you please put that bloody guitar down?'

He did. He then turned dark and angry eyes on Elena. 'What is it you want, Elena? I've already given everything up for you: my time, my sanity, even my job.'

'I never asked you to do that.'

'But it's done all the same.'

'Then undo it.'

'What?'

'Tell Tomi you want your job back. You know he's desperate. He'll give it back to you sooner than spending on advertising for somebody else.'

'Thanks. That makes me feel so much better.'

Elena sighed. 'I didn't mean it like that. You know you'll be missed. The students will miss you. Even Tomi will.'

There was a pause when both of them knew exactly what should be said.

'And I'll miss you,' she said at last, filling the silence with exactly the right words.

'You don't even know I'm around half the time,' Mark said. 'I've been your shadow for months now but you only notice now that the sun has gone in.'

For a moment, Elena wanted to make a joke of his poetic turn of phrase but she felt too sad to say anything at all.

'You have every right to say that,' Elena said. 'If I was you, I'd be saying exactly the same things right now. But I think you should listen to what I have to say.'

Mark made a noise that was mid-way between a sigh and a groan. 'What?'

'Can I sit down?' she asked, looking around the shabby room. There was one other chair opposite the one Mark was occupying but it was covered with newspapers and sheets of music. Elena crossed the room and swept the mess up in one armful, placing it on the floor in a small mountain.

'I was hoping you'd be waiting for me at the hotel when I got back to Venice,' she told him. He didn't say anything. 'No, that's a lie.'

'Why doesn't that surprise me?'

'I was hoping you'd follow me and stop me after I broke up with you - tell me to stop being stupid.' She shrugged. 'But you didn't. And you were right not to because you've been doing that all along, haven't you? You followed me out to Venice and tried to tell me, so many times, that I was being a fool and that I couldn't be happy with anyone other than you. But I didn't want to hear you.'

She paused. He was watching her with an intensity that made her feel nervous. She felt like she was auditioning for her life.

'I guess I didn't want anyone getting as close as you were. It scared me. Do you want to know why? Do you want to know what this is all about?'

Mark frowned. 'Rosanna said there was something I should-'

'I've never told anyone before. I've locked it away. But I've leant that no matter where you run, no matter how you cocoon yourself in your new life and your new self, you can never truly escape your past. It's only ever a blink away. No matter how brash and bold I am, no matter which mask I choose to wear, I'm still the sixteen year-old girl standing in the bend of the road, looking down the cliff face at a billowing cloud of dust.'

Tears swam in her eyes as the words left her mouth.

'Lucio and I had spent the whole summer together. We'd just left school and were celebrating - doing all the crazy stuff you do when you're sixteen. I'd never met anyone like him before but I guess every sixteen year old girl feels like that when she falls in love, and I really believed I was in love. I thought I was going to spend my whole life with Lucio. We didn't talk about that, of course; we were too busy messing about to be serious but I could see my whole future clear ahead - as bright as the summer sunshine. We spent hours doing absolutely nothing but our favourite thing - messing about on his moped. He loved that moped. It was like an extension of him, really, and he insisted on it being an extension of me too! We did some really stupid things - every day - but none as stupid as the day I've tried so hard to forget.'

Elena stopped for a moment but she didn't look at Mark. She was miles away - somewhere in the Italian countryside - somewhere in her past.

'We'd taken the coast road and had stopped for a picnic that I'd made up that morning. And then ...' she paused. 'It was all so unreal. Lucio got on his bike and was fooling around. One moment, we were laughing, and making fun of each other, and then there was the roar of his bike as he took up my dare. He was always a bit of a show-off and I loved him for it.

'I hadn't really believed it had happened because it had seemed more like a scene from a film than anything else. I kept expecting him to appear again - with a huge smile on his face as he laughed at having tricked me. But he never did appear.'

'What happened?'

'His bike had skidded, right on the edge of a cliff. He didn't have time to stop. I couldn't even see him - the land just disappeared into air and then sea. There was nothing there.'

'God, Elena-'

'You see?' she cried. 'Do you see now? I had to get away from that person. I hated myself. I was a murderer.'

'No, Elena -'

'But he died! Because of a stupid, stupid dare! I wanted him to prove himself to me. I was nothing but a vain, self-centred, foolish teenager.'

'It was an accident,' Mark said.

'And I caused it!'

They were both silent for a moment.

'I never want to go through that again,' Elena said at last.

Mark frowned at her. 'But you had two fiancés. Surely that meant doubling the chance of it happening?'

Elena gave a tiny shrug.

'I don't understand you,' Mark said. 'I really don't. If you'd been so scared of losing those close to you, why get engaged at all? That doesn't make any sense. Unless, you weren't ever going to take things further than that. Was that it?'

'I don't know,' she said in a half-whisper. 'Why are you asking me all these questions? I don't have the answers!'

'I'm asking them because you're *here!* Why are you here telling me all this stuff now? How do you expect me to respond?'

Elena looked at him, her eyes dark and full of sadness. 'I just thought I owed you an explanation. That's all. I wanted to say I was sorry. And that I love you.'

There was another pause and Elena's words hung heavy in the air between them.

'What do you want from me, Elena?' Mark asked. 'You want me to promise you I'm not going to die? I can't do that! I wish I could. I wish I could stand here and tell you that everything's going to be just fine between us but I can't. Nobody can guarantee that sort of thing. I can't - you can't - *nobody!*'

Elena let the tears spill from her face. 'I know that!'

Mark bit his lip and sighed. 'Don't cry,' he said.

Elena looked up at him. 'Then tell me you love me!' she said, her voice loud - demanding attention.

It took Mark completely by surprise and made him laugh which made Elena laugh too. The room was suddenly filled with laughter and, before they knew it, they were hugging and kissing.

'God! Elena! You'll never ever fail to knock the wind right out of me!' He wrapped his arms around her tightly as if he never meant to let go.

Elena hugged him back. 'If I were you, I wouldn't want me! I'm horrible. I've lied to you, deceived you-'

'And I still love you! I must be completely mad!'

'Let's be mad together, Mark. Please? Will you give me another chance? I know I don't deserve it. I know I've been impossible and that I should leave you in peace to find somebody nice but I can't do that.'

He smiled at her and pushed her dark hair away from her eyes. 'And I wouldn't let you.'

'Really?'

'Really. I love you, Elena. You infuriate me. You make me want to tear my hair out and stuff it in my mouth until I choke myself. But I love you!'

Elena's eyes filled with fresh tears. 'Then you'll marry me?'

Mark took a deep breath. 'As long as you promise I'm the only fiancé you're going to marry.'

She nodded. 'I promise.'

CHAPTER 46

Elena and Mark got married in the middle of August and the reception was held in the grounds of a small hotel in the Thames valley overlooking the river, just as Mark had imagined it. Barney Malone was there with the newly resurrected *No Name*. He'd jacked in his office job after three weeks and was actually now making a killing playing at weddings.

'It isn't exactly *Top of the Pops*, but it pays the rent and keeps me out of a suit,' he said.

Linda was there too - back in fine singing fettle after giving birth to baby Cher.

Rosanna and Reuben had flown over from Venice to be there and Mark had even shaken Reuben's hand and received a slap on the back in return.

Even Tomi, the skint Finn made an appearance, offering Mark his old job back with a small pay rise as a wedding present.

It was the perfect day. The sky was the colour of forget-me-nots and a gentle breeze from the river was just enough to prevent Elena from overheating in her full-length rose-coloured gown.

'You look gorgeous,' Mark whispered to her when they finally managed to escape the wedding party and sneak down to the river.

'And you look so handsome,' she said. She'd never seen Mark in a suit before and he looked very dashing in his wine-coloured cravat. Very Mr Darcy, she thought.

'We'll have to have a honeymoon, you know,' he said. 'Now I've got my job back.'

'I know,' she agreed.

'Anywhere you fancy?'

Elena looked thoughtful. 'Not Venice,' she said. 'Anywhere but Venice.'

He laughed. 'Agreed.'

Elena felt as if she never wanted to go back to Venice, yet, at the same time, she couldn't shake the place from her mind. She felt as if its labyrinthine streets had found a way into her very soul.

Sometimes, she even dreamed about them: walking over endless bridges and staring into its canals, and each journey would end at Viviana's.

'Where have you been?' Stefano would say. 'I've been worried about you.'

'I'm fine, Stefano! Please don't worry about me. Everything's fine. Absolutely fine!'

And, on waking, she really did feel fine. Perhaps it was because she'd come to terms with the fact that the past was the past. She couldn't erase it but she had to move forward into her future, and that future now contained Mark. She couldn't remember ever feeling so happy before. So they hadn't been able to afford the flat they wanted, so they were still working for appalling wages, but they had each other. Mark was right about not being able to guarantee her the future she wanted but, with Mark beside her, she'd quickly realised that the present was a pretty good place to be.

And the mask?

The mask remains in its box, safely cushioned in its tissue-paper bedding on a shelf in Elena's wardrobe. When she first brought it home, she couldn't stop getting it out and holding it, checking to see if the gold was less gold in the English light. It wasn't, of course. It glimmered and glowed as if alive but not once did she try it on. She didn't need to. The mask had done its job and it deserved a happy retirement but, even though she didn't think she'd ever need to wear it again, she wouldn't part with it for the world. Perhaps it was a comfort thing - just having it there.

No, Elena really doesn't think she'll ever need to wear it again. But you never know, do you?

ABOUT THE AUTHOR

Victoria Connelly was brought up in Norfolk and studied English literature at Worcester University before becoming a teacher in North Yorkshire. After getting married in a medieval castle in the Yorkshire Dales and living in London for eleven years, she moved to rural Suffolk where she lives with her artist husband and a mad Springer spaniel and ex-battery hens.

Her first novel, *Flights of Angels*, was published in Germany and made into a film. Victoria and her husband flew out to Berlin to see it being filmed and got to be extras in it. Several of her novels have been Kindle bestsellers.

If you'd like to contact Victoria or sign up for her newsletter about future releases, email via her website at www.victoriaconnelly.com.

She's also on Facebook and Twitter @VictoriaDarcy

ALSO BY VICTORIA CONNELLY

Austen Addicts Series
A Weekend with Mr Darcy
The Perfect Hero
published in the US as Dreaming of Mr Darcy
Mr Darcy Forever
Christmas with Mr Darcy
Happy Birthday, Mr Darcy

Other Fiction
The Rose Girls
Molly's Millions
The Runaway Actress
Wish You Were Here
Flights of Angels
Three Graces
It's Magic (A compilation volume: Flights of Angels,
Irresistible You and Three Graces)
A Dog Called Hope

Short Story Collections
One Perfect Week and other stories
The Retreat and other stories
Postcard from Venice and other stories

Non-fiction
Escape to Mulberry Cottage
A Year at Mulberry Cottage

Children's Adventure
Secret Pyramid
The Audacious Auditions of Jimmy Catesby

Printed in Great Britain
by Amazon